GRANTA

GRANTA 72, WINTER 2000
www.granta.com

EDITOR *Ian Jack*
ASSOCIATE EDITOR *Liz Jobey*
ASSISTANT EDITOR *Sophie Harrison*
EDITORIAL ASSISTANT *Fatema Ahmed*

CONTRIBUTING EDITORS *Neil Belton, Pete de Bolla, Ursula Doyle,*
Will Hobson, Gail Lynch, Blake Morrison, Andrew O'Hagan, Lucretia Stewart

FINANCE *Margarette Devlin*
ASSOCIATE PUBLISHER *Sally Lewis*
US ASSOCIATE PUBLISHER *Amber Hewins*
MARKETING DIRECTOR *Claire Paterson*
TO ADVERTISE CONTACT *Lara Frohlich* (212) 293 1646
SUBSCRIPTIONS *Richard Sang*
LIST MANAGER *Diane Seltzer*

PUBLISHER *Rea S. Hederman*

GRANTA PUBLICATIONS, 2-3 Hanover Yard, Noel Road, London N1 8BE
Tel 020 7704 9776 Fax 020 7704 0474
e-mail for editorial: editorial@grantamag.co.uk
Granta is published in the United Kingdom by Granta Publications.

GRANTA USA LLC, 1755 Broadway, 5th Floor, New York, NY 10019-3780
Tel (212) 246 1313 Fax (212) 586 8003

Granta is published in the United States by Granta USA LLC and distributed in the United States by
Granta Direct Sales, 1755 Broadway, 5th Floor, New York, NY 10019-3780.

TO SUBSCRIBE call (212) 246 1313 or e-mail: granta@nybooks.com
A one-year subscription (four issues) costs $37 (US), $48 (Canada, includes GST), $45 (Mexico and
South America), and $56 (rest of the world). Toll-free customer service line (US only): 1-800-829-5093.

Granta, USPS 000-508, ISSN 0017-3231, is published quarterly in the US by Granta USA LLC,
a Delaware limited liability company. Periodical Rate postage paid at New York, NY, and additional
mailing offices. POSTMASTER: send address changes to Granta, 1755 Broadway, 5th Floor,
New York, NY 10019-3780. US Canada Post Corp. Sales Agreement #1462326.
Printed in the United States of America on acid-free paper.
Copyright © 2000 Granta Publications.

Design: Random Design.
Front cover photograph: Lise Sarfati/Magnum; back cover photograph: Joseph O'Neill

ISBN 1-929001-02-9

GRANTA 72

Overreachers

"The best book on writing I've read. Ever."
—KAREN SANDSTROM, *The Plain Dealer*

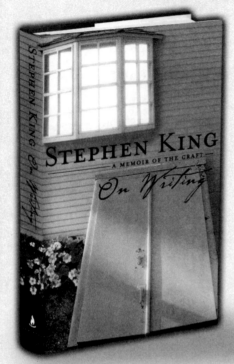

"Memoir, style manual, autobiography—the inspiring *On Writing* seems almost unclassifiable, except as that neatest of rabbit tricks: a one-of-a-kind classic."
—TOM NOLAN, *The Wall Street Journal*

"This warmly conversational book about literary criticism...takes a helpful, nuts-and-bolts approach to the budding writer's basic concerns while giving them a King-like spin."
—JANET MASLIN, *The New York Times*

"As good and as true as anything King has written... *On Writing* rivets attention and inflames admiration."
—*Publishers Weekly* (starred boxed review)

"There's no disputing that Stephen King... can write. What's more, and what's new, is that he can teach you how to do it."
—MAMEVE MEDWED, *Newsday*

"For anyone who wants to write and everyone who loves to read...an excellent memoir and writing manual."
—*Library Journal*

GRANTA

OVERREACHERS

Richard Ford

HUTCHISON

Overreachers

Madeleine Granville was standing at the hotel window of the Queen Elizabeth II, trying to decide which tiny car far below on Mansfield Street was her yellow Saab. Henry Rothman was tying his tie in front of the mirror. Henry was taking a plane in two hours. Madeleine was staying behind in Montreal, where she lived.

Henry and Madeleine had been having a much more than ordinary friendship for two years—the kind of friendship no one but the two of them was expected to know about (if others knew, Henry and Madeleine had decided, it didn't matter because no one *really* knew). The two of them were business associates within a large multinational company specializing in enhanced agricultural food additives. Henry was forty-nine, Madeleine was thirty-three. Together, as business associates, they had travelled a great deal, often abroad, staying together in many beds in many hotel rooms until many late mornings, eating scores of very good restaurant meals, setting out upon innumerable days in bright noon sunshine, then later saying their goodbyes in other hotel rooms or in airports or in car parks, hotel lobbies, taxi stands, bus stops. While apart, which had been most of the time, they had missed each other, talked on the phone often, and when they had come again into the other's presence had felt relieved, grateful, happy, fulfilled. Henry Rothman lived in America, in Washington DC, where he had a comfortable, divorced lawyer's life. Madeleine had settled in a tree-lined suburb with her one child and her architect husband. Everyone who worked with them knew everything and talked about it constantly behind Henry and Madeleine's backs. And yet the feeling was that it would never last, and so whose business was it. Conflicted gossip was very Canadian, Madeleine said.

But now, they'd decided, was the time for it all to be over. They loved each other—they each acknowledged that. Though they possibly were not *in* love (these were Madeleine's distinctions). But they had been in *something*, she understood—possibly even something better than love, something with its own intense and timeless web, densely tumultuous interiors and transporting heights. What that exactly *was* was hazy. But it had simply not been nothing. Affair was the wrong word.

As always, though, other people were involved, no one in

Rothman's life, it was true, but two in Madeleine's. And to these two, life had been promised a steady continuance. So, either what was not an affair ended now—they'd both agreed—or it went much, much further—out on to a terrain that bore no boundaries or markers, a terrain full of hazards. Neither of them wanted that.

It could as easily have stopped six months before, in London, Henry had thought on the plane the day before yesterday. Seated together at a sidewalk cafe on busy Sloane Square one spring morning, with taxis pouring noisily past, he and Madeleine had suddenly found they had nothing much to say, and at the precise moment when they'd always had something to say—a meticulous prefiguring of their luncheon plans, rehearsing their assessments of a troublesome client, discussing reviews of a movie they might attend, some encoded mention of lovemaking the night before—all the engaging, short-range complications of such arrangements as theirs. Love, Henry remembered thinking in London, love was a lengthy series of seemingly insignificant questions whose answers you couldn't live without. It was precisely these questions they'd run out of interesting answers for. And yet, to have ended it then, far from home, would've been inconsiderate. *Then* would've meant something about themselves that neither of them believed: that it hadn't *mattered* very much; that they were the kind of people who did things that didn't matter very much, and either importantly did or didn't know it about themselves. None of these seemed true.

Therefore, they'd kept on. Though over the months, their telephone conversations grew fewer and briefer. Henry went to Paris alone twice. He began a relationship with a woman in Washington, then ended it without Madeleine seeming to notice. Her thirty-third birthday passed unobserved.

And then as he was planning a trip to San Francisco, Henry suggested a stop-over in Montreal. A visit. A chat. It was clear enough to them both.

The evening of his arrival, they'd eaten dinner in a new Basque place Madeleine had read about, near the Biodome. She had dressed up in a boxy, unflattering black wool dress and black tights. They had drunk too much Nonino, talked little, walked to the St Lawrence, held hands in the chill October night, while quietly confronting the fact that without a patched-together future to involve and distract them, life became quite repetitious in a very little time.

Still, they had gone back to his room at the QE II, stayed in bed until two a.m., made love with genuine if self-considered passion, talked an hour in the dark, after which Madeleine had driven home to her husband and son.

Later, lying in bed in the warm, clocking darkness, Henry thought that sharing the future with someone certainly meant that repetitions had to be managed more skilfully, or else that sharing the future with someone was not a very good idea, and he should perhaps realize that once and for all.

Madeleine had been crying by the window (because she felt like it) and Henry had been continuing to dress while not exactly ignoring her, but not exactly electing to attend to her either. Madeleine had re-arrived at nine to drive him to the airport. It was their old way when he came into town for business. She wore fitted blue corduroys under a frumpy red jumper with a little rounded white collar. She was gotten up, Henry noticed, strangely like an American flag.

In the room now neither of them ventured near the bed. They merely had coffee standing up while they passed over small matters about business, mentioned the fall weather—hazy in the morning, brilliant in the afternoon. Typical for Montreal, Madeleine pointed out. She read the *National Post* while Henry finished in the bathroom.

It was when he emerged that Henry noticed Madeleine had finally stopped crying and was watching down the twelve storeys to the foggy, gloomy street.

'I was thinking about all the interesting things you don't know about Canada,' Madeleine said. She had put on a pair of clear-rimmed eyeglasses, perhaps to hide that she'd been crying. It made her look studious. Madeleine's hair was thick and dark-straw coloured and tended to dry unruliness, so that she often just bushed it back with a big clip, which she'd done this morning. Her face was pale, as if she'd slept badly, though her features, which were pleasing and soft with full expressive lips and cheeks and dark, thick eyebrows, seemed almost lost in her hair. Henry went on tying his tie. In the cityscape beyond the window, a big, T-shaped construction derrick with a little green operator's house part-way along the cross-arm seemed to exit both sides of Madeleine's head like an arrow. A tiny human figure was visible in the house. 'All the famous Canadians you'd never guess were Canadians, just for example.'

'Par example?' Henry said. This was as much French as he spoke. They spoke English here. They could speak it to him, was his belief. 'Name one.'

Madeleine looked around at him condescendingly. 'Denny Doherty of the Mamas and Papas,' she said. 'He's from Halifax. Donald Sutherland's from the Maritimes someplace. PEI maybe.' Madeleine looked different from how she actually was—a quality Henry always found intriguing. Generally, he thought, people looked how they were. The world worked well that way. Madeleine, though, looked like her name implied—slightly old-fashioned, formal, settled, given to measured responses, to being at ease with herself and her assessments of others' characters. (She was trained as a chartered accountant.)

But in fact she was nothing like that. She was a strong farm girl from near Halifax herself, and liked to drink schnapps, was once a teenage curling champion, liked to stay up late having sex and laughing. He had thought perhaps this strangeness was just a matter of their ages (he was sixteen when she was born) and that people who knew her didn't find her at all incongruous.

Madeleine looked back out the window at the cars lined along the side of the basilica of the Cathédrale Marie-Reine du Monde. 'It's a hazy day to be flying,' she said. 'I'd rather stay here.'

It was eleven. The room service tray with silver things and a red rose in a crystal bud vase sat on the dishevelled bed, on top of the scattered pages of the newspaper. Henry liked reading the Canadian papers. They made him think about all those important things that were going wrong in the world that weren't very important to him.

Henry Rothman was a large bespectacled man, who when he was young had looked—and he had agreed—something like the actor Elliott Gould in Bob & Carol & Ted & Alice, though he had felt he was more light-hearted than the character Elliott Gould had played— Ted. Rothman was a lawyer and a lobbyist for several firms that did big business in the States and abroad. He was a Jew, like Elliott

Gould, and had grown up in Roanoke, had gone to Virginia and then to Virginia Law School. His parents had been small-town doctors and now lived in Boca Raton, where they were happy in a condominium doing nothing. He practised with a firm that included his two brothers, David and Michael, who were litigators. He had been divorced ten years and had a daughter living in Boston teaching school.

Madeleine Granville was an account executive for Rothman's biggest client, the West-Consolidated Group. Madeleine knew about the cost of things: currency, fertilizer, train transport, containers of soy beans, containers of corn, benefits packages, bonuses, severances. She had gone to McGill and studied economics. She spoke five languages, had lived in Greece, and had wanted to be a painter, until she met a handsome young architect on a train from Athens to Sofia. They had settled in Montreal where he had his practice and where they both liked it. Their story was a story Henry Rothman liked. It seemed young, heady, exciting, but also savvy, solid, smart. Very Canadian. Canada, in so many ways, seemed superior to America. Canada was sane, tolerant, friendly, less litigious, less dangerous, calmer. He had thought of retiring here, possibly to Halifax or Cape Breton, two places he of course had never been. He and Madeleine had even discussed possibly living together by the ocean. It had become one of those magical issues you give your complete attention to for a week, and then later can't understand why you ever considered. In truth, Rothman loved Washington. He liked his life and his big house behind Capitol Hill, his law-school chums and partners, the city's slightly antic, slightly tattered southernness, his brothers, his membership at the Cosmos Club. His access. He occasionally even had dinner with his ex-wife, Laura, who like him was a lawyer and had remained unmarried. Who you really were and what you believed, he realized, were represented by what you maintained or were helpless to change. Very few people really knew that; most people continued to try to become something else. But after a while these personal facts simply revealed themselves like maxims, no matter what you said or did to contest them. Henry Rothman understood he was a man fitted primarily to live alone, no matter what kind of enticing sense anything else made.

Madeleine was writing something with her fingertip on the cool window glass while she waited for him to finish dressing. Crying was over now. No one was mad at anyone. She was amusing herself. He could see light through her yellow hair. 'Men think women won't ever change; women think men will always change,' Madeleine said concentratedly, as if she were writing these words on the glass. 'And, lo and behold, they're both wrong.' She tapped the glass with her fingertip, then stuck out her lower lip in a confirming way and widened her eyes and looked around at him. She was a complex girl, Henry Rothman understood, for whom life was just now beginning to seem confining. In a year she would almost certainly be far away from here. This love affair now was only a symptom.

He came to the window in his shirtsleeves and put his arms around her from behind in a way that felt to Henry fatherly. Madeleine let herself be drawn in, turned and put her face nose-first against his stiff shirt, her arm loose about his soft waist. She took her glasses off. She smelled warm and soapy, her pale skin where he touched her neck under her hair, as smooth as glass.

'So, what's changed?' he said thoughtlessly.

'Oh,' she said into the folds of his white shirt. She shook her head. 'Mmmmm. I was just trying to decide something.'

He held her close, pushing with his big fingers into the taut construction of her body. 'Say,' he said. She would speak, then he could provide a good answer. The window made the air on the back of his hands cool.

'Oh, well.' She paused and took a breath. 'I was trying to determine how to think about all this now.' She rubbed the sole of her shoe over the polished top of his black shoe, scuffing it. 'Some things are always real*er* than others. I was wondering if this would seem very real at a future date. You know?'

'It will,' Henry said softly. Their thinking was not far apart. If their thinking were far apart someone might feel unfairly treated.

'You respect the real things more, I think,' Madeleine said, and swallowed, then exhaled. 'The phoney things disappear.' She lightly drummed her fingers on his back. 'I'd hate it if this just disappeared from memory.'

'Oh, no,' Rothman said. 'I can promise you it won't.' Now was the right moment to get them both out of the room. Too many difficult valedictory issues were suddenly careering around. 'How about some lunch.'

Madeleine sighed again. 'Oh,' she said. 'Yes. I'd like to have some lunch. Lunch would be superior.'

The phone on the bed table began ringing then, loud shrill rings which startled them both, and for some reason made Henry look out the window into the pale autumn haze. Far away on a wooded, urban hillside he could see the last of the foliage—deep oranges and profound greens and dampened browns. In Washington today summer was barely over.

He was startled when the phone rang a third time. It had not rung once since he'd been in the room. No one knew he was here. He stared at the white telephone beside the bed as if he expected it to visibly vibrate.

'Don't you want to answer it,' Madeleine said. They had been embracing, but both were staring at the white telephone.

It rang a fourth time, very loudly, then—as though suddenly— stopped.

'It's a wrong number. Or it's the hotel wanting something.' He touched his black-framed glasses in a way he understood to mean he was jumpy.

Madeleine looked at him and blinked. She did not think it was a wrong number. She believed he knew exactly who it was, and that it was someone inconvenient. Another woman. Whoever was next in line after her.

Though that was not true. There was no one in line. He had no idea who'd called and hoped whoever it was wouldn't call back. It was time to go.

When the phone suddenly rang again Henry went straight for it and hurried the white receiver to his ear.

'Rothman.'

'Is this *Henry* Rothman?' a smirky, unfamiliar man's voice said.

'Yes.' He looked at Madeleine who was looking at him in a way that wished to seem interested but was in fact accusatory.

'Well, is this the Henry Rothman who's the high-dollar lawyer from the States?'

'Who is this?' He stared down at the hotel's name on the white instrument. *La Reine Elizabeth II.*

'What's the matter, asshole, are you nervous now?' The man on the phone chuckled a mirthless chuckle.

'I'm not nervous. No,' Henry said. 'Why don't you tell me who this is.' He looked at Madeleine again. She was staring at him disapprovingly, as if he were staging this entire conversation and the line was actually dead.

'You're a fucking nut-less wonder, that's who you are,' the man on the phone said. 'Who've you got hiding in there with you. Who's in bed sucking your dick, you cockroach.'

'Why don't you just tell me who this is and leave the cockroach stuff behind,' Rothman said in a patient voice, wanting to put the phone down. Abruptly, the man hung up before he could.

He looked at Madeleine. The big black derrick's armature with the little green house attached was still emerging from her head on both sides. The words *Saint Hyacinthe* were written along the cross-arm. 'Who was it?' she said. 'You look shocked.' Then suddenly she said. 'Oh, oh, oh, oh, don't tell me. It was Jeff, wasn't it? He knows I'm up here. Oh, shit.' Madeleine turned and faced the outside and put both her hands to her cheeks as if that would change things significantly.

'I didn't admit anything,' Henry said, and felt immensely irritated. He expected loud pounding to commence immediately from out in the hall, then shouting and kicking, then the outbreak of a terrible fist fight that would wreck the room. All this, moments before he could make it to the airport. He reminded himself he *hadn't* admitted anything. 'I didn't admit anything,' he said again and felt foolish.

'I just have to think,' Madeleine said. She looked pale and was patting the sides of her face, as if this was a way of achieving calm inside her head. It was theatrical, he thought. 'I have to be quiet a moment,' she said again, facing away.

Henry looked around the cramped, little room. The cluttered, unmade bed with the coffee utensils and the silver bud vase, the dresser and the clean mirror, the cloth-covered chair with a blue hydrangea print. Two reproductions of Monet's *Water Lilies* on opposite, otherwise featureless white walls. Nothing promising or even unpromising was in this room. Nothing foretold that things would quickly work out perfectly and he would soon be on his flight, or that none of that would happen. This was a venue, a space, nothing more. He could remember when rooms were different. Better. He thought what he often thought at the moments when things went very bad—and this was bad: that he was a man who overreached. He always had. When you were young it was supposed to be a good quality. But when you were forty-nine, it wasn't.

'I have to think where he might be,' Madeleine said. She had turned and was staring at the phone again as if he—her husband— was inside it and threatening to burst out. It was one of those moments when Madeleine was not how she appeared: not the slightly formal, reserved girl in Gibson Girl hair, but a kid in a bind, trying to figure out what to do. It was less intriguing.

'I suppose maybe the lobby,' Henry said, thinking the words: *Jeff. A man lurking in the hall just outside my door, waiting to come in and cause mayhem.* It was an unpleasant thought.

The telephone rang again, and Henry immediately answered it.

'Let me speak to my wife, you cockroach,' the same sneering, man's voice said. 'Can you pull out of her that long?'

'Who do you want?' Henry said forcefully.

'Let me speak to Madeleine, prick,' the man said. The name Madeleine produced a small shock in his brain.

'Madeleine's not here,' Henry Rothman lied.

'Right. You mean she's busy,' the man said. 'I get it. Maybe I should call back.'

'Maybe you've made a mistake here,' Henry said. 'Madeleine's not here.'

'*Is* she sucking your dick?' the man said 'Imagine that. I'll just wait.'

'I haven't seen her,' Henry lied again. 'We had dinner last night. And then she went home.'

'Yep, yep, yep,' the man said and laughed sarcastically. 'That was after she sucked your dick.'

Madeleine was facing outside again, listening to Rothman's conversation.

'That's not true,' Henry said, feeling disturbed at the man's anger. 'Where are you?'

'Why do you want to know that? You think I'm outside your door calling you on a cellphone?' Henry heard some metal-sounding clicks and scrapes on the phone line. Possibly Jeff had dropped the receiver because his voice was suddenly distant and unintelligible. 'Well, open the door and find out,' the man said, back in touch with things now. 'You might be right. I'll come in and kick your ass.'

'I'd be happy to come talk to you,' Henry said, then stopped. Why had he said such a thing? There was no need for that. He saw himself in the mirror, a large man in shirtsleeves and a tie and a little bit of belly. He looked away. It embarrassed him to look this way.

'You want to come talk to me?' the man said, then laughed again. 'You don't have the nuts.'

'Sure I do,' Henry said. 'Tell me where you are. I've got the nerve for that.'

'Then I *will* kick your ass,' the man said in a haughty voice.

'Well, we'll see.'

'Where's Madeleine?' The man seemed slightly deranged.

'I have no earthly idea.' It occurred to Henry that every single thing he was saying was a lie. He had brought into existence a situation in which there was not one shred of truth anywhere. How could that happen?

'Are you telling the truth?'

'Yes. I am. Now where are you?'

'I'm in my car. I'm a block from your hotel.'

'I probably can't find you there,' Rothman said. He looked at Madeleine. She was staring at him. In just an instant, he had things rounding back under control. He could tell it in her face—a pale face, with bleak admiration in it.

'I'll be at the hotel in five minutes, big man,' the man said sneeringly.

'I'll wait for you in the lobby,' Henry said. 'I'm tall, and I'll be wearing...'

'I know,' the man said. 'You'll look like an asshole no matter what you're wearing.'

'OK,' Henry said.

Madeleine's husband clicked off. Madeleine had taken a tentative seat on the arm of the blue hydrangea chair. Her hands were clasped tightly. He felt a great deal older and also superior to her— largely, he understood, because she looked sad. He had taken care of things, just as he almost always had.

'He thinks you're not here,' he said. 'So you should leave. I'm going to meet him downstairs. You have to go out by some other door.' He began looking around for his suit coat.

Madeleine smiled at him, almost wondrously. 'I appreciate your not telling him I'm here.'

'You *are* here, though,' Henry said patiently. He forgot his coat and began looking for his billfold and his change, his handkerchief, his pocket knife, the collection of non-essentials he carried in his pockets. He could check out of the room later. This was all nuts. He looked at Madeleine, seated prettily on the chair arm in her red jumper over her blue corduroys.

'You're not a bad man at all, are you, Hank?' Madeleine said sweetly. No one else called him Hank. He didn't particularly like it. 'Sometimes I'll be alone,' she said, 'or I'll be waiting for you, and I'll get mad and just decide you're a shit. But you really aren't. You're kind of brave. You sort of have principles.'

These words—principles, brave—made him feel unexpectedly frantic when he did not want to feel frantic. He was not supposed to feel frantic. He felt very large and cumbersome and frantic in the room with her. No longer superior to her or anyone.

'I think it's probably time for you to leave now,' he said, thinking again about his suit coat, trying to still himself.

'Sure,' Madeleine said, and looked to the side of the blue chair for her purse. She felt inside it for keys and produced a yellow plastic springy car-key- loop. Finding it seemed to make her stand up suddenly. 'When will I see you again?' She touched the bushed-up back of her hair like a middle-aged woman, and turned her eyes down. She was so changeable. She could look so many ways. 'This is a little sudden. I'd pictured something different, somehow.'

'I'm sure it'll all be fine,' Henry said and manufactured a smile. They needn't say anything else.

'I'm sure, too,' Madeleine said, 'setting aside the matter of when I'll see you again.'

'Setting it aside,' Henry Rothman said. 'Setting it aside for the moment.'

Flipping the yellow, springy key loop back and forth across her fingers, Madeleine started across the room toward the door, going past where Henry stood waiting for her to leave and feeling marooned. 'He's not a violent man,' Madeleine said. 'Maybe you two'll like each other. You have me in common, don't you?' She smiled at the door.

'That probably won't be enough for a long friendship,' Henry said. He wanted to sound flippant. It was one of a number of possible ways he could sound now. None of them was really the right way.

'I'm really sorry this is ending this way,' Madeleine said quietly, and let herself out, permitting the door to shut with a click.

'Me, too,' Henry Rothman said, but he was certain she didn't hear it.

Standing in the elevator vestibule, where a stale cigar aroma hung in the silent air, Henry began thinking that he was on his way now to meet the irate husband of a woman he didn't love but who he had nevertheless been fucking. This would be a man he didn't know but who had every right to at least hate him and possibly want to kill him. It was a man whose life a certain Henry Rothman had entered uninvited and possibly spoiled, but now wanted out of, thank you. Anyone could argue that whatever bad befell him was what he deserved, and that possibly nothing was really bad enough. In America, of course, people sued for relief, but probably not in Canada. He thought about what his father would say, his father in Boca Raton. His father was also a large man, gone bald, with a great stomach and an acerbic manner from years of treating cracker anti-Semites with fatal diseases in Virginia. 'At the bottom of the mine is where they keep the least amount of light,' his father liked to say, which was how Henry felt now—in the dark, at the bottom of something, with no idea how he should go about finding the light.

Though just blundering in as though he understood everything and letting events happen willy-nilly was certainly the wrong course. He didn't need to know much about Jeff—it wasn't necessary—but knowing nothing was unlawyerly. On the other hand, he felt that there was something so profoundly unserious about all of this that a sudden urge he recognized as similar to lunacy made him want to burst out laughing just as the mirrored elevator slid open. Still, though, as long as Madeleine was discreetly out of the hotel; and as long as Jeff hadn't kicked in the door and caught them in the middle of something, which had now not happened—then what could this possibly be about? The lawyer Henry Rothman said it was all about something that a man he didn't know might dream up, versus what he himself didn't admit to. Nothing added to nothing. He would simply tell as many lies as necessary. That *was* lawyerly: a show of spurious goodwill being better than no show of any will; the goodwill, in essence, being represented by the trouble of inventing a lie to cancel out the bad will of having an affair with Madeleine in the first place. And since their relationship was now over, Jeff could claim the satisfaction of believing he had caused it to be over. Everybody gets to think he wins, though no one does.

Stepping out of the elevator into the long, brightly-lit lobby, Henry concentrated on the light and sudden crowded atmosphere, the throng of hotel guests pulling suitcases on wheels and moving in groups toward the revolving door to the street. Many were smiling, slow-moving elderlies with plastic cards strung around their necks and little fanny packs jammed with valuables. They were speaking indecipherable French. He felt, he realized, absolutely calm.

Otherwise, the lobby offered up a pleasant inauthentic festive feeling with its big gold chandeliers. It was like a stage lighted for a musical, waiting for the principals to appear. He strolled out toward the middle of the humming concourse where expensive clothing stores and gift shops with bright showcase windows lined one side, and the people gazing in the windows looked prosperous and well cared for, as if they were all expecting something happy to occur soon. It reminded him of the fancy lobby of the old Mayflower in Washington, where he often met clients, and at the same time it felt foreign in the half-intriguing way Canada always felt foreign; as if the world had been tilted five degrees off from what you were used to, the floors at an angle, the doors opening from a different side. Nothing, of course, that you couldn't negotiate. New York, run by the Swiss.

In the middle of the lobby under one big glass chandelier he at first observed no one who might be a Jeff. A group of small American-sounding children trooped past in a ragged line, all wearing bunchy white tae kwon do uniforms and holding hands. They were headed toward the revolving doors. Some large, elderly black ladies, eight of them, dressed in big quilted fall frocks with matching expensive-looking hats, walked past. They were Southerners. He realized this because they were all talking too loud about taking their bus trip down to Vermont this afternoon. Plus, something that had happened the night before had been scandalous and was making them laugh.

And then he saw a man who was watching him, a man standing outside the glass and metal entrance to the English sweater shop. He could not be Madeleine's husband, Henry surmised, because he was too young—no more than mid-twenties. The man wore black jeans and white sneakers and a black leather jacket, and had a rough crew cut, blond hair, and was wearing yellow aviator glasses. He looked like a savvy college student who'd taken extra time graduating because of some exotic side adventures. Not an architect. If the man weren't staring at him so intensely, Henry felt he would never have noticed him.

When he caught the man's eye a second time, the man abruptly began walking straight toward him, both hands thrust inside his black jacket side-pockets, as if he might be hiding something there, and Henry realized with a small start that this man was in fact Madeleine's husband, could only be him, except that he looked ten years younger than Madeleine, and twenty-five years younger than himself. This would be different from the rendezvous he'd anticipated. It would be easier. The husband wasn't even very big.

When he was ten feet away, just at the verge of the crimson carpet, the young man he took to be Madeleine Granville's husband stopped, his hands still in his pockets and simply stared, as if something uncertain about Rothman—something unassociated with his identity—needed to be certified.

'Do you think I'm who you're looking for?' Henry said across the space between them. He was actually looking at the tae kwon do kids filing out toward the street still holding hands.

Madeleine's husband, or the man he thought was Madeleine's

husband, didn't say anything but began walking toward him again, only slowly now, as if he wished to give the impression that he was intrigued by something. It was all too ridiculous. More theatricality. They should go have lunch, where he could tell the man a lot of lies and then pay the check. That would be good enough.

'I saw your picture,' the young man said and actually seemed to sneer. He didn't remove his hands from his pockets. He was much smaller than expected, but very intense. Possibly he was nervous. His aviator glasses emblematized intensity, as did this black jacket zipped up to his neck so you couldn't tell what he had on under it. Madeleine's husband was handsome but in a reduced, small-featured, vaguely spiritless way, as if he'd once failed at something significant and hadn't forgotten it. It was odd to think she found them both—himself (the big cumbersome Jew) and this small Frenchy-seeming man—attractive.

'I'm Henry Rothman.' Henry extended his large hand, but Madeleine's husband ignored it. What picture had he seen? One she'd taken, he supposed, and rashly kept.

'Where the fuck's Madeleine?' he said. He didn't seem the least bit like a young man who would say a thing like he'd just said, or whatever he'd said on the phone. Cockroach. Sucking your dick. It was absurd. Henry felt completely in control now.

'I don't know where Madeleine is,' he said. And it was technically true, which made him relax even more. He was tempted to offer to take the man up to his room as proof. But Madeleine had a habit of leaving earrings, toiletry essentials, articles of underclothing wherever she'd been. Too risky.

'I have an eight-year-old son,' the intense, bespectacled young man said, and seemed to set his shoulders inside his bomber jacket. He blinked at Henry very intently and leaned forward on the balls of his feet, making himself appear, oddly enough, even more reduced. His eyes behind the yellow lenses were the blandest uninflected brown, and his mouth was small and thin. His skin was soft and slightly olive-tinted, with a faint flush of emotion in his cheeks. He is like a pretty actor, Henry thought, clean-shaven and actorishly fit-looking. Madeleine had married a pretty boy. Why indeed ever have a Henry Rothman in your life for two years if this boy appealed to you? It made him feel as if his qualities as a human had been *employed* for some purpose he didn't understand. It was not a very good feeling.

'I know you do,' Henry said about the business of the child.

'So, I don't want to fuck with you,' the young man said, reddening. 'I'm not about to let you fuck up my marriage and keep my son from having two parents at home. Do you understand that? I want you to.' His soft boy's mouth became unexpectedly hard. He had small, tightly-bunched squarish teeth that detracted from his beauty and made him seem vaguely corrupted. 'If it wasn't for that, though, I wouldn't give a goddamn what you and Madeleine did together,' he went on. 'Fuck in hotel rooms all over the planet and I couldn't give a shit.'

'I guess you've made your point, then,' Henry said, feeling ready to go, hoping he'd made his point.

'Oh, am I making a point?' Madeleine's husband said and widened his eyes behind his idiotic glasses. 'I didn't realize it. I thought I was just explaining to you the facts of life, since you're way out of touch with them. I wasn't trying to persuade you. Do you understand?' The boy did not remove his eyes from Henry's eyes. An aroma of inexpensive leather had begun filtering off the black jacket, as if he'd bought it that day. Henry Rothman had never owned a black leather jacket. In Roanoke, doctors' sons didn't go in for those. Their style then had been madras sports coats and white bucks.

'I understand what you mean,' Henry said in what he hoped would seem like a fatigued voice.

Madeleine's husband glared purposefully at him, and Henry again realized how he himself wasn't the least bit serious about any of this. He would be willing, he felt, to bet money Madeleine's husband wasn't serious either, though he perhaps didn't know it and believed he felt great passion about all this baloney. But neither of them were truly up against anything here. Everything they were doing, they were choosing to do. He was choosing to be here, and Jeff was choosing to put this unconvincing ferocious look on his face. They should talk about something else now. Hockey, maybe.

'I admit I may like Madeleine more than I ought to,' Henry said and felt satisfied with it. 'I may have acted in some ways that aren't entirely in your interest.'

The young man blinked his lightless brown eyes upon hearing this.

'Is that so?' he said and blinked again. 'Is that your great admission?'

'I'm afraid it is,' Henry said and smiled for the first time. He wondered where Madeleine actually *was* just at the very moment he'd admitted to her boy husband, in his own way at least, that he'd been fucking her. He'd only said it so that something that passed between himself and this man could have a grain of substance. 'What kind of architecture do you do?' Henry asked comfortably. Some people were speaking French close by. He looked around to see who. It would be nice just to be able to start speaking French now. Or Russian. Anything. Madeleine's husband said something he wasn't sure he understood. 'Excuse me?' He smiled again.

'I said fuck you,' the young man said and stepped closer. 'If you persist with this I'll arrange for something really bad to happen to you. Something you don't want to happen. And don't think I won't do that. Don't think I won't. I will.'

'Well, I can certainly believe you,' Henry said. 'You have to believe that when someone says it. It's the rule. So, I believe you.' He looked down at his own shirt front and saw a tiny black decoration of Madeleine's mascara from when she had stood close to him by the window after crying. It made him feel fatigued all over again.

The young man stepped back. His face had lost its blush of red and looked cold and pale and clammy and mottled. He had never removed his hands from his jacket pockets. He could have a gun. Though this was Canada. No one was murderous here.

'You American assholes,' Madeleine's husband was saying now. 'You've got divided inner selves. It's all part of your history. You have a choice about everything. It's pathetic. You don't really inhabit anything. You're cynical. The whole fucking country of you.' The young man shook his head and seemed to want to look disgusted.

'Take all the time you want. This is your moment,' Henry said.

'No, that's enough,' the young man said and looked tired himself. 'You know what you need to know.'

'I do,' Henry said. 'You made that clear.'

Madeleine's young husband unexpectedly turned and without speaking again went striding across the festively lit, gilt and red lobby and out through the revolving doors where the tae kwon do children had gone, disappearing as they had amongst the passers-by. Henry

23

looked at his wristwatch. It had all occupied fewer than five minutes.

Back in his room he changed his smudged shirt and arranged his few clothes and toiletries back into his suitcase. The room was cold now as though someone had turned off the heat and opened a window down a hallway. Two message slips lay on the carpet just inside the door. These would be messages from Madeleine, or else they were second-thought threats from the husband. Somehow, these message slips triggered a strong desire in him to make up his bed, straighten the room, urges which always meant life was becoming messy in some pointless way. He decided to leave the messages alone.

Standing for a moment exactly where Madeleine had stood earlier, at the window across from the big T-shaped crane which was slowly lifting a heavy concrete-filled bucket toward the top floor of an unfinished building's high silhouette, he wondered again where, out in this strange disjointed city, she was. Having a coffee, possibly, with a girlfriend she could regale with all this; waiting for her son to be let out of school, or for the husband to arrive and for some brittle, unhappy bickering to commence. Nothing he envied. On the plate-glass window he saw where Madeleine had been writing with her finger. It showed up now that the room was colder. It seemed to say 'Denny.' What or who was Denny? Maybe it had come from someone earlier, some other hotel guest.

He felt suddenly exhausted to the point of being dazed. Sometime, too, in the last hour, he had cracked a sizeable piece off of a molar. The jagged little spike caught at the already tender tip of his tongue. The broken part he'd swallowed without even knowing it. The day had worked its pressures. He took off his glasses and lay across the newspapers on the unmade bed. He could hear the muffled TV in another room, an audience laughing. There was time to sleep for a minute or five.

About Madeleine, though: there had been a time when he'd loved her, when he'd said so, felt so rather completely. None of the foolishness about love or being *in* love. One definite time he could remember had been on a pebbly beach in Ireland, near a little village called Round Stones, in Connemara—on a trip they'd made by car from Dublin where they'd seen some investors, negotiated significant advantages for the client. They'd laid a picnic on the rocky shingle and staring off that night had declared that the lights they could see out in the night were the lights of Nova Scotia, where Madeleine had been born, and where life would be better—in true geography, of course, they'd been facing north and were only espying the opposite side of the bay. Behind them in the village, there had been a little fair with a lighted merry-go-round and a tiny row of bright arcades that glowed upwards and upwards as the night fell. There, that time, he'd loved Madeleine. And there were other times, several times when he knew. Why question it?

Though even then there had been the *is this it?* issue. Thinking of it made him think of his father again. His father had been a New Yorker, and had New Yorker ways. 'So, Henry. Is this it for you?' he'd say derisively. His father had always felt there should be more, more for Henry, more for his brothers. More than they had, more than they had accepted. To accept, to not overreach was to take too little. And so, in his father's view, even if all was exquisite, unequalled, which it might've seemed, would it still get no better than this in life? He'd helplessly wondered that, even when he and Madeleine had felt love's force the purest and strongest. Life always *had* gotten better. There had always been more coming. Although he was forty-nine now, and there were changes you didn't notice—physical, mental, spiritual changes. Parts of life had been lived and would never be again. Maybe the fulcrum's tip had *already* come, and something about *today*, when he would later think back from some point further on, *today* would seem to have been when 'things' began going wrong or else were already wrong, or even when 'things' were at their pinnacle. Then, of course, at that later moment, you *were* up against something. You were up against the fact that you'd reached, or almost reached, your destination point and had no more interesting choices—only less and less and less interesting ones.

Still, at this moment, he didn't know that; because if he did know it he might decide just to stay on here with Madeleine—though of course staying wasn't really an option. Madeleine was married. Though the husband had been right about choices, merely wrong in his appraisal. Choices were what made the world interesting, made life a possible place to operate in. Take them away and what difference did anything make? Everything became Canada. The trick was simply to find yourself up against as little as possible. Odd, Henry thought, that this boy should know anything.

In the hall outside the room he heard women's voices speaking French very softly. The housekeepers, waiting for him to leave. He couldn't understand what they said, and so for a time he slept to the music of their strange, wittering language.

When he turned away from the cashier's, folding his receipt, Henry found that Madeleine Granville had been waiting for him, standing beside the great gold pillar where luggage was stacked. She had changed her clothes, pulled her wet hair back severely in a way that emphasized her full mouth and dark eyes. She looked jaunty now in a pair of nicely fitted brown tweed trousers, a houndstooth jacket and expensive-looking lace-up walking shoes. Everything seemed to emphasize her slenderness and youth. She was carrying a leather knapsack that seemed to anticipate a trip. She also looked extraordinarily pretty, a way he'd seen her look other times. He wondered if she was expecting to go with him, if matters with the husband had come apart.

'I left you two messages.' She smiled at him in a mockingly amused way. 'You didn't think I'd let you take a taxi.'

Some of the people he'd seen earlier were still present in the lobby—a child sitting alone in a big throne chair, wearing his white tae kwon do get-up. A black woman in a brocaded fall suit having a present wrapped in the sweater shop. It was past noon. He had missed lunch. 'Are you going fox-hunting?' he said, hoisting his suitcase, unsure what to do now.

'I'm taking Patrick to see the last of the fall foliage after school.' Patrick was her child. She held one arm stylishly out, extended a foot. 'Don't I look autumnal?'

'You're standing right where I had a truly ridiculous conversation about an hour ago,' Henry said. He looked toward the revolving door. Traffic was silently moving on the street just beyond. He wondered if Jeff was lurking somewhere nearby.

'We'll put up a plaque,' Madeleine said and seemed in gay

spirits. '*Here the forces of evil were withstood by*…what?' She patted her damp hair with her palm.

'I don't mind getting a taxi.'

'Screw you,' she said brightly. 'It's my country you've been kicked out of.' She turned to go. 'Come on… *Were withstood by the forces of dull convention. Alas.*'

From the passenger's seat of Madeleine's Saab, Henry watched out at the big construction cranes. There were many more cranes and superstructures than he'd seen from his room's window. *Saint Hyacinthe* had been his. They made the city feel uninteresting, indifferent. For this reason alone a taxi would've been better. A taxi alone to an airport, never looking right nor left, was always a comfort.

'You look beat up,' Madeleine said. Driving too fast usually put her in an aggressive good humour. Together they had always been driving someplace good. He liked speed then. Now, he liked it less, since it threatened getting to the airport. And there was nothing to say about looking 'beat up.' He seemed to know her, and now he also seemed not to know her. It was part of the change they were enacting. When they were in the thick of things together, Madeleine couldn't drive without looking at him, smiling, remarking about his excellent qualities, cracking jokes, listening to his comments. Now she could be driving anybody—her mother to the beauty parlour, a priest to a funeral.

'Do you realize what the day after tomorrow is,' she said, manoeuvring skilfully through the traffic's changing weave. She was wearing some sort of scent that filled the car with a dense rosy aroma he was already tired of.

'No,' he said.

'It's Canadian Thanksgiving. We have it early so we can get a jump on you guys. Canada invented Thanksgiving, *eh*?' Madeleine quite liked making fun of Canadians but didn't like it at all if he did. He had never really, of course, thought of Madeleine as Canadian. She just seemed like an American girl to him. He was not exactly sure how you considered someone Canadian—what important allowances you needed to make.

'Do you observe it for the same reason we do?' he said, watching traffic without noticing it. He still felt slightly dazed.

'We just *have* it,' Madeleine said happily. 'Why do you have it?'

'To solemnize the accord between the settlers and the Indians who might have murdered them. Basically it's a national gesture of relief.'

'Murder, murder, murder. It's your big subject down there, isn't it?' Madeleine looked pleased. 'We just have ours to be nice. That's enough for Canada. We're just happily grateful. Murder really doesn't play a big part.'

The old French university buildings passed below and to the left. The little Frogs-only fantasy world. He considered how he and Madeleine would function together following today. He hadn't really thought about it. Still, everybody had a past. It would be a relief to the people who knew about them to have this over with. Plus, not having him in her life was going to be much better for Madeleine. The world would open up again for both of them.

'I've got something to tell you,' she said, both hands firmly on the leather steering wheel.

'I probably already know what it is,' Henry said. His tongue sought the sharp little spike of his broken molar. The tender flesh was debrided and sore from going there. He could get it fixed in San Francisco.

'I really don't think you do,' Madeleine said. A great white Japanese 747 slowly descended out of the sky ahead, and across the autoroute in front of them. 'Do you want me to tell you?' she said.

'I don't have to. It can wait forever.'

'That guy wasn't your husband,' Henry said and quietly cleared his throat. The thought just came to him—why, now, he didn't know. Lawyer's intuition. 'Did you think I was stupid? I mean...' He didn't care to finish this sentence. It finished itself. Most sentences could. So much that was said didn't need to be. Aristotle was right about it. The subject actually embarrassed him.

Madeleine looked at him once, looked away then looked again. She seemed impressed. And she seemed happy about feeling impressed, as if this was the best of all outcomes. The big white jet sank from sight into an unremarkable industrial landscape. No big ball of flaming explosion followed. Everyone safe. 'You're guessing,' she said.

'I'm a lawyer, what's the difference,' he said.

She liked this too and smiled. He understood it was impossible for her not to like him. 'How'd you know?'

'Among other reasons?' Freeway traffic was now standing back for the airport exit. He looked out at the high concrete sides of the highway. 'He acted more serious than he felt. Something he said…"divided inner somethings?" Plus, he looks like an actor. He wore those glasses. Are you sleeping with him, too? I don't mean "too." You know.' He noticed the scuff on the toe of his shoe where she had stood on it.

'Currently, no,' Madeleine said. She touched her brass hair clip with her little finger and cocked her head slightly. She appeared to be on the verge of realizing something. What that might be, he thought, would be worth knowing. 'I knew you'd go see him,' she said. 'I knew you couldn't resist it. You always want to seem to be so forthright and brave. It's your disguise.'

Henry watched the clean industrial landscape passing along more slowly. The green sign was visible. AEROGARE/AIRPORT. What an exertion. Everything said twice.

'He's an American,' Madeleine said. 'His name's Bradley. He *is* an actor. We worried you'd know he wasn't Canadian.'

'No worry there,' Henry said. She was taking the AEROGARE/AIRPORT SORTIE/EXIT and looked across at him and seemed slightly tricked herself. Perhaps, he thought, she was thinking about patting her face when they were in the room, or saying, *I'd pictured something different.* These might seem excessive now. He reached and took her hand and held it loosely. She was nervous. Her hand was moist. This whole business had required something of her, too. They had been in love, perhaps were still in love. 'Is someone filming all this?' he said and glanced to the side, at a pickup truck speeding along beside them on the autoroute. For a moment he expected to see the truck bed full of cameras, sound equipment, smiling young cineastes. Everything trained on them.

'For once, no,' she said glumly.

Up ahead the D'EMBARQUEMENTS/DEPARTURES area was

jam-packed. Cars, limos, taxis, people loading golf bags, collapsible cribs and taped-up coolers from the backs of idling vans. Policemen with white oversleeves were waving everyone through. He had only a suitcase, a briefcase, a raincoat. It had become a wonderful autumn day. Clouds were being cleansed from the sky—a perfect day to take in the fall spectacle.

He continued holding her hand, and she grasped his back in a way that felt important. What would it be like finally, he wondered, to grow uninterested in women. The things he did—going here, going there, deciding this, that—he'd always had a woman in mind. Their presence animated everything. So many things would be different without them. No more moments like this—moments of approximate truth vivifying, explaining, offering silent reason to the choices you made. And what happened to those people for whom life wasn't that way? They certainly achieved things. Were they better, their accomplishments purer? Possibly, of course, when it was all out of your reach—and it would be—you wouldn't even care. You could hope for that.

On the curb side, amid skycaps and passengers alighting and baggage carts nosed in at reckless angles, a family—two older adults and three nearly grown blond children—were having a moment of prayer, standing in a tight little circle, arms to shoulders, heads bowed. These were Americans, Henry realized. Only Americans would be so immodest with their belief, so sure a quick prayer was just the thing to keep them safe—at once so careless and so prideful. Not the qualities to make a country great.

'Do you think if we asked them, they'd include us in their little circle,' Madeleine said, breaking their silence, as she pulled to the curb, exactly beside the praying Americans. She meant to annoy them by stopping so close.

'We're represented already,' he said, looking out at the pilgrims' hefty, strenuous backsides. 'We're the forces of evil they think so much about. The terrible adulterers. We worry them.'

'Life's just a record of our misdeeds, is that it?' she asked musingly, still clumsily grasping his hand. He couldn't open his door for the praying Americans.

'I don't think that,' Henry said, holding her warm, soft, moist hand casually. She was just letting the other subject go now—the lying, tricking him, having a joke at his expense. Though why, for God's sake, not let it go?

He sat for a moment, facing forward, unable to exit. He said, 'Have you decided you don't love me?' It was of course the thing he wanted to know. His version of a prayer.

'Oh, no,' Madeleine said. 'I wanted us to go on. But it just won't. So. This seemed like a way to seal it off. Exaggerate the difference between what is and what isn't. You know?' She smiled weakly. 'Sometimes you can't believe the things that are taking place are actually taking place, and you need to believe it. I'm sorry, though. It was too much.' She leaned and kissed him on the cheek, then took both his hands to her lips and kissed them.

He liked her. Liked everything about her. Though now was the wrong moment to say so. It would seem insincere. Reaching for too much. Though how did you ever make a moment be worth as much as it was in fact worth, if you didn't reach?

Outside, the American Christians were hugging each other, smiling big confident smiles, their prayers having reached a satisfactory end.

'Are you trying to think of something nice to say,' Madeleine said jauntily.

'No,' Henry said. 'I was trying not to.'

'Well, that's just as good,' she said, smiling. 'It might not be good enough for everybody, but I understand. It's hard to know how to end a thing that didn't altogether begin. Isn't it?' He pushed open the heavy door, pulled his suitcase out of the back, stepped out into the cool fall light, looked quickly in at her. She looked up through the open doorway. 'Wouldn't you agree with me about that, Henry?' she asked. 'That'd be a nice thing to say. Just that you agree with me.'

'Yes,' Henry said. 'I do. I do agree with you. I agree with you about everything.'

'Then rejoin your fellow Americans,' she said. He closed the door. She did not look his way again. He watched her ease away and quickly disappear into the traffic that was heading back to town.

☐

31

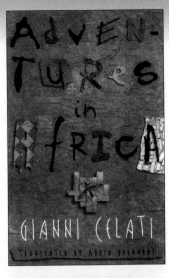

GRANTA

THE HOTEL CAPITAL

Olga Tokarczuk

TRANSLATED FROM THE POLISH BY
TERESA HALIKOWSKA-SMITH

LISE SARFATI/MAGNUM

The Hotel Capital

is only for the rich. For them there are porters in uniforms, long-legged, tailcoated waiters with Spanish accents; for them the silent lifts with mirrors on all sides; for them the brass door handles which must never be allowed to show any fingerprints, the door handles which are for this reason polished twice a day by the petite Yugoslav woman; for them the carpeted stairs to be used only in case they should be assailed by the claustrophobia of the lift; for them huge sofas, heavy quilted bedspreads, breakfasts in bed, air conditioning, towels whiter than snow, soaps and beautifully scented shampoos, toilet seats of real oak, new magazines every morning. It is for them that God created Angelo of Soiled Linen and Zapata of Special Orders, for them the chambermaids in white and pink uniforms, scurrying along the corridors, myself among them. But perhaps to say 'myself' is already to say too much; not much of myself is left when, in the little service room at the end of the corridor, I put on a striped apron while, at the same time, taking off my own colours, my body smell, my favourite earrings, my warpaint make-up and high-heeled shoes. At the same time I take off my exotic language, my strange name, my sense of humour, my face lines, my taste for food not appreciated here, my memory of small events—and I stand naked in this pink and white uniform as if emerging from the sea mist. And, from this moment on,

The whole of the second floor of the hotel is mine

every weekend, that is. I start here at eight o'clock and I don't have to hurry since, at eight o'clock, all the rich people are still asleep. The Hotel snuggles them inside, rocking them gently, as if it were a big seashell in the world's depths and they the precious pearls inside it. In the distance the traffic awakens and the underground train makes the grass tremble gently at its tips. A cool shadow lingers in the hotel's yard.

I come in through the back door and immediately I become aware of strange intermingled smells of cleaning materials, freshly laundered linen and the walls sweating with the excessive turnover of people. The poky little lift stops in front of me, ready for service. I press the button for the fourth floor and proceed to my supervisor,

Miss Lang, to collect my orders for the day. Every time, somewhere halfway between the second and third floors, I am touched by a panicky sensation lest the lift should stop and I should stay here forever, enclosed like a bacterium inside the body of the Hotel Capital. And once the hotel awakens, it will set to work, unhurriedly digesting me, it will even get at my thoughts and absorb all that is left of me, it will feed on me before I noiselessly disappear. But the lift mercifully lets me out.

Miss Lang sits behind her desk, with her spectacles balancing on the tip of her nose. She looks just like what the queen of all chambermaids, the resident of all eight floors, the dispenser of hundreds of bed sheets and pillowcases, the chamberlain of carpets and lifts, the equerry of brushes and vacuum cleaners, should look like. She eyes me from behind her spectacles and takes out a card prepared especially for me, on which, laid out neatly in rows and columns, a plan of the whole second floor is drawn, indicating the status of each room. Miss Lang does not notice guests in the hotel. Perhaps she considers them to be the concern of the higher management, difficult as it is to imagine someone higher, more distinguished than Miss Lang.

For her, the hotel is probably a perfect structure, a living, if inert, being which we have to take care of. Sure enough, people flow and fly through it, warm its beds, drink water from its brass nipples. But they pass on, go away. We and the hotel remain. That is why Miss Lang describes the rooms to me as if they were haunted places— always in the passive tense, as *being* occupied or dirty or free for the last few days. As she does this, she looks resentfully at my own clothing, at the traces of my too hurriedly applied make-up. And almost straight away I am walking along the corridor with a note in Miss Lang's beautiful, slightly Victorian handwriting, planning the strategy of how best to use my strength.

It is then that, unconsciously, I cross from the domestic part of the building to the Guests' Quarters. I can tell this by the smell—I only have to lift my head to recognize it. Sometimes I score ten out of ten: the scent is that of Armani, or Lagerfeld for Men, or of the seductively elegant Boucheron. I recognize these scents from the free samples in *Vogue* magazine. I am familiar with the look of their containers. I also catch the scent of powder, of anti-wrinkle cream, of silk, of crocodile skin, of Campari spilled over the bedding, of Caprice cigarettes for subtle brunettes. This, to me, is the specific smell of the second floor. Or rather, not the complete smell, but only the first layer of that special smell of the second floor which I recognize instantly the way one recognizes an old friend, while on my way to the changing room where

A transformation

takes place. Clad in the pink and white uniform, I find myself viewing the corridor with different eyes. I no longer trace the scents, I cease to be drawn by my own reflection in the brass door handles, nor do I listen for the sound of my own steps. What I am singularly interested in now are the numbered rectangles of doors in the corridor's vista. Behind each of these eight rectangles there is a room—the four-cornered, prostituted space which every few days gives itself to someone else. The windows of four of the rooms look on to the street where a bearded fellow in Scottish attire stands playing his bagpipes.

I suspect he is not a genuine Scot. He exhibits too much enthusiasm. Next to him—a hat and a coin meant to attract offerings.

The next four rooms, whose windows overlook the yard, are not as sunny and seem to be permanently bathed in shadow. All eight rooms are lodged in my brain, even before I can see them. My eyes search out the door handles. Some of them have DO NOT DISTURB notices attached to them. I am pleased at this as it is not in my interest to disturb either the rooms or the people in them, and I prefer that they do not disturb me as I contemplate my sole possession of the second floor. Occasionally, a notice declares the room is READY TO BE SERVICED. This notice puts me in a state of alertness. There is also a third kind of information—that supplied by the absence of any notice. This energizes me, makes me slightly anxious. It switches on my chambermaid's mind which until then has remained inactive. Sometimes, when the stillness behind such a door is too palpable, I have to put my ear to it and listen intently, and even peep through the keyhole. I prefer this to suddenly finding myself inside with an armful of towels and stumbling upon an alarmed guest covering his nakedness or, even worse, finding a guest so deep in helpless sleep that he scarcely seems to be there. That is why I obey the notices on the doors: they are visas granting me entry into a miniature world,

The world of numbers

Room number 200 is empty, the bed rumpled, a few bits of debris and a bitter smell of someone's hastiness, of their turning over in bed, of their feverish packing. This somebody must have left early in the morning, probably had to rush to the airport or maybe to a railway station. My job consists of removing the traces of this person's presence from the bed, the carpet, the wardrobes, the cabinet, the bathroom, the wallpaper, the ashtrays and finally the air itself. This is not at all easy. It's not enough just to clean. The vestiges of the personality left behind by the previous occupant have to be overcome by my own impersonality. This is what Transformation is all about. It is not enough to wipe away with a piece of cloth the traces of the reflection of that face in the mirror, but the mirror has to be filled with my pink and white facelessness. That smell left behind by distraction and haste has to be stifled by my complete absence of smell. This is what I am here for, as someone in an official capacity who is therefore a non-person. And this is what I do. It is always hardest with women. Women leave behind more traces and I don't mean simply that they forget their knick-knacks. They instinctively try to remake hotel rooms into ersatz homes. They root wherever they can, like seeds carried on the wind. In the hotel wardrobes they hang some of their deep-seated longings, in the bathrooms they shamelessly divest themselves of their desires and deprivations. Light-heartedly they leave the imprint of their lips on glasses and cigarette butts, as well as their hair in the bath. On the floor they sprinkle talcum powder which traitorously reveals the mystery of their footprints. Some of them do not wipe off their make-up before going to bed and then the pillowcases, like Veronica's veil, retain the image of their faces. They never leave tips, however. For this the self-assurance of men is needed. Men tend to view the world more as a marketplace than a theatre. They prefer to pay for everything, even in advance. It is only when they pay that they feel free.

The next room is

The Hotel Capital

Number 224, occupied by a Japanese couple

They have already been here for some time and I feel quite at home in their room. They get up very early, probably in order to go on an infinite round of visits to museums, galleries and shops; gliding gently and quietly through the streets and giving up their seats in the underground train, they multiply the city in their photographs. Their room is an elegant double room. It gives the impression of not being occupied at all. There are no objects left by mistake on the chest of drawers under the mirror. They use neither TV nor radio; there are no fingerprints on the brass switches. There is no water in the bath, no steam on the mirror, no fluff on the carpet. The pillows do not retain the shapes of their heads. No black hair sticks to my uniform. And, what is alarming, they have left behind no scents. The only scent is that of the Hotel Capital itself. By the bed, I can see two pairs of neat, clean sandals tidily arranged, momentarily released from their service to the feet. One pair is bigger than the other. A guidebook, the bible of every tourist, rests on the cabinet, and in the bathroom there are toiletries—functional, discreet. All I have to do is to remake the bed and, in doing so, I create more disorder than they would make in a month.

I feel moved while cleaning here, amazed by this mode of being which seems like not being at all. I sit on the edge of the bed, absorbing this absence of theirs. It touches me that the Japanese always leave a small tip—a few coins neatly stacked on the pillow—which I am obliged to take. This is a kind of letter, a newsletter; a kind of correspondence between us. They give me this tip as if they were apologizing for engaging so little with me themselves; the tip is for the absence of noise, for not being part of the chaos around them. They are concerned that this may disappoint or anger me. This small tip is the expression of their gratitude that I allow them to be themselves. I try to appreciate this, their way of meeting me—when I make their bed, I do it with love.

I plump up the pillows, I caress the sheets they are unable to crumple—it is as if their slender bodies were less material than the bodies of others.

I do it slowly, savouring it, feeling that I am giving of myself. I dissolve myself in giving, I forget myself, I caress their room, I touch things with tenderness. And they quite possibly sense this caress on their skins as they travel on the underground to yet another museum, on yet another excursion into the unrecognizable city. For a moment they hold in their heads the image of the hotel room; they are overcome with an unspecified longing, a sudden desire to go back, but there is no trace of me in that image. My love, which they may well call sympathy, has no face, no body under the pink and white uniform. So when they leave the tip it is not for me but for the room, for its silent continuance in the world, for its constancy amid the inexplicable inconstancy. The two coins left on the pillow preserve the illusion that such rooms exist even when nobody looks at them. The two coins dispel our only essential fear—that the world exists only in the act of seeing and there is nothing beyond this. And so I sit and smell the coolness and emptiness of this room, full of respect for the Japanese couple known to me only from the immaterial shape of the footprints left in the abandoned sandals.

I must now take my leave of this small temple. I do it quietly, as if sighing, and go downstairs on to the landing since by now it is

Time for tea

The white and pink princesses of other floors are already sitting on the stairs, biting into their buttered toast and drinking tea. Next to me Maria who has the looks of a native American, a little further Angelo of the Soiled Linen and Pedro of the Clean, probably as he is so serious. He has a pepper-and-salt beard and thick black hair. He could be a missionary, or a monk who has just paused for a moment on his spiritual journey. He is reading *Lord of the Flies*; some words he underlines with a pencil, the others he sips with his coffee.

'Pedro, what is your native tongue?' I ask.

He lifts his head from the book, hums and haws as if woken from a dream. It is apparent that he is translating my question in his head into that tongue of his. You can tell from his temporary absence. He must have time to retreat into himself, look around, name this rhythm of his, define it in a word, translate it and finally say:

'It is Castellano.'

Suddenly I feel intimidated.

'So where is this Castile?' asks Ana, an Italian girl.

'Castile—Bastille,' pronounces Wesna, a beautiful Yugoslav girl, philosophically.

Pedro draws a shape with a pencil and, tripping over his words, reaches back to the times of old, when—for some reason—people were criss-crossing the huge land masses which today we call Europe and Asia. During their wanderings they mixed and settled and then moved on again, carrying their languages like banners. They formed great families, although they did not know each other; only the words were permanent. We light cigarettes while Pedro draws graphs, proves similarities, pulls out the roots from words as if stoning cherries. For those who understand this lecture, it slowly becomes apparent that all of us sitting on these stairs, drinking coffee and eating toast, spoke the same language long ago. Well, perhaps not everybody. I do not dare to ask about my own language; also Myrra, who comes from Nigeria, pretends not to understand. When Pedro stretches a dark, swirling cloud above our heads, we are all trying to squeeze underneath.

'It is like the Tower of Babel,' Angelo sums up.

'You could say that,' the Castilan Pedro nods, sadly.

But here is Malgosia. She rushes in late as usual. She is always short of time, always lagging behind. Malgosia is one of my own; she speaks the same language, so her fresh blushing face appears to me joyfully close. I pour her tea and butter her toast.

'*Czesć,*' she rustles, and this becomes a signal for the conversation to split into all the possible languages.

And from this moment on, all the white and pink ladies hum in their own tongues; words rattle like wooden building blocks, rolling down the stairs to the kitchen, laundry, linen storerooms. You can hear the foundations of the Capital vibrating in sympathy.

Unfortunately, the break is over and we have to go back to our respective floors where the remaining rooms are awaiting us. We scatter, still chattering, but soon the long corridors impose their silence on us. And so it will remain. Silence—the virtue of chambermaids in all the hotels of the world.

Room 226 looks as if it has only just been occupied. Luggage still unpacked, newspaper untouched. The man (judging by the men's cosmetics in the bathroom) is probably an Arab (Arabic labels on the suitcase, an Arabic book). And almost instantly, a thought: what is it to me where this next guest in the hotel comes from and what he's doing here? I encounter only his belongings. A person is merely the reason why these things have found their way here, just a figure which relocates them in space and time. In fact, we are all transitory inhabitants of things as trivial as clothes and as big as the Capital. This Arab and the Japanese, myself and even Miss Lang. Nothing has changed since the times referred to by Pedro. Hotels and luggage might look different, but the journey is the same.

There is not much to do in the room. The guest must have arrived at night, he didn't even go to bed. He's probably gone out on business and will unpack on his return. Or he'll continue on his journey, allowing himself to be carried along by the itinerary on which his belongings take him. In the bathroom I observe with satisfaction that he hasn't washed and that instead of toilet paper he used face tissues.

He must have been nervous—or careless, which comes to the same thing. He must have suddenly felt out of place when the taxi brought him from the airport at night. In such circumstances, a sudden surge of desire assails one. Nothing tames the world as surely as sex. Perhaps he slipped out in search of women's or men's bodies, those fragile vessels which are capable of taking one painlessly through any anxiety, any fear.

Room 227 is exactly the same as 226. The same single room. But here the guest has been staying for longer. I would not be aware of this if it wasn't for the familiar smell of cigarettes, alcohol and disorder. The mess horrifies me. Half-empty glasses everywhere, cigarette ash, spilt juice, the waste paper bin overflowing with vodka, tonic, cognac bottles. The smell of a vicious circle, of hopelessness. I open the window, I switch on the air conditioning but this only deepens the atmosphere of a no-hope situation, sharpens the contrast between the fresh and healthy and the stuffy and sickly. This fellow (dozens of ties thrown over the wardrobe door) is different from the rest of the guests. Not only because he drinks and makes a mess, but because he forgets himself. He does not respect the limits of what it is permissible to communicate through one's belongings. He has no care for appearances. He pours all his inner disorder into the hands of someone like me. I feel like a nurse and, in a way, I like it. I dress the bed wounded by the night's sleeplessness, I wash the scars of the juices spilled over the table top, I draw out the bottles from the room's body as if I were pulling out thorns. Even vacuuming is like cleaning wounds. Carefully, I arrange in the armchair the new and expensive toys, probably bought only yesterday—a cover-up of painful guilt. This fellow must have stood there before the mirror for a long time, trying out different ties or perhaps even suits, but each change filled him with disgust. After which he went to the bathroom—there is an unfinished drink on the side of the washbasin. He was helpless and clumsy, he spilled shampoo on the floor and tried to wipe it up with a towel. I will forgive him this. I rub out the stains, I arrange his cosmetics. I know he is terrified of old age. Here is a wrinkle cream, powder, eau de cologne of the best quality. There is also rouge and an eye pencil. Each morning, terrified by the unfamiliarity of his face, he must stand before the mirror and with trembling hands try to restore to it its familiar looks. He falters, cannot see clearly, draws closer to the mirror, smearing it with his fingers. He pours out the shampoo, swears, attempts to clean it up, and then swears in English, French or German. He is all ready to confront the world as he is, but then he catches sight of himself in the mirror, changes his mind, returns and finishes the job. The make-up fluid covers the lines of disappointment round his lips, and the bags under his eyes which betray his sleeplessness, and the dark spots on his chin which reveal pill taking. A touch of eyeshadow masks the redness of his eyes. In the end he manages to take his leave, and, when he returns, he should find the bathroom free of any sign of his downfall. It is up to me to dispense forgiveness. It even occurs to me to leave him a note with the words: 'I forgive you'. He would accept these words as if they were a message from Providence itself and he would return to where his children are awaiting the soft toys, where his ties are neatly stacked in the wardrobe, where—with a face swollen from drink, a glass in hand—one can go out on to a terrace and bellow to the whole world: 'Fuck it!'.

But it's reality which is Providence and therefore everything that happens is likely to have a reason. I leave the room to its forever provisional occupant.

Olga Tokarczuk

In the corridor I pass Angelo carrying sacks of dirty linen. We smile. I open the door to room number 223 and at a glance I am sure that the people in this room are

Young Americans

None of us relishes the thought of cleaning the rooms in which young Americans lodge. This is not just prejudice. We have nothing against America, we even admire it and long for it although many of us have never set foot in the place. But young Americans who alight at the Capital make a thoughtless, stupid mess in which there is no rhyme or reason. It is a chaotic kind of untidiness and dealing with it gives you no satisfaction. In fact you can't ever get rid of it; even after you have arranged everything neatly and in order, after you have removed all the stains and traces of mud, after you have smoothed all the bed covers and pillows, after you have let out the whirling smells, this mess will disappear only momentarily, or rather it will hide somewhere underneath and wait there for the return of its owners. It will awake at the very sound of the key turning in the lock and immediately hurl itself into the room.

It is only children who can create such a mess: a half-peeled orange on the bed, bathroom tumblers filled with fruit juice, a tube of toothpaste squashed on the carpet. Scraps of paper arranged like a collection, clothes tags from the best shops, pillows stuffed into the wardrobe, a hotel pencil broken in half, the contents of a suitcase spilled over an armchair, addressed postcards with no greetings on them, the TV on, the curtains flung open, socks and underwear drying on the air conditioning, cigarettes scattered around, ashtrays overflowing with watermelon seeds. The room in which the Americans live is compromised, stripped of all dignity, pseudo-friendly. That it should be this lovely pink and beige room number 223 which is despoiled in this way! It looks like a serious old gentleman dressed up as a clown.

When I enter it, I feel pain. I stand still for a while contemplating the scale of this disaster. The room looks like a minor battlefield. The expensive silk dresses thrown carelessly over the arms of the chair, the scent of luxury perfumes, of money, of physical prowess, of a six-footer—the smell of carelessly ignoring the order which is the integral nature of things. All this frenetic activity, which in its inattentiveness to the present fails to comprehend that contained in it is the germ of the sacred future, frightens me. It is like an assault mounted against room number 223. In this assault, the room stands for something stable, graspable, rooted in the present and unchangeable, and in this assault I take the side of the room.

Slowly and systematically, I set about tidying up, taking care not to touch Private Things. Perhaps they are accustomed to not being in their rightful places.

Time flows in leaps and bounds and I feel more and more anxious. The TV buzzes, CNN hurls news at me from the whole buzzing world, and the world reassures CNN that it exists somewhere and is always full of young Americans. My anxiety is growing, my gestures become more sweeping and exhausting, I begin to rush, keep looking at my watch—I am emerging from the 'here and now' and just beginning to place one foot in the moment 'later'. I swear to myself, 'Shit!'. I sing, Yankee Doodle Went to Town. I leave a damp cloth on the wooden table top. This is serious negligence, as the wood gets stained from the damp. The air of disorder must be catching. I have to escape to the bathroom where I cannot be pursued by all this buzz, and where, after a while, after I've finished picking up the towels, the flannels, the soaps and the containers strewn about the floor, after I've shut the door to the bathroom and concentrated on the details, stillness finally descends.

The bathroom is the bottom line of the room, the underside of life. After having a bath, we leave hair in the bathtub, dirt from our skin settles on its sides. The waste paper basket is full of used tampons, tissues and cotton wool pads. Here is a shaver for the legs, there a little mirror useful for squeezing out blackheads and applying the make-up which serves as a cover-up for all the indecisions. Here is the talcum powder for the feet, the gadget for making an enema, and a cosmetic bag stuffed with contraceptives. The bathroom cannot hide this other side of life. I clean around roughly, as if afraid of destroying these relics of the transitoriness of the people who live here. Perhaps they should be aware of it. Perhaps they did not have a chance to see it on TV, nor read about it in magazines which mix everything together, one thing on top of another like in a hamburger; perhaps they have not learned about it at school, they did not see it in the movies, Armstrong did not find it on the moon. So they have not yet understood that, with every passing moment, we disintegrate. That amidst life, we die. They as much as I.

This thought brings me closer to them, to these rich, energetic Americans, so different from me. They have their unimaginable country, a different rhythm of life, an orange juice for breakfast every day. Two thousand years ago, they would be Romans and I would be an inhabitant of some distant province of the Empire, Gaul perhaps, or Palestine. But both they and I have bodies made of clay, or is it ash, the body which loses hair, which ages and wrinkles, and leaves a deposit of dirt on the smooth sides of the bath. When I put out clean towels and hang up new bathrobes, I have such a strong feeling of the shared insignificance of our existence, that I freeze, motionless, as when I found an old teddy bear worn from care and dressed in babies' clothes in the bed of a rich and important woman, who came here to attend a high-powered scientific conference. Or when the bedding in the suite of some VIP is damp with sweat. It is Fear, this bony chambermaid, which makes their beds. Thank God, it exists, fear. Without it, they would be like the gods of old—strong, confident, proud and stupid. And now, when they lie in their beds, after days filled up with business affairs, money, excursions, shopping, important meetings, and they cannot go to sleep, when they survey some complicated pattern on the wallpaper, their tired eyes begin to spot a flaw, a hole, an irrelevance in that rhythmical pattern. They begin to notice in it some scratch, some discolouring, the kind of dirt which cannot easily be wiped off, washed out. In such moments, carpets go bald like women when they get ill, and the freshness of a muslin curtain reveals a hole burned by a cigarette. The satin of the pillows comes adrift at the seams, rust is creeping on to the door handles and locks. The edges of the furniture become blunted, the tassels of the curtains get tangled. The travelling rug loses its fluffiness and becomes matted. There is a musty smell of dust. I can guess just what those people do then. They get up, shake their heads and have a stiff drink or swallow a sleeping tablet. Lying there with their eyes shut, they count sheep until sleep rescues their threatened thoughts. In the morning, that fleeting moment in the night appears to them unreal and barely distinguishable from a nightmare. Don't we all suffer from them occasionally?

I lean against the bathroom door. The work is finished. I feel like having a cigarette.

Now the choice is between rooms number 228 and 229. I settle on 229, as its Kabbalistic sum of numbers equals

Thirteen

This is a number of excess and trickery, and so is this room. Room 229 possesses special qualities. It entices, makes promises, brings surprises. In itself it seems like any other room—on the right-hand side a bathroom; a short passageway; and then all the rest: the bed covered with a brown counterpane, wallpaper in greyish shades, flowery curtains, a chest of drawers and a mirror. And yet it gives off the impression of being emptier than all the others. I can hear my own breath, I see my hands swollen from the water, the mirror gives back my reflection in a less coincidental fashion. Whenever I walk into this room, I stiffen. Last week there was a couple of lovers here, perhaps a newly married couple. They rumpled the bed, threw around the towels, spilled the shampoo. What was left after them were yellow stains on the sheet and a huge bouquet of flowers, the witness of vows of love I was sorry to have to throw away. It is harder to bring this room into a state of readiness to receive guests as it has its individual face. It receives people with consideration. I suspect that that one night spent here is enough to get them trapped, to bring unquiet dreams, to hold them a little longer, to bring out desires and overturn carefully laid plans. A fortnight ago, the occupants forgot to turn off the taps in the bathroom. The water flooded into the corridor, submerged the fluffy carpets, seeped up into the gilded wallpaper. The guests, terrified, stood there wrapped in blankets, while the staff were running around with torches. 'It's nothing! It's nothing!' Zapata kept repeating as he wrung out the wet cloths, but his face communicated a different message—that something terrible had happened—stupid, thoughtless people had raised their hands against the Hotel Capital.

And it is always in room number 229 that something like this happens.

Olga Tokarczuk

This room is different, that's for sure. I think that the people in Reception know that, and they allow it to stay unoccupied more often than the others. They direct the traffic to the lower-numbered rooms, at the nearer end of the corridor, closer to the lift, the stairs, nearer to the world.

When the room stands empty all I do is to check that everything is in order, that dust has not accumulated on the furniture, that the air conditioning works. I do it particularly carefully. I smooth the counterpane, I run my finger along the top of the wall panelling, I air the room and then I sit for a moment in an armchair and listen to my own slightly agitated breathing. The room encloses me within itself, cradles me. It is a most tender if non-physical caress, this embrace which only an enclosed space can give you. At such moments I feel distinctly that my body exists and is contained fully in the pink and white uniform. I am conscious of the feel of the collar on my neck and the coolness of the zip between my breasts. I feel how tightly the ties of my apron hug my waist. I am aware of my skin, conscious that it's alive and breathing, that it has its own scent, and I can feel my hair where it touches my ears. I like then to get up and look at myself in the mirror which never spares me a surprise. Is this me? Really me? I touch my face, tighten the skin on my cheeks, blink my eyes, pull my hair tighter with a grip. This is how I see myself in dreams—always in the mirror, always a different face.

I stand there and long to immerse myself in the immaculately clean bathtub, then dry myself with all these white towels and afterwards stretch on the brown counterpane and listen quietly to our breathing—my own and the room's, the room's and my own.

But today room 229 is occupied and there is a note on the door handle saying that it is ready for service. I turn my key and go in, pulling my cleaning kit behind me. And I freeze in alarm, since the room is not empty. At the desk a man is sitting bent over his electronic notebook. I regain my voice, apologize and make as if to leave, thinking there must be some mistake, he has put out the wrong sign. He, however, apologizes in turn and invites me in, asking me not to take any notice of him.

It does happen from time to time. I heartily dislike it, though. It means I must hurry and do what I have to do under the gaze of the guest. Now the guest becomes a host and myself a guest. The established order is inverted. My cleaning is no longer omnipotent, it becomes emptied of meaning. The rooms are not meant to contain a cleaner and a guest—we are in each other's way. I must quickly and nimbly make a double bed, which means I have to move it away from the wall. There's not much space to do this. The fellow at his computer is a sufficient obstacle to the efficient carrying out of that task. I already know that I don't like him. He is shockingly alive.

First I take off the sheet and the four pillowcases. I put on the clean undersheet. To smooth it out I have to go round to the other side of the pulled-out bed. I feel the man's eyes on me. I do not dare look at him in case I meet his gaze. I would have to smile, he might ask me something, I would have to answer. I try to be quiet, not to make a rustling noise. Now I put on the top sheet. I have to squeeze between the furniture to tuck in the edges. When I pass the man's outstretched legs, I tense up in order not to touch them accidentally and I start to hurry and rush what I am doing. The fellow looks at me quite openly now. I can feel it. His outstretched legs are a provocation, they're in my way and make me shy. The hurry and agitation make me hot. My tensed-up calf muscles hurt when I lift the heavy mattress. I put on the clean pillowcases, but I don't quite succeed and a pillow slips out of my hand and drops on the floor. I stumble over it and lose my balance. I fall straight into his curious gaze.

'Are you Spanish?' he asks.

'Oh no, no.'

'Jewish?'

I deny it.

'So, where are you from?'

I reply, and he looks disappointed. I arrange the pillows and start tackling the counterpane. He follows me with interest as I fight with the heavy bedspread. Again I am close to him, this time with my back to him. As I arrange the pillows I sense his eyes on my calves. I move towards the wall and hide my legs behind the bed. Suddenly, I feel embarrassed about my flat, black shoes and, before I know it, I raise myself on tiptoe. At once I regret having to wear this ugly, unflattering uniform with the apron and a bunch of keys at my waist and not one of those elegant dresses I saw in the Americans' room.

I feel grubby, sweaty, tired. I know that the man at the computer is staring at me quite unashamedly. His gaze touches me somewhere around the collar and the zip, but I am already on the other side of the bed. I should go past him once more in order to lay out the small cushions, but I would have to stand with my back to his voracious gaze, so I simply toss the cushions on to the bed. Crouching down to pick up the dirty linen, the linen of the fellow who is staring at me, I feel that my body is swelling as if wanting to jump out of its uniform. Would I have to excuse myself? And in what tone, what language, why? I back towards the door with my eyes lowered. I collect my cleaning materials and rush to the door.

'Thank you,' I say, knowing that there is nothing I have to thank him for. It is he who should bow courteously and kiss my hand. And I would curtsy or something of the kind.

I see that the fellow nods his head forgivingly and in the very slight smile of his there is something which makes me reach for the door handle with relief.

'See you,' he says, but I don't want to see him ever again.

I am already outside the door.

I stand there for an instant and listen. I feel hot, my legs are hurting, my muscles tremble from exhaustion. I've hurried so much that I have a lot of spare time now. It would be good to go downstairs and cool down.

I leave my bucket next to the wall and go to the third floor, where there is a small passageway to the annex, a twisting side stair and where

The mysterious part of the hotel

for the permanent guests starts. I go down a few steps, pass one or two doors and stop in front of the banister separating a stairwell two or three storeys high. I look down and see only the ground floor from here. And—as usual—not a soul about.

Only the half darkness and the quiet. This is the best relaxation: to look down to where everything becomes progressively smaller and more distant, less clear, more illusory. The annex is really the most mysterious part of the hotel. You have to be very clever not to get lost here. It is all stairs, passages, landings and bends. It is a kind of tower with additions, three storeys high. On each storey there are two rooms, and each room number always begins with a seven. I know that there are eight rooms in all, but I cannot imagine where they squeezed in the two remaining ones. Perhaps they are being occupied by misanthropes or inconvenient wives, dangerous twin brothers, shady women lovers. Perhaps they are rented out by the Mafia for the purpose of illegal transactions, or to heads of state who, in the enclosure of this spiral space, can try to be someone ordinary for a while.

In this part of the hotel, the rooms are different; they are, in fact, apartments. They are in some ways less elegant, or have a different kind of elegance, with their built-in wardrobes, covered balconies, curious furniture and fake books: whole shelves of them: Shakespeare, Dante, Donne, Walter Scott. When you take one of these in your hand, it turns out to be an empty box mimicking a book cover. Libraries of emptiness.

When you go down to the staff toilets you have to be careful not to lose your bearings. It used to happen to me at the beginning. I used to open a familiar door but it did not lead to where I expected. I used to leave my cleaning kit on the stairs and then not be able to find it again. I admired the reproductions of still lives on the wall and then thought that I saw them in a dream. Something strange happens to space here. Space does not like spiral stairs, chimneys and wells. It tends to degenerate into labyrinths. The best way is to hold on to the handrail as I am doing just now. Not to look down or up, but straight ahead.

Suddenly, I catch a sound. Somewhere below me something is going on which sounds suspiciously rhythmical—puff, puff and a squeaking noise. I descend one floor, tense as a cat. A groan, a squeak, a groan, a squeak. What is it? I approach the door which is just like any other door in the hotel. Except that it is a little ajar, and through the crack I can see metal buckles, and I can clearly hear these strange noises and this groaning. Carefully, I put my ear to the door and now the groaning becomes quicker, more violent, and the squeaking more terrifying. I jump away, feeling suddenly hot; the keys attached to my belt clank. On the other side of the door everything stops. Quietly, I run up the stairs to the floor above and look over the railings. There's a click of buckles being released and a man wearing nothing but shorts puts his head out of the door. In his hands he has a gadget made of springs, like a complicated expander. I step back to the wall. It's not easy to calm the imagination, once it is aroused.

I climb down the dark spiral stairs once more to the cellar where the staff toilets are located. Here it's bright owing to the vulgar strip lighting. I reach the toilet and close the door behind me. I splash my face and hands in cold water but this does not bring any relief. I sit down on the toilet seat. Not a sound is to be heard here. It's sterile, calm, secure. With great attention I examine the box of cleaning powder, paper towels, a big roll of the toilet paper and the notices written out in Miss Lang's handwriting which amount to A Short History of Civilizing the Staff.

First Miss Lang wrote: WHY DO YOU THINK DISPOSABLE BAGS HAVE BEEN INSTALLED HERE BY THE HOTEL? and signed it: MISS LANG. But evidently none of the girls was able to answer this question, and hence the notice underneath: WOULD YOU MIND USING PAPER BAGS TO DISPOSE OF SANITARY TOWELS. But this request must also have gone unheeded since below, in red letters, Miss Lang has written categorically: PLEASE DO NOT THROW SANITARY TOWELS AND TAMPONS INTO THE TOILET!

Now I sit on it, contemplating the shape of each letter. Then I pull the chain, adjust my hair and go back to my floor, since I still have to clean the last room.

It's past two o'clock in the afternoon and the hotel is busy. The official lift goes up and down, there is a clanking of doors being opened and shut. Guests are going out into town, their stomachs demanding lunch. Angelo of the Soiled Linen has settled in his little service room and is packing linen into big sacks.

'How many left to do yet?' he asks.

'Just one,' I reply and once again, I become aware that Angelo's proper place is not in a hotel, not even a hotel as elegant as this one, but in 'The Song of Songs'. That is where he might be wandering, leaping from mountain to mountain like a young deer. Because Angelo is as beautiful and imposing as the mountains in his native Lebanon.

He nods his head, indicating an elderly couple leaving room 228. I saw them once before on the way to the lift. He is tall, with a slight stoop, but in much better shape than she is. Perhaps he is younger, or perhaps he is just cheating time. She is small, wrinkled, trembling, barely able to walk.

'They are Swedish. She has come here to die,' says Angelo knowingly.

Angelo may be joking, but when I look at them as they go past, I see that this old man is more than supporting her, he is practically carrying her. If he stepped aside, she would fall on the floor like a discarded garment. They always wear beige and faun, the colours of the hotel. They are both grey, with the kind of greyness which has long left all sins behind.

When they've disappeared into the lift, I go into their room. I like doing this room. There is not much to do here; things are all in their places as if rooted to the ground. The air is not reverberating with bad dreams, groans, excitement. The pillows, barely showing any indentation, testify to a good sleep. In the bathroom towels are tidily hung, toothbrushes neatly arranged, the shine of the tumblers is reflected in the mirror. Cosmetics are basic—an ordinary cream, mouthwash, discreet perfumes and eau de cologne. When I make the bed I am struck by the absence of any tangible smell. It's like it is with children. Children's skin does not have any smell by itself, it only captures and retains outside smells: the air, the wind, the grass crushed by an elbow and the wonderful, salty smell of the sun. This is what this bedding smells of. When one sleeps with no sin, no long-term ambitions, no angst and no despair, when the skin becomes thinner and thinner, paper-like, when life is escaping slowly from the body like air from a rubber toy, when one sees one's past as something completed and closed up, when in the night one begins to dream about God, then the body ceases to mark its presence in the world with a smell. The skin receives smells from outside and savours them for the last time.

On the bedside table two books are resting next to each other. I listen for sounds from the corridor and then do something which I am not supposed to do. I open the first of the books, a thick one which might be a diary since each page is marked with a date and below it trembling rounded letters in a language totally unfamiliar to me. The book is almost finished, there are only a few pages left to the end. The other book is the Bible, in Swedish. I cannot understand anything and yet all seems so familiar. A red bookmark marks the Book of Ecclesiastes. I run my eye along the page and I have the impression that I am beginning to understand it. First individual words and then whole phrases float out of memory and mix with the print. *'That which hath been is now; and that which is to be hath already been; and God requires that which is past.'*

The most mysterious words of the Holy Book.

When the cleaning is done I sit for a moment on the freshly made-up bed. It is very pleasant to suspend one's existence in such a way. Then I look at my hands, roughened by the bath-cleaning fluids, at my already swollen feet in their black slippers. But my body is alive and fills the skin to the brim. I sniff the sleeve of my uniform—it smells of tiredness, sweat, life.

With deliberation I leave some of this smell in room 228.

I close the door and go to the service room. I put away the vacuum cleaner and the cleaning kit and divest myself of the pink and white uniform. For a moment I stand there naked, without qualities. For the Transformation to take place in reverse order, I must put on my earrings, a colourful dress, ruffle my hair and put on make-up.

As I walk out into the sunlit street I pass the Scotsman who is changing in the doorway. The kilt is resting on the bagpipes while he buttons up a pair of fashionable jeans.

'I knew you were only pretending,' I call to him.

He smiles mysteriously and winks at me. ☐

GRANTA

KILTYKINS
Ved Mehta

Ved Mehta, 1970

When I was seeing Kilty (how, even today, the word 'seeing' mesmerizes me), the fact of my blindness was never mentioned, referred to, or alluded to. My recent friends cannot believe that could have been the case—indeed, from my present vantage point, I myself can scarcely believe it, especially since Kilty and I were so intimate in everything else. But in this respect my relationship with Kilty was not unusual; I was equally reticent about the subject with practically everyone else. The silence must have been a testament to the force of my will.

I now understand that, at the time, I was in the grip of the fantasy that I could see. The fantasy was unconscious and had such a hold on me, was so intense and had so many ramifications, that my girlfriend's indulgence in it was the necessary condition of my loving her. Indeed, if I got interested in a woman and she interfered by hint or gesture with it, I would avoid her, feeling sad and frustrated. Yet there was hardly a day that I did not feel defeated, patronized and humiliated—when I did not wish to be spared the incessant indignities that assaulted me. To give a fairly innocuous example, I still come across a man I have known since my university days, several days a week, in a club to which we both belong, and every time I see him he tells me his name. I have gently told him many times that I recognize him by his voice, but to no effect. Although this man is a historian of international stature, he seems to lack the sensitivity to realize that a voice, in its way, is as distinctive as a face. Could it be that the fantasies that sighted people have about the blind are based less on reality than those that blind people have about the sighted?

I needed to be accepted on my own terms by Kilty and anyone else I was close to—it was easier for me to conduct myself as if I could see. So the fantasy was not wholly irrational. In order for me to live as if I could see, it had to remain largely unconscious. I had to function as if I were on automatic pilot. Talking about the fantasy, analysing it, bringing it out into the open would have impeded my functioning. Or, at least, that was my unconscious fear. I went overboard. I allowed the fantasy to pervade every part of my life: the way I dressed myself, wrote books and articles, collected furniture and paintings. But even when I was most under the influence of my fantasy, I maintained the habit of checking external reality. I never walked off a cliff, for instance. Without such continual verification, I could not have survived in the sighted world.

Over the years, I have often asked myself, How was it that my girlfriends all played along without once slipping up? Was my fantasy contagious? Did I seek these women out because they were susceptible to my reality and, in their own way, could take leave of that reality and mould themselves to mine? Anyway, isn't that the sort of thing that all people do when they are in love—uniting, as it were, to become, as Genesis has it, 'one flesh'? Yet I wonder if, in my case, their accommodation prevented them from really getting to know me and me from really getting to know them, thereby condemning me to devastating isolation. But then, the fault was mine. I no doubt impressed them with my mastery of my surroundings. I did not feel limited in any way, and I think I must have felt that from the moment I became blind, two months short of my fourth birthday, as a result of an attack of cerebrospinal meningitis. When I was twenty-three, I published a youthful autobiography, which dealt with my illness and my blindness, but by the time I met Kilty eleven years later I had all but disowned the book as juvenilia, so I never mentioned it to her.

When I bounced back from my bout of meningitis, which lasted some two months, I probably forgot in my conscious mind what it had been like to see. Unconsciously, I assumed that I could do everything that anyone else could do—indeed, I was scarcely aware of any change, for I was incapable of distinguishing between sight and the absence of sight. Keats says that in 'darkness there is light,' but the entire experience of darkness and light became, in a sense, meaningless to me. As a four-year-old child, I imagined that my world was everybody's world. If I had been older, I might have experienced my blindness differently—hesitating, perhaps, to put one foot in front of the other, moving about with outstretched hands, or clinging to the end of my mother's sari. Had that been the case, I would have experienced blindness as frightening, tragic, debilitating. As it was, I laughed and played, jumped around, ran about, hopped and skipped, climbed up and fell down—much as I had done when I could see.

This happened in Lahore, in then undivided India. At the time, my four sisters and one brother were all younger than twelve, and, like children anywhere, they made no concessions for me. My westernized father, a born optimist, did not curtail his aspirations for me. Instead of equating me with the blind beggars outside the gate, he took inspiration from what Milton had attained and wished the best for me. Only my mother, a religious woman with very little schooling, was unable to extend herself to my new condition. Believing that blindness, like poverty, was a curse for misdeeds done in a previous incarnation, she would search my face for some sign of my bad deed and, finding it innocent, was sure that my blindness was merely a passing curse of the evil eye. No matter how much or how often my father, a medical doctor, explained to her that the long, raging fever had damaged my optic nerves and that I would be permanently blind, she insisted that my condition was temporary. She carted me around to healers and astrologers who prescribed Ayurvedic or Unani treatments, along with a variety of penances. She tried all of them. That was her form of denial, and it must have reinforced my own denial—my habit of living as if I could see. Within seconds of meeting a woman, I was able to surmise what they looked like—even the shade of their lipstick. But what they were not to know was that I had reached that level of mastery only after years upon years of using alchemy to transform my ears into my eyes—of developing, in Keats's words, 'blindness keen'.

At that time, in India, the blind were considered uneducable, and there were years at a time when I was not sent to school. Eventually I went to a school for the blind in Arkansas and then to college in Southern California and then to Oxford and Harvard. I became a writer. Paradoxically, in order to live in the world, I had to live as if I could see, and yet that very way of living was a hurdle to acceptance by others, especially by any woman I loved, for, as long as I continued to hide from myself, how could I expect her to truly know and love me? Still, I met women and fell in love with them. One such case was Kilty.

It was November 1968 when, as if to soften the edge of a miserable wintry day, a shy young woman whom I had encountered at parties around town walked into my office at the *New Yorker* magazine. When I was first introduced to her I'd remarked on her unusual first name and she had told me that actually it was Katherine, but then when she was being brought home from the hospital her mother had proposed several nicknames, including Kathy, Katrina and Kat, but her father had said that the baby looked too uncommon for any of them, and had come up on the spot with 'Kilty.' It had stuck.

'I see you're busy,' she now said, backing out of my office and starting quickly down the hall.

I dashed after her and caught up with her near the elevator.

'Don't go away, Kilty.'

'I don't want to disturb you,' she said.

'You are not disturbing me—you're brightening my day.' I was surprised at my words, but her shyness encouraged me.

Kilty laughed in a girlish, high-pitched way, and her laughter rippled along the corridors. As we walked back to my office she would, now and again, fall behind or step ahead, to make way for curious colleagues, who had come out of their offices to look at the source of the laughter.

Sitting down and facing me across my desk, she said, 'I think you know my father from the Century.'

Every now and then, I had indeed encountered her father, Timothy Chaste, at the Century, a men's club for writers, artists and amateurs of the arts, situated on West 43rd Street.

'I am a fan of yours, and I wonder if I could trouble you to read my poems,' Kilty said, and pushed a folder across the desk. She had a little girl's voice.

'I'd love to read your poems,' I said, and asked where I should return them to her. I seemed to remember she lived somewhere outside the city. She said she used to live in Pleasantville, but her parents had recently bought a co-op apartment, with a big mortgage, on Fifth Avenue. Last spring, when she graduated from college, she had moved in with them. She added quickly, 'Maybe instead of your just sending your comments by mail we could have coffee somewhere near here and talk about my poems.'

We agreed to meet at Schrafft's the next day, and I walked with her to the elevator.

Kilty's poems turned out to be all about love and were rather elegaic. The voice was that of a confused college girl. The verses seemed formless and incomplete. Still, when we met for coffee, I had no trouble saying encouraging things about them.

'Thank you—you can't imagine how much your opinion means to me,' she said. Her little girl's voice, though shy, sounded to me like the jingling of bangles on a beckoning hand.

'Gosh, I wouldn't have thought my opinion would be so important to you,' I said, and then, realizing that I seemed to be inviting compliments, I looked away.

'I think of you more than you know,' she replied.

Christmas was approaching. Kilty persuaded me to install a Christmas tree in my apartment—I had never had one before—and came round one evening to decorate it. She arrived with a sewing basket containing, among other things, pipe cleaners and colourful scraps of fabric and pieces of felt. While we sat and talked, she started stitching together some birds. Her sitting on my Italian-silk sofa and bending over the sewing in her lap—even as my mother, my sisters and my aunts had done, knitting, stitching and embroidering at home—gave the room a family touch.

When she had an assemblage of colourful birds, she showed me how to bend their little pipe-cleaner legs around the branches of the tree and we worked rapidly until much of the front of the tree was alive with the small, auspicious things. Now and again, by design as much as by accident, I touched Kilty's hand: it was long, shapely and competent.

On Christmas Eve she invited me to dinner with her parents and her younger sister, Bronwyn, at their apartment. Mr Chaste seated me between Kilty and himself and talked to me as a friend, while his wife went through all the correct motions of a cordial hostess and treated me as one of the family. Nevertheless, the evening seemed a little stiff and forced, especially because Kilty acted as if I were her parents' guest, conspicuously avoiding speaking to me. Yet the more she ignored me the more I felt drawn to her.

Early in the New Year we had dinner with two friends at a German restaurant. When I walked her home, she seemed excited, almost hyper.

As we approached her building, I cautiously put my arm around her, and fully expected her to disengage herself gently. Instead, she turned her face toward me and rested her head on my shoulder.

I found myself kissing her. We circled the block, kissed again, crossed over to the park side of Fifth Avenue, kissed again and yet again.

In the morning, just as I walked into my office and was wondering about the appropriate time to call Kilty, the telephone rang.

'It's me,' Kilty said. Perhaps because of her little girl's voice, the greeting sounded very intimate. 'Beware,' I told myself. 'Go slow. It takes you forever to recover from a love affair.'

'Last night was wonderful,' I said, not quite certain whether I was saying the right thing.

'What are you doing tonight?' she asked.

That's a question that I should have asked, I thought.

'I'm taking you out to dinner,' I said quickly.

In speaking to her, I seemed to veer from caution to boldness, from one extreme to the other.

'Same German restaurant?' she asked.

'I thought you might like a change.'

'This little mouse is a homebody. She likes the same nibbles again and again.'

I found the way she talked in her little girl's voice about nibbles both exciting and threatening. I was reminded of my mother, who had a girlish side, and who, like a child, was by turns sweet and arbitrary. I recalled how the atmosphere of the household would change from rational discourse to arbitrary fiat whenever my father went away and we were left under my mother's thumb. One moment she'd be very cuddly when all I wanted to do was go outside and play, and the next moment she would start shouting at me for no reason I could imagine.

When Kilty and I went out to dinner that night, we happened to get the same table and the same waiter that we'd had the night before.

'The same as before,' she said. 'This little mouse—'

'I know. The mouse doesn't like change.'

'Yes!'

We both laughed.

Over dinner, Kilty told me that at boarding school and at college in Toronto she had painted posters and watercolours and sold them to fellow students in order to help pay for her education. When she came to New York, she felt that she had no practical skills for getting an ordinary job, so for the first month or two after graduation she had tried out painting as a career, and had made the rounds of galleries in SoHo and Greenwich Village. Although the gallery owners were very taken with her paintings, she didn't sell any. Her father then suggested that she try modelling—she was stunning, with a delicate face and deep blue eyes set off by long jet-black hair—and that was what she was doing now.

Modelling: what an odd suggestion for a father to make, I thought, and I asked her if she liked being a model.

'No, I don't—it's horrible. Many of the models I have to hang around with at the agencies have never set foot in a college, and they shamelessly offer themselves to slimy hustlers just to get one measly little job. Outright prostitution would be more honest than modelling.'

'Doesn't your mother object to your modelling?' I asked.

'What's wrong with people admiring a beautiful body? It makes me happy that God has given me good looks to share.'

I was taken aback by her abrupt change of stance. I quickly turned to another subject, and asked her whether she had ever thought of going to graduate school.

'After you've lived and worked in New York City as an adult, it's hard to go back to campus living,' she said.

'I suppose anything would be better than the dreary life of a graduate student,' I said, trying to be agreeable.

'How can you say that?' she asked sharply. 'I thought that, as an Oxford man, you had the highest regard for academic life. As it happens, I've been seriously considering going on to Yale for a PhD. I love studying. I could even become fond of New Haven.'

Glossing over her contradictions, I told her about my experience as a graduate student—how I had loved Oxford but found Harvard cold and uncaring.

'What was Oxford like?' Kilty asked eagerly. 'Bronwyn talks about going there when she finishes college.'

There was so much to say about Oxford that I could think of

no one concrete thing. I finally said, 'I had my happiest years there.'

'What were your friends there like?'

I told her about Dom Moraes, a vivid poet friend of mine, and, on an impulse, described the funny way we'd sometimes talked, inserting 'tiny' before certain words and attaching 'kins' to others.

She suddenly became excited. 'You mean I might say to Dom, "I'm having a tiny dinner with Vedkins"?'.

'That's about right. And sometimes, if we were especially silly, we would call each other "ducks". I think that was a take-off on "duckie", which is what English shop assistants used to call us.'

'How wonderful! Can we talk like that to each other?'

'You don't scorn such talk as precious and adolescent?'

'I'd love calling my tiny boyfriend Vedkins.'

Gosh, what have I let myself in for? I thought. That stuff had sounded pretty silly even at Oxford when we were undergraduates.

'I don't think that kind of fatuous Oxford talk would go over in America,' I said.

'Why do you always think in big categories, like women and America? The "tiny" stuff will be our private talk, just between you and me. You know, I still call Bronwyn "Roo", and she calls me "Piggy-winks". And sometimes when we really don't want anyone to know what we're saying, we talk pig Latin, lickety-split. So you see that we Americans have silly talk, too.'

'What are you thinking?' Kilty said a moment later.

'I was just wondering if you minded that I wasn't an American.'

'You are such a wondrous bird. Don't you know that we Americans are all originally immigrants?'

'So you don't mind?'

'I find you very exotic—like baklava!'

On the street corner, I hesitated between turning south and taking her to her parents' apartment and turning north and inviting her to my apartment. Kilty instinctively turned north, and I fell in step.

Once we were inside my apartment, she sat down on the sofa. I sat down next to her, and we embraced.

Later, as I switched off the lamp on the bedside table, I remembered an episode with Gigi, my first serious girlfriend, when I had suddenly become impotent. I started shivering.

'Why are you shivering so?'

'It's no good!' I cried, pulling away from her. 'I'm good for nothing.'

'Shhh.'

'You should have nothing to do with me,' I cried into the pillow.

'Shhh.'

'I can't stop shivering. It's all over.' I was getting maudlin. 'You don't know awful things about me,' I said. 'I'm not a man.'

I expected Kilty to say, as Gigi had done, that I shouldn't worry, that it didn't matter—I wanted her to console me—but she did nothing of the kind. Instead, she said, 'First-time jitters.' She threw herself on me and wrapped herself around me, biting and licking me. I remember thinking that she was as voluptuous as a Zola heroine.

I revived in a rush. She was initiating me into making love with my whole body. My relief, however, was momentary. Her wild passion stirred a new fear in me, different from the earlier, paralysing one but equally intense—that she would be demanding and uncontrollable. I never stopped to think whether she was actually wild or I simply perceived her that way, because I was still ignorant of the true scope of a woman's passion and needs. Even as I was delighting in her unrestrained lovemaking, I worried that I might not measure up to her expectations, and so a more desirable man would materialize and tear her away from me.

'You're scowling. What's the matter?' she asked.

'Nothing. Just for a moment, I had a bad thought.'

'What was it?'

'I was remembering some losses.'

'You are my strange, tiny Vedkins. My very own tiny Vedkins.'

I take things too seriously, I thought. I must learn to enjoy things. She's being playful. That's part of lovemaking.

I fell asleep with my cheek resting on her shoulder.

W here shall I put the question?' I asked myself. The apartment? There's no romance in that. In a restaurant? That's a public place. On the Top of the Sixes, with a stunning view of the city I love? That's touristy. On a boat on the Circle Line? That's certainly romantic, but also public and a bit tacky. Take her away to an inn somewhere in the Catskills? That's sort of middle-aged—OK for divorcées and widowers but not right for young love. Walking along the Brooklyn Bridge? That's all right for spring, but not for the winter. Still, I didn't want to let another day go by. We'd been together now for only a few weeks, but I was deeply and irrevocably in love. Trying to learn from what I thought of as mistakes with other women, I was determined not to be tardy and casual. I felt that I had to take control and act quickly.

When I was in high school, I had fallen under the spell of J. D. Salinger and his toy epic, *The Catcher in the Rye*, and had been mesmerized by Holden Caulfield's ingenuous question to a New York taxi driver: 'You know those ducks in that lagoon right near Central Park South? That little lake? By any chance, do you happen to know where they go, the ducks, when it gets all frozen over?' In my adolescence, I had identified with those migrating ducks.

I decided that as soon as Kilty and I got together that evening, I would coax her to take a walk with me in Central Park and steer her to the duck pond. We had generally been meeting for dinner at my apartment after she finished her day of modelling—or, what was more likely, looking for modelling jobs. But that day she was held up during some modelling session and didn't get to my apartment until about nine-thirty, by which time it was dark and not safe to be out in the Park. It was also fiercely cold. I had to put off my proposal until the next day, and I thought that that was just as well, because it happened to be Saturday and I could take her to the Park in the afternoon, when the sun might be out.

After we'd had a potluck—since I was incompetent in the kitchen, she always did the preparing—she slumped down on the bed, uncharacteristically neglecting to wash the dishes, and said, 'I hate my body. I hate men gawking at me. It makes me shy all over. When I'm posing for the camera, I always squirm and fidget, and then they have me start all over again. That just makes the sessions longer and more agonizing.'

'You are tired, sweet—just close your eyes and rest,' I said, lying down next to her and reaching for her.

'Leave me alone,' she said, and she turned to the wall and began crying into the pillow. 'I hate you,' she sobbed.

'You can't mean that,' I said, trying to get close to her.

She edged away from me, toward the wall.

'Has something happened?' I asked weakly.

'You should know.'

'Kiltykins,' I said, 'what has happened to my tiny girlfriend?'

'Don't you dare call me that.'

She had never spoken to me that way before, and she seemed so remote that I myself started crying.

'Please turn to me, please look at me,' I pleaded, but she kept her face averted and pressed into the pillow. I ventured to stroke her back, but she didn't respond.

'I hate being a kept woman. Why haven't you asked me to marry you?' she demanded, her voice muffled by the pillow.

'Oh, no! Is that what's rankling you? This very evening, I was going to ask you to ma-ma-marry.' I still couldn't say the word without stammering, so the sentence remained unfinished. I was now almost thirty-five. The long years of wanting to be married hadn't helped me overcome the feeling that I could never be married.

'You were really going to ask me?' Suddenly warm and tender, she wiped my tears away with the end of the bed sheet and snuggled up next to me, as abruptly as she had earlier turned her back on me. 'I feel like a bad girl. Will you forgive your tiny Kiltykins? Sometimes demons take hold of me. I don't know where they come from, but they come and go like dog days.'

'I was going to propose to you this very night, and then we could have tied the knot whenever you wanted.'

'What were you going to say?'

'Some sweet things,' I said, and I told her of my plans.

'Well, let's go there tomorrow, just as you planned—by the duck pond,' she said.

'You don't think I've ruined the surprise?'

'But I haven't given my answer. A lady needs to be properly wooed and given time to think.'

She then threw herself on me passionately.

The next day I took Kilty for lunch at a little Italian restaurant on Madison Avenue, and afterward we walked over, through a cold, sunless afternoon, to the pond. It was windswept and bleak, and there was not a single duck or child in sight.

'Well?' she prompted.

I was flustered. 'Will you marry me?' My words came out in a single breath. I wondered whether I had surrendered to her what should have been entirely my initiative.

'In books, men kneel on one knee.'

I knelt down, and she seemed happy.

'But I'm waiting for your answer,' I said.

'You know so little about me. I gave you my answer when I slept with you.'

'I was hoping for a definitive response, sweet.'

She flung her arms around me and kissed me powerfully, murmuring, 'Yes...yes...yes...yes.'

As Kilty and I were walking back to my apartment, after the formalities at the duck pond, I said to her giddily, 'The moment we get home, I'm going to telephone my parents in New Delhi, and Jasper and Miriam, my friends in Oxford...'

Her hand in mine went rigid.

'Are you all right?'

'Yes,' she said, in a distant voice. Then she said, 'You aren't to breathe a word about marriage to a soul.'

'I won't if you don't want me to—but why not?'

'Don't ask me any questions unless you want me to flip.'

'I won't,' I said accommodatingly.

Her spell—or whatever it was—passed, but the rest of the way home I stepped along in a gingerly fashion, as if my very balance had been shaken. Finally, in the evening, when she was her relaxed, flirtatious self again, I asked her the reason for the secrecy.

'I must speak to Pappy and Mother before anyone else hears about our marriage. You can't have any idea how much persuading it will take to get them to agree. I'll have to find just the right moment, or everything may go kaput.'

'I don't understand,' I said. 'You talk as if your parents regarded me as a pariah.'

'The problem is not with you, sweet. It's with them. You don't know my parents. Mother is so moral, with such strict principles, that she would never give her consent—never accept you into the family if she knew that you'd already slept with me.'

'Why does your mother have to know anything about that?'

'She has her ways of finding out. Ever since I was small, she has been able to look right through me and know whether I'm lying.'

I tried another approach. 'Maybe I could have a word with your father in the club.'

'You don't know Pappy. He's very possessive of me. Only Mother can bring him around.'

'I know he's eccentric,' I said, 'but he has always been friendly to me at the club. I think I can talk to him man-to-man.' I realized as I spoke that I owed such self-confidence to Kilty.

'Please don't even think of talking to Pappy,' she protested. 'If you love me, you will let me handle my parents in my own way.'

'I will, but I need to understand what I'm up against.'

'If you must know, Pappy and Mother want for their daughters blond, blue-eyed, tall, all-American boys, who are good Protestants like themselves. And you are dark, and unconventional in looks and on top of it, an Indian and a Hindu. Another thing against you is that you are a writer. Pappy has had so little success with his drawings that he never wanted us girls to go near anyone who was in the arts. He wants us to marry doctors or lawyers.'

I said to Kilty, 'You've got to lead your own life. It may take your parents some time but they are good people and they will accept anyone you love.'

'I know that. And time is the very thing I want to give them. All I ask of you is patience.'

Patience, I thought. How can I forget how patient she was on our first night together?

So it was that what should have been our joyous news became our miserable secret. When we were together near my apartment, we'd skulk around in case her parents might catch sight of us and she even stopped meeting me anywhere in the vicinity of the club, in case we should run into her father.

At the time Muriel Spark had an office across the corridor from mine at the *New Yorker*, and we became fast friends. Hardly anyone was more fun to be with than Muriel. She dressed like a schoolgirl but had a muscular intelligence, and was full of tart observations and laughter. I was so taken with her and her books that within a few weeks of meeting her I'd read nearly all her novels.

I told Muriel about Kilty, and after that Muriel would always ask me, 'How are you and Kilty getting along, Veders? When am I going to hear some wedding bells?' Not knowing that all the resistance came from Kilty, she used to badger me for holding back.

One evening, she had dinner with Kilty and me in the apartment, and after she had gone Kilty said, 'I found your friend Muriel cold and frightening. I couldn't wait for her to leave. I'm sure she has X-ray eyes and she could see right through me.'

'I don't think she has X-ray eyes at all,' I said. 'Nor is she particularly cold.'

'If you say so,' Kilty said in a resigned tone. Then she picked up and opened Muriel's novel *The Bachelors*, which Muriel had brought as a present. 'Look, she has inscribed it to you: "To my favourite bachelor." What a wonderful inscription.'

'Actually, it's a bloody insult, à la Muriel,' I said. 'She's comparing me to the criminal-protagonist of the novel. As she sees it, I am leading a barren life. She's as acerbic with her pen as she's sweet with her tongue. On second thought, maybe she just wishes me well and is trying to hasten me on toward marriage.'

'So she guessed our secret?'

'It's no secret that we are seeing each other,' I said.

'I'm sure she thinks I'm a witch.' Kilty's voice quavered so eerily that I almost had the illusion that it belonged to someone else.

'I'm sure she thinks no such thing,' I said.

One evening, soon after Muriel Spark's visit, both Kilty and I got off work a little early, and we walked over to a market and bought shrimp, rice, asparagus, onions, thyme and bay leaf. When we got home, laden with our purchases, I put *Don Giovanni*, a favourite opera of ours, on the gramophone while Kilty prepared an East–West combination of shrimp curry and wild rice. As always, it was exciting to have Kilty puttering about in my kitchen and filling the apartment with homey aromas. She deftly cut, mixed and ground—at every stage cleaning up after herself, so that the kitchen was almost as neat as when she started. Perhaps because for most of my life I had been living in a solitary environment, I was disturbed by disorder and so was especially taken with her standards of neatness.

When Kilty finished in the kitchen, we went into the living room, turned the opera down and ate at the dining table. After dinner I poured a little brandy into a couple of crystal snifters and we settled down together on the sofa.

'Coby called today, and I'm going to Philadelphia to see him tomorrow,' she said without any preliminaries. 'I broke up with him last October, just before I went to Paris with Michael.'

I knew about Michael—he was a good friend of mine—but Coby was news. I was stunned.

'You've never mentioned Coby before,' I said.

'You've never mentioned any of your ex-girlfriends to me, either.' Her tone was defiant—one of tit for tat.

Why had I never stopped to think about her earlier involvements, I wondered. Why hadn't I learned something from my experience with Gigi? Why had I simply assumed that I was Kilty's first love, even though every woman I had previously been involved with seemed to bring with her the memory of another lover?

'But there hasn't been a woman in my life for a long time,' I protested.

'I know,' she said, putting her head affectionately on my shoulder. 'Don't be alarmed.'

'But I am, very alarmed. How many beaux have you had?'

'You know about my liaison with Michael, and I had a beau when I was at boarding school, but Coby, whom I started dating in college, was the only serious one.'

'How long were you together?'

'Two, three years, but why is that important?'

'Do you still think about him?'

'I still sometimes wake up from dreaming about him.'

'Do you dream much about me?'

'Do you feel competitive with him?'

'Yes, and desperately jealous.'

'I can't swear that you have no reason not to be.' She cuddled up to me. 'Sweet, don't put me through an inquisition.'

'I must know, Kilty. I can't—' I broke off.

'Before I can be really all yours I must take leave of Coby properly. I will have no peace unless I do.'

'Kilty, I've gone through this business of waiting for a girlfriend to say goodbye to an old boyfriend before,' I said. 'I'm not going through it again.'

She pulled away and half stood up. 'You want me to walk out the door and never come back?' Her voice quavered, as it had after she met Muriel.

Her threat was so unexpected and so at variance with my perception of her character that I wondered in passing whether I knew the woman I had so recently proposed to at all.

'Please don't talk like that,' I said. 'I'll do anything you want. Sit back down. Relax.'

On the gramophone, Leporello was singing '*Madamina, il catalogo è questo*'.

'There is no way I could ever be happy with you—or with anyone else—unless I squared things up with Coby,' she said, sitting down and sounding like a little girl again.

I didn't want to hear anything more about Coby. Images of her kissing him were already disturbing me. I felt as though I needed a Wailing Wall. I told myself that instead of sweeping away thoughts about Coby I should try to learn every last thing about him.

Inwardly, I was crying, but I said, in my most encouraging voice (the one I used for interviewing reluctant subjects), 'Tell me more about Coby. He sounds fascinating.'

'You know the way people refer to Frank Sinatra as "Old Blue Eyes?" Well, everyone at Toronto used to refer to Coby as "Bedroom Eyes".'

The nickname was so unexpected that I flinched.

'What does "Bedroom Eyes" mean?' I demanded. 'It tells me nothing about his eyes. Are they restless, or deep, or penetrating, or seductive? Is his gaze so intense that you feel you are in his power? Are they those X-ray eyes that can see through you, unclothe you?'

'Don't overdo it,' she said. 'I know how you feel.'

'I'd really like to know who my competition is,' I said.

'To begin with, he's not your competition. Besides, you must control your jealous impulses.'

'It's only fair that I should know something about him,' I said. 'What did he major in? What is he doing in Philadelphia?'

'Please, don't. Not so fast.'

'Who is he? How long have you known him?' I knew I was beginning to sound prosecutorial, but I couldn't seem to check myself.

'If you must know, we met at Toronto. We were taking the same class and he started passing notes to me.'

Exchanging billets-doux right under the nose of the unsuspecting professor—how sly and intimate.

'Now Coby's at the University of Pennsylvania Law School,' she said. 'He's the top student there.'

Oh, God! Unlike me, he will have a real profession, I thought. He can give her financial security, while I can only struggle to make ends meet.

'Why do you look so sad?' she asked.

'Is Coby very handsome?' I asked.

'When I first saw him, I ran in the other direction, because he looks like a movie star. But, sweet, don't torture yourself. I've broken up with him, and that's the end of it.'

'But it's not the end of it if you want to go and see him.'

'I want to go and be with him, not for my sake but for his. He can be really violent, and I want to make sure he doesn't do harm to himself.'

'Why couldn't you just talk to him on the telephone?'

'As I told you, I am finished with him, but he's not finished with me. I have to help him get over me.'

'If I were you, I'd make myself scarce—cut off all communication,' I said. 'Otherwise, you'll simply be reminding him of what he's lost, and prolonging his misery.'

'How little you understand about women.'

Understand women! Was I as ignorant about them as she seemed to think I was? And how different from men were they, really?

'It's true. I don't have much knowledge of women,' I said.

'But at college you must have gone on a lot of dates.'

'I didn't,' I said. 'I must know where you will be staying if you go to Philadelphia.'

'In Coby's apartment.'

'Why do you have to stay with him?'

'Why not? I've always stayed with him. If you think Coby would let me stay anywhere else, you're crazy.'

I could contain myself no longer. 'Kilty, I'll go mad if you stay with Coby. It's cruel. It's unbearable.'

I half expected her to get up and head for the door, but she didn't make a move. Instead, she said, in a bantering tone, 'I thought that as a writer you would have a greater range of sympathies—that you'd be tolerant of people who are quirky and do unconventional things.'

'I might like to write about someone who's quirky and does unconventional things, and I might even be drawn to such a person, but it doesn't follow that I would want to live with her.'

'So my Vedkins doesn't want to live with me.'

'Kilty, be serious. You know that's not what I was saying. I just find the idea of your staying with Coby insane.'

'I am disappointed in you.'

'*I* am disappointed in *you*.'

'I'm going.'

Kilty went to Philadelphia on Friday without giving me Coby's number. She asked me merely to wait for her calls, and then she didn't telephone until Saturday afternoon. She explained that she hadn't been able to call earlier, because she couldn't talk privately to me from Coby's apartment.

'Where are you calling from, then?' I asked.

'From a telephone booth.'

I knew that I was being blunt, but I asked her, 'You aren't sleeping with him, are you?'

'What do you think?'

'Of course not.'

'Then why do you ask?'

'Look, Kilty, I'm going crazy. Just swear to me that you're not.'

'I swear.'

'Do you cuddle?'

'What kind of question is that?'

'Kilty, I have to know.'

'He tries, but I tell him I'm spoken for. Don't you trust your Kiltykins?'

'I do, but I grew up hearing my father say, "All men are wolves."'

'Then your father has Coby's number.' She laughed.

'Don't you see why I have these head-splitting images? Can't you just say goodbye to Coby and get on the next train and come back?'

'I gave Coby my word that I would stay with him for three days.'

'Tell him that your fiancé is about to check into the mental hospital—that he needs you.'

'Shhh. I told you that has to be a secret.'

'What? My going into the loony bin?'

'No, silly, the duck pond.'

'Why can't you say "our engagement"? Coby isn't there, is he?'

'I think of it as "duck pond". Do you mind?'

'But why does that have to be a secret from him?'

'Because he's my mother's pet. He still talks to her. Or when he's feeling lonely he calls Bronwyn. They call each other Buddy, and they're very close.'

'I myself need some comforting.'

'Why don't you take Bronwyn out to lunch?'

My anger was mounting.

'I'm sorry I'm putting you through all this, but it's necessary,' she said. 'Do you know why I love you so much? Because you're the strongest man I've ever known. Stronger than Coby, stronger than Pappy. Just let me get through this in my own way.'

'But I don't feel strong. I have these nightmares. I seem to be always shivering.'

'In a little more than two days, I'll be back, dear heart.'

'Where do you sleep?'

'You know that law students are very poor. He just has a studio apartment.'

'How many beds does he have?'

'One.'

'One? So where do you camp out?'

'He has a sofa.'
'Where do you get dressed?'
'In the bathroom.'
'What do you wear when you sleep?'
'A nightie.'
'Does he turn off the lights, or does he see you in your nightie?'
'Of course, he sees me in my nightie. I told you, he lives in a one-room apartment.'
'Is there a lock on the bathroom door?'
'What questions you ask! I don't know. Vedkins, I trust him. He would never do anything stupid. If he did, that would be the end of everything.'
'But I thought everything had already ended.'
'I mean, after something like that we couldn't even be friends.'
'I don't think you can be friends with someone with whom you had a deep involvement. There is too much history.'
'Most of the time, I forget you're not an American, but sometimes you really talk like an Indian.'
'I am an Indian.'
'But you're living in America.'
'Your toilet things.'
'What about them?'
'Do you keep them in a toilet bag or are they spread around the bathroom?'
'I don't have a toilet bag. When have you ever seen me with a toilet bag?'
'I don't want your toothbrush to be touching his toothbrush.'
'What did you say?'
'Dammit, I don't want him to be mucking around with your toilet things.'
'He would never do that. I must go. Coby is calling me.'
'I thought you were telephoning from someplace other than his apartment.'
'I'm calling from a bank, but he's waiting outside the booth.'

When she finally came back from Philadelphia, I asked her, 'Are you over and done with Coby?'

'You talk as if I'd gone to bury him.'

'Kilty, you know what I mean.'

'I don't.' There was a sharpness in her voice that made me wince. 'Do you think you can finish a relationship over a weekend? Is that how you finish your relationships? You should have warned me if that's the kind of person you are.'

'But, Kilty, you told me—'

'I told you that I will be all yours, but only after I have nursed Coby through this terrible black period.'

'You don't mean to say you'll have to go back to Philadelphia?'

'I think I can handle it over the telephone, and take care of things when he comes to New York—or, at least, that's what I think now. But I must be free to do whatever I think is right.'

'Why in hell would he be coming to New York?'

'To see me, Bronwyn and Mother. Besides, he has some family here.'

'Did your mother find him suitable for you?'

'Of course. He is so handsome and presentable.'

'In other words, I'm not.'

'What do you expect? He looks like a movie idol.'

'Then your mother is dumb to prefer him to me. I mean "would be" when she gets to know about us.'

'Now you're getting personal. In America, we are not rude about people's mothers.'

Listening to her, I sometimes felt that she was the reasonable one and I was the unreasonable one. How could I expect Coby to stop loving Kilty, just like that? Would I have Kilty treat Coby with any less kindness than my last girlfriend had treated me? The truth was that I was beginning to discover in myself sympathy for Coby. I told myself, 'You've been behaving like an ogre. Stop persecuting Kilty. Show some understanding for Coby.'

'You must help him to get over you,' I said. 'In his place, I would expect nothing less from my Kilty.'

Summer came and went. Every two or three weeks either Kilty would go to Philadelphia or Coby would turn up unexpectedly in New York. And she so arranged matters—unconsciously, I presumed—that I was never able to meet Coby and judge for myself how much of a threat he really was. On top of all that, she would frequently swear that she was going to talk to her parents about our engagement and would later come up with an excuse for not doing so. Whenever I pushed her on the subject, her voice would harden and her hands would tense up. At first, I didn't know what to do, but eventually I caught on that if I hugged her she would immediately relax, almost as if she had been playing a little game.

One Saturday evening, when I was walking Kilty home after dinner, she was especially warm and forthcoming and I seized the opportunity to bring up something that had been puzzling me about her.

'I sometimes feel that I know two Kiltys. I mean, there is this Kilty I am walking with. But there is also the other Kilty, who, without any warning, can become as stiff as a poker.'

'You're talking about the demon Kilty. I'd like to be free of her, too, but I have no control over her.' There was an undertone of deep distress in her little girl's voice.

'Why don't you have control over those demons?' I asked, gently.

'Because Libbie takes me over.'

'Who is Libbie?' I pressed.

'Libbie was our little sister.'

'I've never heard you mention her before.'

'We never talk about her, because Pappy was watching her on the beach. She was just a little girl when she drowned. Maybe Pappy's attention wandered, or maybe Bronwyn and I distracted him. Please don't ask me for any more details.' She seemed on the verge of tears.

As I was kissing Kilty goodbye just outside her building, she said, 'I'll be leaving for New Haven tomorrow. I've been accepted at Yale.' She was going to study for a PhD in English literature.

I berated her for never telling me about her plans.

'I applied just as a lark. I was sure I wouldn't get in.'

'I can't bear the thought that you'll be in New Haven while I'm in New York. If you want to go to graduate school, why don't you go to Columbia?'

'It's too late to apply anywhere else now, and Yale is giving me money.'

The next day, I took Kilty to Grand Central Station, and hauled her suitcase full of clothes and books from the taxi to the platform.

'It won't be too bad for you, sweet, will it?' she asked.

I felt like yelling, 'What do you think? Why are you doing this to us?' But instead I said, 'No, it won't be too bad. I'll try to come up on weekends.'

'Wouldn't that be very disruptive to your work?'

'It will be OK.'

'It will be expensive—what with taxis, trains, hotels and restaurants.'

'I'll manage,' I said.

'So you'll come up next Friday?'

I hadn't planned on it, but I said yes.

'So we'll be separated for only five days—right?'

'Right.'

'And every night I'll call you and wish you goodnight.'

'Yes, of course.'

'Once I get used to graduate school, maybe I'll be able to come down for weekends and spare you the trouble. And, you know, I don't have to stay at Yale the whole year. Your Kiltykins might be fed up to her gills by December.'

'Since you're going, you should make the best of it,' I told her. Why am I saying things that I don't mean, I wondered. By not being honest about my feelings, I'm playing games with her. But what choice do I have?

'Dealing with my parents will be so much easier once I'm not living under their roof. I could announce our wedding to Mother and Pappy over the phone, and if they didn't agree we could just go down to City Hall in December and get married.'

'Yes, of course.' I felt old and tired.

Within hours of her departure, Kilty sent me a telegram saying that unless I objected she would arrive in New York City the following Friday evening. That made me wonder why she hadn't waited until the end of the day, when we would be talking on the telephone.

Kilty arrived in the city late that Friday. I suggested that the next day we go to Cartier so that I could get her an engagement ring. 'Even if you shouldn't wear the ring, it would be a testament of our promise at the duck pond,' I said.

Kilty agreed with such alacrity that I reproached myself for not having suggested the expedition earlier.

At the jeweller's, the salesman, a vice-president of the company, announced in a manner both deferential and unctuous, 'I have never failed to satisfy a bride with just the right ring.' As he brought out a tray of rings with ornate settings of single diamonds flanked by smaller diamond baguettes, he added, 'Diamonds are forever.'

Kilty shyly slipped one or two of the rings on to her finger but then said firmly, 'I don't like diamonds.'

The salesman was clearly surprised but, turning to me, he said, 'Madam is right. Diamonds are not for everybody.' He turned to Kilty and asked her if she had a favourite stone.

'Gravestone,' she said to me, under her breath in pig Latin, but brightly asked the salesman if he could show her some rubies, and he brought out another tray of rings. Kilty chose a modest platinum ring discreetly set with a blood-red stone, and, putting it on her finger, examined it, back and front.

'I love it,' she said. 'I think I read somewhere that this is a stone of passion.' Taking it off and playing with it, she asked the salesman if there was any danger of the stone's falling off while she was washing the dishes.

Another educated girl might look down on domesticity, but my Kilty thrives on it—goes public with it, I thought. Maybe we really are on our way to being married.

'I can guarantee, Madam, that the ruby is well set and that the ring can undergo a lot of punishment,' the salesman said.

'We'll take it,' I said, without asking the price.

'Spoken like a bridegroom,' the salesman remarked.

I started. The word 'groom' made me think of someone taking care of a horse, rather than a woman, and, in any case, it did not quite fit me.

I made out a cheque for $1,102.40. While the salesman was writing the receipt, with his back to us, Kilty put the engagement ring back on her finger and said, in a whisper, 'This tiny duckie now has a duck-pond souvenir.'

She might go about things in a light-hearted way, but she fully savours them, I thought. Her way is much better than my serious approach.

We were hardly out of the shop when she said, 'My mother's engagement ring is antique.'

'Then would you rather have an antique engagement ring?'

'I think so,' she said. 'But I don't want to part with this one.'

'You can have as many rings as you like,' I said. 'I'll get you an antique one the next time I'm in London.'

Before the end of the day, I wrote a letter to the wife of a friend in London describing Kilty and asking her to be on the lookout for an appropriate antique ring. In due course she wrote back that she had come upon an unusual Georgian item, with a heart-shaped frame of tiny emeralds holding a miniature portrait of a Jane Austen-like lady.

'The ring sounds rather delicate,' I told Kilty. 'It certainly couldn't be worn while washing up. It seems very impractical.'

'It would be nice to have a second ring, however delicate, as an alternative,' she said.

In a way, I didn't like the thought of her having two engagement rings, but I made the necessary arrangements to get the antique ring. She thought it was just right, but wouldn't allow me to get it sized for her until she had spoken to her parents.

One day in early October, Kilty announced on the telephone, without any preliminary, 'I may never be able to do it.'

'Do what, sweet?'

'Marry you.'

For a moment, I imagined that she was in the middle of one of her demon fits.

'You're not being serious,' I said soothingly.

'I am too,' she said petulantly.

As we talked on, it appeared that she had made up her mind to call the whole thing off.

'Is there another man in the picture?'

'Boys are constantly ogling me in the classroom and on the streets. It's very flattering. But you know your Kilty isn't fickle.'

Your Kilty—the words confused me.

'You don't know what you are saying,' I said.

'I need time, lots of time.'

'If you are so unsure, maybe we should stop seeing each other,' I responded, but as soon as my words were out I regretted them.

The last thing that I imagined was that she'd take me up on it, but she said, 'If that's the way you feel, I think we should stop seeing each other, but remember the onus is on you.' She hung up.

I was too proud to call her back, and she didn't call me. A few days went by. All that time, I kept thinking that this was merely a lover's quarrel—a temporary impasse, which we would somehow soon get over. Then I received a letter from her with a protruding object, which turned out to be a pink seashell. Its outside was so crinkly and knotty that it could have been a piece of bark, while the inside was so smooth and fine that it could have been a piece of glass. She might have had any number of reasons for choosing that particular seashell—she liked it, she'd just been to a beach, and so on—but I imagined that she was telling me to take the rough with the smooth. Her letter, however, said that she loved me.

I felt I could now initiate a call to her without injury to my pride.

'Are you very sad?' These were the first words from her on the telephone.

'Overwhelmingly so,' I said.

'I know,' she said. 'I can't help it. I'm very sorry. I'll be a good girl from now on, I promise. But I warn you, sometimes those roaming demons take over your Kilty, and it's as if I had no control over what I say and do.'

One weekend I took a train to New Haven and there, on a glorious day in late fall, we sat under a tree on the campus with students sprawled all around us—eating, talking, or simply basking in the warmth of a brief Indian summer.

'Being in these surroundings reminds me of my failures at Harvard,' I said, and then, thinking that I was being too gloomy, I added, 'I'm told that in Japan people glorify failure, as if success were ignoble.'

'Maybe, after we get married, we should go and live in Japan. I'm ready for something different.'

Her mention of marriage, unprompted, lifted my spirits, and set the tone for the rest of the weekend.

A day or two later, in New York, I received a letter from Kilty. It was written on a sheet torn from a Latin notebook with declensions of the three pronouns ego, nos, and vos on one side and on the other this message:

> Darling, I love you. I miss you. I could only be writing this to you. Do you believe me? The radiator bings. Also a cold draft hits our legs. Our heads are hot. For the class, he has put aside his pipe. The dullest are in the class. He wears a college blazer, consumes our time with impossibly dull genius. Because of him, us are uniformly restless. How can we let him know that he is bound by the social contract to be quiet.

The letter, if a little incoherent, was so evocative of damp New Haven and self-absorbed Yale, that it seemed sheer poetry to me. Another delightful and loving letter followed. I wrote and told her that I could no longer go on living without her, that she had to take her parents into her confidence and stop wavering. She immediately responded with two telegrams, dispatched within a half an hour of each other. Because they were sent to the office over the weekend, I didn't get them until the following Monday. The first telegram read,

SATURDAY NOVEMBER 22 SORRY TO SEND THIS TO THE OFFICE CANT REACH YOU BY PHONE I LOVE YOU AND WANT TO MARRY YOU NOW OR WHEN EVER YOU CHOOSE IF YOU DONT CALL BY MONDAY NIGHT I WILL KNOW THAT YOU HAVE DECIDED NO LOVE KILTY.

And the second telegram went,

DARLING PLEASE TELEPHONE I LOVE YOU AND WANT TO BE WITH YOU FOR ALWAYS KILTY

On the one hand, her telegrams filled me with hope and excitement, but, on the other, they made me weary. Could she really think that my failure to call her within forty-eight hours would indicate that I didn't want to marry her? And why send the telegrams on a weekend to my office rather than to my apartment? Was she just being absent-minded or did she consciously want me to miss her deadline? I should have noticed a kind of danger signal in these telegrams, but as soon as I read them I got her on the telephone. She said that she was determined to get married before Christmas and would be coming down to New York on Friday to make all the necessary arrangements.

Kilty had vacillated so much that I didn't allow myself to take her coming for granted until she actually arrived on Friday November 28. This was such a heady period that for years afterward I remembered each date as if I were marking off days in an Advent calendar. That weekend, she talked about quitting Yale, arranging the wedding, and going on a honeymoon to Merano, in northern Italy; her friend Sophie had been there, and reported that it was an incomparable place. For myself, after all I had lived through, I had trouble thinking beyond the wedding, especially since Kilty had still not broken the news to her parents. I had come to share her dread of approaching her parents, so that I now imagined they had the power to abort our plans.

'You leave Pappy and Mother to me,' she would say stubbornly whenever I brought up the subject. 'They lost Libbie, and they won't want to lose Kilty. But I have to get at them in my own way and in my own time. Actually, I'm sure they have already guessed, and reconciled themselves to everything.'

As luck would have it, I won a free trip to New Delhi in an airline raffle the same Friday that Kilty came down to the city to set our marriage plans in motion. Since coming to the West, I had had such limited funds that I had been able to go home only twice in twenty years. And just then my father, who had heart trouble, was not keeping well. I mentioned the free trip to Kilty and asked her what she thought of it.

Before the words were out of my mouth, I regretted them. Kilty would not hear of my passing up the trip.

'You have to go,' she said. 'It would be easier for me to talk to my parents if my Vedkins wasn't sitting around waiting for an hour-by-hour account.'

Even as Kilty is tackling her parents, I will be giving the good tidings to my family, I thought. For many years, my relatives had been waiting for the news of my marriage. I had now turned thirty-five and, in their eyes, was long past the Hindu stage of a householder—of becoming a family man in my own right. The Hindu life cycle calls for a man to devote his first twenty-five years to learning, his second to raising a family, his third to doing community service, and his fourth to preparing to take leave of worldly cares.

'I'll just go for a week,' I said. 'Two days and two nights will be taken up by flying there and back, but I will have five days at home. That will be plenty.' I remember noticing that she seemed to be relieved that I was going, but I told myself that that was natural, given the pressure of making wedding plans in such a short time.

On Monday December 1, in order to fulfil a requirement for the marriage licence, Kilty and I got our blood drawn by my doctor. The next morning, furnished with the blood-test reports, we rode down in the subway to City Hall and obtained a marriage licence, stamped 'December 2, 1969, 11:53 A.M.' It admonished us, 'The marriage SOLEMNIZATION may NOT be performed within 24 HOURS AFTER THIS DATE.' If the date had been left up to me, we would have returned to City Hall on December 3 and got married. But Kilty wanted a proper wedding, so we settled on December 20—the Saturday before Christmas and almost a year to the day since she had trimmed the Christmas tree in my apartment. She thought that would give her enough time to find a wedding dress and to invite the few guests we wanted. We got in touch with Judge J. Howard Rossbach in Riverdale, a friend of mine, and he agreed to save the date and perform the ceremony.

'The marriage plans are going lickety-split,' Kilty said. 'Now I feel we are going to be married, for real.'

'I feel that, too,' I said.

On Thursday December 4 I flew out, and as I was saying goodbye to Kilty I made her promise three things: she would talk to her parents promptly; regardless of what they said, she would telephone the guests and invite them; and she would keep me informed by cable. Since at my home people routinely opened mail that wasn't addressed to them, we decided that whenever we had something private to say we would sign our cables with the names of our respective close friends, Jasper and Sophie.

Just as I was getting settled in my seat on the plane, the hostess handed me a box containing long-stemmed yellow roses and this little card:

To dearest Ved and Kiltykins—from you know who.

I held the roses in my lap all the way to New Delhi.

The very first day, in the midst of all the family excitement of my coming home, I slipped off to the telegraph office and cabled Kilty:

NEW DELHI 5 12 69 SWEETHEART MY FATHER IS WELL STOP KEEPING UP MY SPIRITS BY THINKING OF YOUR THREE PROMISES STOP CABLE HOW YOU ARE LOVE VED

She cabled back,

NEW HAVEN 12 6 69 VED SOPHIE MISSES JASPER AND LOVES HIM ENORMOUSLY

My second cable to Kilty went,

NEW DELHI 7 12 69 KILTY DEAREST MADE MY DAY TO HAVE NEWS OF YOU STOP DREAMT OF YOU ALL NIGHT LONG STOP FAMILY ARRIVING FROM EVERYWHERE STOP WISH YOU COULD BE HERE STOP LOVE AND KISSES VED

And hers went,

NEW HAVEN 12 8 69 HELLO SEMINAR PRESENTATION WENT WELL STOP MISSED JASPER IMMENSELY PLEASE SEND NEWS LOVE

This was the first time I had heard of any seminar, and there wasn't a word about her parents. I tried to keep a lid on the cauldron of my anxieties, and sent a cable reminding her of her promises and asking her for some concrete news.

Kilty replied,

NEW YORK 12 10 69 VED SOPHIE HEARD UPSETTING STORY ABOUT JASPER FROM A MRS QUINCY HOWE CONCERNING HER DAUGHTER STOP EVEN THOUGH THE INCIDENT WHICH INVOLVED AN INVITATION WAS SEVEN YEARS AGO SOPHIE ASKED ME TO FIND OUT BECAUSE SHE IS SAD ABOUT IT STOP MUCH LOVE

I think the fire went out of me when I intuitively grasped that Kilty hadn't spoken to her parents, and that the ostensible excuse was a seven-year-old incident I could scarcely recall. Had I stood up Tina, the daughter of the newscaster Quincy Howe? Or had I made—God forbid—a pass at her, which she had reported to her mother, and which her mother had remembered for seven long years only to inform Kilty of it now? Did Kilty really want me to believe that she was so fragile that a mere unconfirmed rumour had shattered her? In any event, could she hold something against me that had happened long before she came on the scene, especially when, despite my protestations, she had continued to see Coby even after we were engaged?

I was relieved that I hadn't given an intimation of my pending wedding to anyone at home. In some part of my mind, I must have known that when it came down to it she would welsh on her promises. The fact that I was able to put a rational face on things I ascribe to my knowledge of Kilty and to my history of emotional disappointments. As I was leaving New Delhi, I picked up a blue silk suit that I had ordered on the day I'd landed to be made up for her as one of my wedding gifts: it matched the shade of her eyes. I now intended to give it to her and pretend that I had casually picked it up as a travel present—glossing over the fact that so very recently it had signified my hopes and expectations.

From the airport in New York, I reached her on the phone at her parents' home and we arranged to meet that night at my apartment. Kilty entered with a heavy step and returned my embrace a little self-consciously.

'Is it because of Tina?' I asked.

'Who is she?'

'The daughter of Mrs Quincy Howe, the person you cabled me about.'

'Let's not talk about that, please.' She seemed very edgy.

While outwardly I was calm, inwardly I was fretting about the embarrassment of telling Judge Rossbach at the last minute that the wedding had been put off.

I said, a little offhandedly, to make her relax as much as anything, 'I suppose you were too busy with your seminars and papers and such to do much about the preparations.'

'My Vedkins understands everything.'

One weekend early in January 1970, a couple of weeks after our missed wedding date, I went up to New Haven. Kilty met me at the station, we got into a taxi, and I gave the driver the name of the hotel I had booked myself into. I noticed immediately that she wasn't her usual ebullient self. At first, I thought she was preoccupied with the upcoming semester exams, but when I reached for her hand she jerked it away but then let me take it.

'What's the matter?' I asked.

'A lot.'

'What?'

'Not in the taxi,' she said, her eyes tearing. Then she snuggled next to me. 'How is my Vedkins, my sweetiekins?'

Her changes of mood were always abrupt; in fact, that was one of the things I found most enticing and most terrifying about her. There was something so delicious about kissing and cuddling her that for the rest of the ride we cooed and talked gibberish as if we were young lovers.

In my hotel room, she slumped into the armchair in what I could only call a catatonic state.

'Come and sit here and tell me what's the matter,' I said, patting a place next to me on the couch.

'No.'

'Kilty—'

'I hate you.' She said hurtful things like that sometimes,

especially after we had made love and had been deliriously happy, and later she always apologized, saying that such seemingly angry statements were mere ejaculations, her way of coming down to earth. I had learned to brace myself against them, especially since her demon moods passed quickly. But this time there was a vehemence in her voice that stung me.

It was some time before I could get her to talk at all. And then she said, 'I've missed my period.'

'So?'

'I've always been regular to the minute. I'm warning you that I'm getting an abortion.'

I thought of Coby. 'Oh, Kilty, you haven't been seeing him, have you? You promised. I trusted you.'

'What are you talking about? If I'm pregnant, it's with your baby.'

'Oh, no!' The idea that Kilty could think of getting rid of the baby was so upsetting that I barely knew what I said.

'You mean you wouldn't want it, either?' she said, brightening.

'I don't think I'll survive your having an abortion,' I said. I knew that it sounded like a form of blackmail, but I couldn't help it.

'Let's not talk about unpleasant things, sweetheart. Your bunny is not in the mood. She just wants to snuggle up next to you.'

'But, Kilty, this is very serious.'

'Vedkins is a very serious fellow, but Kiltykins has been put here by God to lighten his spirits.'

Toward the end of the week, I received a typed letter from Kilty addressed to me at my office. I had never received a typed letter from her before, and I was frightened by its portentousness. Moreover, it was so different in tone from her other letters that, although its contents were meant to be reassuring, I was anything but reassured. She wrote:

Tuesday morning

Dear Ved:

Since you left Sunday, I have been trying to think so as to arrive somewhere other than the state of confusion in which I was left.

Sunday and Monday nights have been difficult; it is during the night that my own demons roam most freely. In addition, I have been worrying about you.

I want to get this letter off quickly to you, because I think that whatever you think about its contents, it will make waiting more endurable.

I have decided that if I am pregnant we should marry and have the child. I would like to finish one semester here, and then leave for wherever your next piece of writing would take you.

I think that we would both die slow deaths if either one of us allowed me to destroy something that was made by love. When I think that the something is (if it exists) a human being, that course of action just saddens me beyond expression.

Besides that, how could we delude ourselves into thinking we had a hope for a happy life together if we could not nurture our own creation, but killed it instead? It frightens me to think that either of us could be so impervious to the most basic...oh, I am sick of these words.

This decision being made, I can't imagine what it would be that would stop me from being a good mother.

On Monday I was given back my English test. It had a huge A on it. As soon as I looked at it, tears were sliding down my face. I didn't know what to do with my stupid, stupid A.

Please, for my sake, get sleep and nourishment. It would be a lovely triumph if you could be happy as well.

At the bottom of the paper, she had written 'I love you' and had drawn the usual smiley face. Kilty arrived at practically the same time as the letter and came to my apartment weeping. She told me right off that she had had second thoughts after sending me the typed letter, and that under no circumstances would she now have the baby. Her declaration upset me so much that I told her that if she went ahead with an abortion I would leave her, and, no matter what she said or did, I would never be there for her. She thereupon got so upset that she clung to me, swearing that she would have the baby, come what may. At that moment, she seemed so vulnerable and helpless that I almost regretted my threat, but I felt that I couldn't go back on it—

that it was my only hope of bringing her to her senses and making her do the right thing, as I saw it.

But I was also beginning to realize, if tardily, that whatever she asked for, I would slavishly give to her—that, despite my threat, I would never have the will to leave her.

Kilty called me from New Haven. In the course of the conversation, she casually mentioned that her pregnancy had been confirmed by the medical tests and that she had already made an appointment at the hospital for a 'D and C'.

'That sounds ominous,' I said. 'What is "D and C"?'

She was squeamish about the subject, and it took her some time to explain to me that D and C stood for 'dilation and curettage'— a medical procedure for scraping the uterus, which was legal at the time as abortion was not.

'You mean for terminating your pregnancy?' I said bluntly.

'Yes.'

'But, Kilty, you can't do that. Don't you remember what you said in your typed letter? You'll be killing "our own creation".'

'But I don't love you any more.'

'What?'

'You don't mean anything to me.'

'I'm sure that's not what is in your heart. You are just under tremendous stress. I am taking the next train to New Haven. You are not to do anything until I get there.'

In the hotel in New Haven, Kilty said, 'I don't care what you do, but I'm having this thing out.' She sounded broken up.

'You mean you are not ready for a baby?'

'I'm not ready for your baby.'

'You don't feel anything for the baby?'

'Zilch.'

'How would you feel about seeing a psychoanalyst?

'I'd like to, but I don't have any money.'

'I'll pay for it, but I myself don't have any experience of psychiatry.'

'I do, but I don't know any doctor in New Haven.' She told me that she and her sister had off and on seen a psychoanalyst named Dr Aldridge in Scarsdale since they were fourteen.

I suddenly felt disenchanted with her in a way that I had never felt before. I was so ignorant about psychoanalysts that I thought the people who went to them were either pathetic lunatics or rich wastrels. My way of getting through life was with the British stiff upper lip, and I couldn't imagine myself being involved with a woman who didn't take the same approach. Still, living in New York City in the Sixties, I knew many people who went to such doctors and all of them were evangelists for the Freudian method, each of them talking as if his or her doctor were the best. It was always 'everyone needs a shrink to grow up', and 'my doctor says' this or 'my doctor says' that. They seemed to subscribe to one view of the world, one model of the mind, one way of doing things—something that was intellectually and emotionally repugnant to me. Yet I was now suggesting that Kilty see a psychoanalyst.

'Why don't we call up Dr Aldridge?' I said.

'Going back and forth from New Haven to Scarsdale would take up a lot of time in travelling. You know, Dr Aldridge only sees patients on weekdays. And, besides, I don't know if he has any time free—he's very much sought after.'

'Then we have to try to find a good doctor for you in New Haven.'

'I need time to clear my head—I'm going for a walk.' And before I knew it she was gone.

I scurried after her, but she said over her shoulder, 'Please leave me alone.'

I went back into the room and dropped down into the armchair. When Kilty was with me, whatever the provocation, I held back my tears. I seemed unable to cry in front of her. But now I cried like a child.

I generally came out of depression by exerting myself to do something active. Remembering that I had a mission—to find a New Haven doctor for Kilty—I picked up the telephone and called my editor at the *New Yorker*, William Shawn.

'I need to see a doctor, badly,' I said. I covered the mouthpiece with my hand so that he wouldn't know I was sobbing.

'Have you had an accident? Where are you?' he said, apparently sensing that I was crying.

'I am falling apart. It has to do with Kilty.'

Mr Shawn gulped audibly. He had met Kilty with me, and had more than an inkling of my romantic predicament.

'Do you know a good psychoanalyst—one in New Haven?' I asked him.

Within an hour or two, he had found us Dr Shortt.

W e made an appointment with Dr Shortt for the next day. He turned out to be a tall, rather wasted man in his seventies, who greeted us at the door from a wheelchair. He was reputed to be a leading psychoanalyst in New England. I was immediately drawn to him. As a disabled man, he knows about suffering at first hand, I thought. He'll bring Kilty to her senses and make her do the right thing.

'Come in! Come in!' Dr Shortt said kindly.

'It's Kilty who needs the treatment,' I said after we were in the doctor's house.

'Do you want to see me, Kilty?' the doctor asked, as if he wanted to confirm the fact for himself.

'Yes, I do,' she said sweetly. For the first time since I had come up to New Haven, she sounded like her old self.

I was about to follow Kilty into the doctor's consulting room— it didn't occur to me that she would be seeing the doctor alone—but Mrs Shortt, who had appeared to help her husband with his wheelchair, firmly directed me into an adjacent room, which seemed like a little study. I sat down in a wing chair, but not for long. I stood up, paced back and forth, opened and closed the window, and looked at my watch repeatedly. Now and again, I could hear a rumble of voices from the other room, but I couldn't make out any words. At one point, I thought I heard Kilty laughing, then screaming. Her eerie outbursts recalled my own visit to a *hakim*, or healer, in Lahore when I was a small boy. My mother had taken me to him, thinking that a neighbour had cast the evil eye on me, and he had applied a few brisk strokes of birch to my backside, then announced, 'There! That's the end of the curse.' I wondered if, even as the *hakim* had exorcized the evil eye with his mumbo-jumbo, the doctor on the other side of the wall was now cuffing and pummelling the demons out of Kilty. Indeed, I thought I heard Dr Shortt say the word 'trepanning', which made me imagine that he might be about to perform that procedure on her in order to dissuade her from the D and C. (As I write this, the idea seems outlandish, but at the time I had never grasped the fact that people went to psychoanalysts only to talk.)

Sometime later, however, Kilty walked into the room where I was waiting, and she was cheerful. 'He's a good daddy,' she said glowingly. 'And you know what? He's very wise. He reads Marcus Aurelius. He quoted some ancient lines from him to me: "Herein is the way of perfection...to live out each day as one's last, with no fever, no torpor, and no acting a part." Isn't that wonderful?'

'But did he tell you to have the baby?' A little like her, I had already begun to think of Dr Shortt as a father figure, and to imagine that he would counsel her to get married and to become a good mother.

'He told me I should do whatever feels joyous to me. Dr Shortt is waiting for you. He'll tell you everything himself.'

I hurried in.

Dr Shortt was seated behind his desk in his wheelchair. Far from sounding infirm, he exuded authority.

'I know it's bad manners, but I should tell you that I don't believe in psychoanalysts,' I said, pulling a chair up to his desk and sitting across from him.

'We can talk about all that some other time, but we need to get Kilty into treatment immediately.'

'Have you convinced her that she should have the baby?'

'She's in no condition to have any baby, mentally—or even physically. She has a date to go into the hospital tomorrow for a D and C. You shouldn't interfere.'

I almost stood up and walked out of his office, for my surge of good feeling toward him was turning to hatred. What am I doing, listening to this crippled, wizened man, I thought, and asking his opinion about anything? My father brought us children up saying, 'Think for yourself.' I am my father's son. I've always been self-reliant.

'What right do you have to make such an absurd judgement, Dr Shortt?' I cried. 'Didn't she tell you that I'm the father?'

'Whether or not to have the baby is the mother's decision only,' he said coolly.

'Are you telling me that I don't count?'

'No. I'm only saying that in this particular decision you can't have any say.'

'Don't I have any rights?'

'Look, we are talking about her body. She has full control to do what she likes with it. Anyway, since you love her, you don't want to make her feel guilty about not having the baby. Guilt is a very destructive emotion.'

'Are you bringing up the guilt business because we are not married? As far as I am concerned, we are as good as married.' I started to tell him about the wedding arrangements that Kilty had bolted from a couple of months earlier. I wanted to know if there was anything I could do to help her change her mind about the baby.

'I don't think so.'

'What did I do wrong? Where did I fail her?'

'I don't know enough about the situation to give you a meaningful answer.'

'Do you think that if I stand by her through the D and C she will then do the right thing and start a family with me?'

'I wish I could I tell you that she would marry you, but I'm not a prophet, merely a doctor. It's clear from talking to her that she finds herself under tremendous pressure and is on the verge of snapping and having a full-scale nervous breakdown. She's going to need a lot of time to think through things and work them out.'

'While she was with you, did you manage to exorcize some of her demons?'

'What did you say?'

'Never mind,' I said. I worried that by having mentioned her demons I might have betrayed her confidence. 'Do you have any specific advice for me?'

'Not really. Just be totally supportive of her. And after the D and C we shouldn't lose a day in getting her to a good psychoanalyst for regular treatment.'

'Will you be treating her?'

'I'm sorry to say that I'm not taking any new patients, but I have an excellent young colleague, a Dr Washburn, who could see her on a regular basis.'

'What will he charge?'

'He has an arrangement with a foundation to take one or two Yale students as patients, so he can see her for a nominal fee.'

Then Dr Shortt told me kindly that he couldn't give me any more time.

In the morning I went with Kilty to the hospital.

A nurse directed us to a private room, and after Kilty had put away her things and changed into a gown another nurse came, prepared her for the operating room, and shifted her on to a cot with wheels. I kissed Kilty, but her lips felt inert.

The nurse rolled Kilty out of the room and down the hall. When the whirr of the wheels subsided, I closed the door and sat down in the armchair. While Kilty was with me, I hadn't noticed the miasmic air of disinfectants and drugs. Now I choked on it, and remembered the scourges of my childhood—the attack of meningitis, and recurrent bouts of typhoid, paratyphoid and malaria. In those early years, having spent so much time in the hospital, I had imagined that I was cursed. Now I imagined a doctor scraping Kilty as if she were a dirty plate and I started groaning.

I couldn't sit still, and soon I was shuttling back and forth between the chair and the bathroom. I felt dizzy and lay down for a couple of minutes on the recovery bed. I started shivering and got under the covers, telling myself as I slipped off to sleep that I must immediately get up and make the bed before Kilty returned.

Suddenly, Kilty was lying next to me, her breath warm against my cheek and her limp arm around me in a half embrace.

'It's you,' I said, waking with a start. 'How do you feel?'

'It's over. That's all I can say. But how is my sweet?'

'Dead.'

She took my hand and put it under the blanket on a sort of diaper she was wearing. 'Isn't it ironic?' she said.

I winced.

'My poor Vedkins, I'll get married to you in June, after I've finished the school year, and then we'll start again, in the right way.'

I was thrilled to have her next to me, talking so optimistically, even if I had trouble believing any of it.

'Don't look so sad,' she said.

Back in New York, I woke up every morning crying and would not be able to stop. I would take refuge in the bathroom basin. After I had somehow washed my face, brushed my teeth and shaved, I would bend over the basin and, putting my hand under the cold-water tap, direct the icy stream into my eyes until they were numb. My tears would stop only to start up again. Somehow, I would get dressed, all the time feeling grateful that I was alone and unwitnessed.

I would arrange my face into a smile and set out, telling myself that I was the son of a woman whose capacity for endurance was awe-inspiring. Most of the time while I was growing up, my mother was sick, and subject to severe asthmatic attacks. Sometimes, as we children listened to her struggling to catch her breath—wheezing and coughing—we would think that she was going to die. Yet, no matter how poorly she felt, she would tie on a colourful sari and put on bright lipstick and get ready to set out cheerfully into the world. What was my psychic pain to her physical suffering, I would ask myself, and, defiantly, I would go down in my apartment-house elevator, take the bus, and arrive at the door of my office generally before any of my colleagues did. I would work through the day, careful not to betray the real state of my mind by a twitch or a gesture. I dreaded the approach of the evening and my return to the apartment.

Soon after the D and C, Kilty started going to Dr Washburn twice a week for psychotherapy. One evening, late in the spring, she called me and said, 'Dr Washburn says that if I want to get married and have children one day, psychotherapy isn't enough: I have to go into deep psychoanalysis.'

'I don't understand. What's the difference?'

'In psychotherapy, a patient sits and talks to the shrink twice a week, but in psychoanalysis, the person lies down on a couch and goes four times a week.'

'That sounds wonderful,' I said. 'It means that you will be finished with all these doctors very quickly.'

'How little you know. Psychotherapy is short-term, but

psychoanalysis takes many years, and, once I start it in New Haven, I will have to stay put here because I won't be able to leave my shrink. And I will not be able to make any major decisions or make any changes in my life at all until it's finished.'

'You mean you will have to suspend your whole life—it sounds like a jail sentence. How horrible. You shouldn't go near it.'

'But you are the one who wanted me to get married.'

'Not to a wretched doctor.'

'But I have no choice. I have to get my life together. Dr Washburn thinks that even when I'm in New York this summer I must continue with Dr Aldridge in Scarsdale. Otherwise, those demons in me will run riot. I will be going back and forth to Scarsdale two, three times a week.'

I listened to her in complete disbelief. I had taken her to Dr Shortt as a sort of quick fix.

'How do you know that Dr Washburn is right about your needing psychoanalysis?' I asked her. 'Since he is a psychoanalyst, he probably thinks everybody needs it. Isn't that what they all think?'

'I trust Dr Washburn, totally,' she said. 'He's already done so much for me. But I am worrying about how I will find the thousands of dollars to pay the nominal fee next year.'

When Kilty came down to New York for the summer and moved back in with her parents, I fancied that, always ethereal, she would now also be psychologically frail and I would have to nurse her along. But she was her old self—lissom and playful, demonstrative and competent, and we resumed our old life as a New York couple, glossing over the New Haven year and all its pain. When I was at the office, she might be at her parents' apartment sewing fall clothes—skirts and shirts and dresses—in order to save money. When I finished work, we might have dinner and go to a play or a concert, or to a nightclub for jazz. Then she might get the idea that we should throw a dinner party. Within a matter of hours, she would have invited a dozen people—my colleagues and her school friends—and shopped, cooked, and set the table. She would preside and serve and then wash up with such finesse that one felt that giving dinner parties was second nature to her. Maybe when she feels psychologically strong and better about herself, everything will fall into place, I thought.

One afternoon when we happened to be walking in Central Park, I guided her to the duck pond, thinking that it would be pleasant to revive our old associations with it.

'The duck pond has so much meaning for me,' I said.

'These ducks drive everything out of my head,' she said. 'Just listen to them quacking.'

'Do you remember when I knelt down on one knee at the edge of this pond?'

'How could I forget that? But then there were no ducks in the pond. Anyway, I was talking to Dr Aldridge the other day about this duck pond, and he said, "Isn't the reality that it is just a miserable, murky artificial lake with some ugly, incontinent birds in it?"' She laughed shrilly.

'But aren't all the other things we felt and thought reality, too?' I said, trying to rally my spirits.

'Yes, but what have they to do with feather-brains?'

'What else do you talk to Dr Aldridge about?' I asked, disheartened.

'Everything. When I see him tomorrow, I'll tell him about this conversation. That's how therapy works.'

At the end of the summer, Kilty took a train back to New Haven. This time, I didn't see her off because the previous week she told me that Dr Aldridge had counselled her not to be involved with me any more. 'We can still talk on the telephone, and I'll write to you,' she said. 'You needn't worry that I'll be involved with anyone else. I'll be living like a nun.'

I laughed out loud. There was something of the buccaneer in her but nothing of the nun, I thought.

'You laugh because you don't think I'm serious, Ved,' she said. Her voice was cold and judicial. 'Through my therapy, I have been discovering that we have been in a destructive relationship from the very beginning, and that you must look to your mental health and I must look to mine. I think it has all been a mistake. It took Dr Washburn and Dr Aldridge to make me realize it.'

I had long felt that no doctor could make sense of our relationship just on the basis of Kilty's perceptions, and I tried to make that point now. 'But neither of them knows me. Neither of them should be passing judgement on us. It's not right.'

'But they are like daddies to me.'

'Damn your daddies.'

'Dr Aldridge said that you'd be angry, and that if you were I shouldn't be upset, because that's a healthy emotion for you to have in this situation.'

'I'm coming with you to your next session, to convince him that he's wrong about us.'

'But that's my last session, and I have a lot to talk to him about.'

'But what I have to say to him is important. I'm going to tell him that I love you, and that, for whatever reason, he has not got things right.'

'He may not see you.'

'I'll force myself into his office.'

The next day, I insisted on taking the train to Scarsdale with her. We sat beside each other, but she wouldn't let me get close to her— hold her hand, or touch her at all. She sat inert, staring out the window—it was as if we were going to the hospital all over again for her D and C. I couldn't stop crying. I knew that my snivelling behaviour was contemptible, but I felt exposed and vulnerable and I would cry at the slightest provocation.

At the Scarsdale station, Kilty got off, ran ahead, jumped into a taxi and sped away, leaving me to find my own way to Dr Aldridge's office.

I caught up with her in the waiting room, just as a door on the far side of the room opened and a disembodied voice called out, 'Kilty!'

I tried to follow her in, but she said, 'It's my hour. You'll have to wait till I finish,' and she closed the door behind her.

When almost an hour had gone by, Kilty came out and said, in gentle tones she hadn't used for some time, 'You can go in now.'

I composed myself and walked into Dr Aldridge's office. The doctor was standing by the door. I thought he would ask me to sit down, but he himself remained standing—towering over me. Either he was a foot taller than I was or I just imagined that he was, because

I suddenly felt shy and confused. I couldn't even remember why I had barged in and what I could possibly say to a psychoanalyst that could make any difference.

'What have you been telling Kilty?' I finally cried. 'You are ruining our relationship!'

That was the extent of my tirade, and it took so much out of me that afterward I felt spent.

'I am Kilty's doctor,' he said, as if he were speaking to a child. 'You are not my patient, and I'd like you to leave now, so that I can get ready for my next appointment.'

His voice—as flat as a robot's—sent a chill through me. He is supposed to be a doctor of the soul, I thought, but he talks to me mechanically, as if I meant nothing to him or to Kilty. I left his office crushed and angry, and took the return train to the city with Kilty. All the way back, she dozed. That was just as well, because I didn't feel like talking.

At Grand Central Terminal, she said, 'I wish everything good for you,' and hurried toward the subway entrance.

Postscript: Dr Bak

It was thanks to Kilty—in my despair of her—that I became a patient myself. For two years I went for psychotherapy for two hours a week at forty dollars an hour. For two years after that, I went for deep psychoanalysis for four hours a week at the same hourly rate. For those four years, I saw Dr Bak at his office on the thirteenth floor of a building at the corner of 87th and Park. Bak, a pillar of the New York psychoanalytic establishment, was a large, dark, imposing man; he had the authoritarian air and debonair manner of a European aristocrat. He seemed always to have a Monte Cristo No. 2 in his mouth and the cigar was always lit, which gave me the impression of Dr Bak as a dragon breathing fire. He had a basso voice and an elusive, confusing way of speaking. I fancied that he spoke that way either because English was not his first language (he was a Hungarian Jew who had escaped to the US in 1941) or because, as a psychoanalyst, he thought that he could keep his patients off-balance by making them struggle to understand him, and thereby get them to yield more unconscious material. But his English pronunciation was good—with the exception of guttural consonants such as 'k' and 'g' which he often transposed. In sessions with Dr Bak, Kilty became Gilty.

'I feel I'm talked out about Kilty today,' I said at one point in my third session. 'I can't think of anything more to say about her.'

'You have a lot to say about Gilty. That's my impression from the other two times you've come here.'

'It's hard to talk about her to a complete stranger,' I said.

For a couple of minutes he just puffed at his cigar and leaned back in his big chair, waiting for me to go on. 'Maybe all you needed were these three consultations with me.'

For the next three years I talked endlessly about my past loves, among other things. I talked about Kilty and Lola, Vanessa and Gigi, but I never referred to my blindness, just as the women had never referred to it. The subject just never came up; even the word itself was never mentioned. When the dam eventually broke—that's another story—I flooded Dr Bak with questions. Did I fall for these women because, like my mother, they denied my blindness? Or did they fall in love with me because I was blind? By falling in love with me, were they denying their own beauty? Did they think that in some magical way I could tell they were beautiful, despite the fact that I couldn't see? Was it their fantasy that I could actually see, and did their love turn to ashes when it clashed with reality? Since the fantasy had served me well in my writing, did I assume that it would serve me well in love?

I asked Dr Bak, 'Why didn't you bring up the subject of my blindness months or years ago? I wasted all this effort coming here and paying my hard-earned money by talking about everything else but the most obvious subject.'

Dr Bak replied, 'But if an insight doesn't come from within you, it is like reading a book. You feel that it is about someone else—not you. It doesn't get integrated into your psyche. You continue to resist the insight.'

'What do you mean?'

'You are forcing me to be very pedantic. Resistance is a psychological defence mechanism that we all have, but it is also a way of fending off unpleasant truths.'

'And of course it could be that my blindness played no role in any of those women falling in love with me or leaving me.'

'Yes, it could be.'

'But then I suppose you would say that if I had been reconciled to the fact of my blindness I would have fallen for a different kind of woman. Maybe a woman who wouldn't have ended up hurting me.'

'Yes, it could be.'

One June day, Kilty telephoned and told me that she had gone into deep psychoanalysis with Dr Aldridge and that he had reached the conclusion that she was 'unanalysable'.

'Dr Aldridge says that, though unusual, sometimes that is the case,' she said. 'I feel that a stone has been lifted from my head. Now that I am free of these shrinks once and for all, I can go on, as I always have, like a blunderhead.' She laughed as if she were making a joke, but rather demonically, I thought, as if also to underscore the fact that, in contrast to her freedom, I would be a slave to psychoanalysis for many more years.

I reported Kilty's call to Bak in my penultimate session before the summer break. Like most psychoanalysts, he took a vacation from his patients in July and August.

'Blunderbuss,' he laughed, from his chair at my head. 'Unconsciously, she wants to shoot dead the person who dares to fall in love with her.'

'Utter nonsense.' He didn't rise to the challenge.

'The galling thing is that Kilty is free from psychoanalysis, and I will have to go on with this hateful stuff, until God knows when.'

'How can you justify that, after three years of coming here, you still have intimate conversations with her? Do you see her? Does she write to you?'

'Yes. The other day she sent me a book about Russian literature because she wanted me to have something "valuable" from her. She said she thought of me because she saw me at a party from across the room at a mutual friend's house. She thought I had "the purest, sweetest smile of anyone", that she deeply regretted the "destruction and suffering" that I had gone through out of love for her, and that she wished for the return of my natural strength and energy. But I feel like a heel telling you this, and betraying her trust.'

'As I've often told you, what you think of as betrayal is an inescapable part of therapy and psychoanalysis. Everything you tell me stays with me. You still seem to love her, but maybe she's just a —'

'I didn't catch the word. What did you say?'

'You heard me.'

'I didn't.'

'What do you think I said?'

'It sounded like "itch" or "witch"…'

'It sounds as if you did hear—your unconscious just doesn't want to acknowledge it.'

Bak stood up—his signal that my hour was up.

I got up from the couch, but instead of walking out of his office as I generally did, I hung back.

The telephone rang. Bak often got calls as I was leaving, as if his friends knew to telephone him during the ten-minute break between patients.

'Go!' Bak said irritably, walking around his desk and picking up the telephone.

'I'm not leaving until you tell me the word,' I said truculently.

He covered the mouthpiece and spat out, 'Bitch.'

Until that moment, I had thought I was over Kilty, but I suddenly had such a surge of anger against Bak that I felt like throttling him. But, being the good patient that I was, I left, quietly closing his office door behind me.   □

GRANTA

PRONEK IN HISTORY

Aleksandar Hemon

Aleksandar Hemon

Dawn

This happened on a night train to Linz: swarthy-faced robbers startle Adolf and strip his felt jacket halfway down his arms so he cannot move them (their long nails scratching him just above his elbow). They slap his cheeks a couple of times, extinguishing any thought of resistance, and then tear the wallet out of his inside pocket. They open the door of the speeding train, and a moist deluge of night air bathes Adolf's face. They throw his easel and portfolio, in that order, out of the train—Adolf can hear the easel and the portfolio echoing it, slicing through the obscure verdure. Then they throw him out— the jacket bundled below his elbows—and he follows the trajectories of the easel and the portfolio. Adolf tumbles down the embankment, the gravel ripping through his pants (recently bought from the money he got for one of his landscapes), skinning his knees and elbows. He eventually stops the revolution and lies still, the gravel ferociously pressing his cheeks. He can only see the rear red eye of the train in the distance, winking away at him, as if all this were a kind of benign joke. Adolf sits up. He can feel bruises spreading like ink blotches all over his white thighs and shaven cheeks. He can feel the skin on his knees and elbows tightening, trying to close quickly over the bloody wounds and cover them up—and there just isn't enough skin.

So there he sits in a throne of pain, at the bottom of the embankment, vexed at the ease with which despair invades every cell of his being (including the bruised areas), and the calmness with which he accepts it, as though it were the moment of relief after an explosive sneeze. His easel gone, his landscapes gone, his elbows gone, his suit gone, the train, with his money, gone. He doesn't even know where he might be—he was dozing, just about to enter a dream populated by fair and fecund Nibelung maidens, when the robbers startled him. Hoping that slumber might dissolve the mountain of problems, or at least allow him to re-enter the maiden dreamland, he closes his eyes, but his heart throbs and throttles, it will not let him rest. An owl hoots (he opens his eyes), sending a signal to nocturnal creatures, and they respond, one by one, and then all together, eager to provide the needed information—saying, perhaps, there is a large, weak body, close to the railroad. Adolf swallows a hefty gulp of dewy darkness, as if it were a magic potion, and crawls up the embankment, the gravel writhing and biting beneath his hands and knees. He reaches the rails and stands up—whichever way he looks, the rails narrow and disappear into a dark, uncertain horizon.

He walks for a while between the rails: the gravel monotonously crunching; the endless crossing of the same threshold; the steady pain in the parched knees and elbows; the tightening of the tired thigh muscles—he looks up, and the sky is wide and bright.

You cannot see the sun yet, just the forest below the embankment, and the glistening, pale mist hovering on top of the deeply green trees, and the verdant ravine with a couple of brawny does grazing solemnly, looking up occasionally, as if expecting important news from afar. 'This is divine,' Adolf thinks. 'The Nibelungs must have roamed forests such as this one.' He stands petrified in the exhilarating moment, fretful to move, lest the landscape crumble into the daily banality of a country morning. It is at this moment that a choir of sparrows breaks out into a hysterically festive chirruping aria. The does scurry back into the forest, the trees ruffle their leaves petulantly, the mist dissipates, the ravine is an empty space, now.

Adolf keeps going, drowsily aware that a decision has been made for him, but does not know what in the world it might be. He walks and stumbles and walks again, storing away his fatigue and despondence as a character-building experience. At last he sees a puny railroad station way ahead of him, but he doesn't hurry up, as if he doesn't want to let those watching him (wherever and whoever they might be) know how close to a defeat he has been.

There is a railroad man stretching up on a ladder leaning against the station wall, extinguishing the lantern above the door. He descries Adolf approaching the station; he touches his forehead with the inner brim of his right palm, narrowing his eyes. His face is round, gathered around a tubby nose with vast oval nostrils. He climbs down the ladder and waits for Adolf, his arms akimbo, his fists resting on his stolid hips, as if he were an angry mother.

'You seem to have missed your train,' the railroad man says, glancing at Adolf's tattered suit. 'Good morning to you.'

'It is a good morning after all,' Adolf says. 'I was just admiring the ravine down this way, and it is beautiful.'

The railroad man smiles and nods. His uniform is dark and neat and reliable, with glimmering badges in the corners of his collar and an array of pens in his chest pocket.

'Beautiful country, makes you happy to have been born here,' Adolf says and scans the landscape around the train station—there is not much to admire around there, but a moment of pensive solidarity is created. 'I wouldn't mind camping here some day.'

'Indeed,' the railroad man says. 'Indeed.'

Adolf attempts to stretch out his arm and offer his hand, but the move is hampered by a swollen elbow.

'I am Adolf Hitler, from Linz,' he says. 'I am a painter.'

The railroad man leans forward to reach Adolf's hand—he seems about to fall forward, but he grasps Adolf's hand and shakes it heartily, as Adolf grimaces in passive pain, and then recovers his balance. 'I am Joseph Pronek, from the railroad,' he says. 'Would you care for a glass of warm milk?'

'Certainly,' Adolf says, and follows Pronek to the door. He can smell the oily railroad-and-coal scent, and he can see the sun ascending behind the forest, long shadows extending behind him.

'I hope you don't mind me asking,' he says, 'but are you Jewish?'

'Oh, I am many things,' Pronek says and opens the door. 'More than I can handle.'

As they step into the warmth of the station office—the fire in the stove belching and crackling, as if happy to see Pronek back— the ground gently rumbles, adumbrating the oncoming train, the rumble growing stronger and stronger, until it tickles Adolf's feet, so he has to make a few tiny steps, this way and that way, as if surreptitiously dancing.

This all happened a long time ago.

The Drawer

History has shown that there were few more joyous daily rituals for Joseph Visarionovich than going through the contents of his dark-wood desk drawer. And rightly so, for the drawer is a little cabinet of historic wonders: behold the bullet that nearly killed Vladimir Ilich, a puny nugget of lead; hear Yagoda's teeth rattle in a little red velvet pouch, always ready to amuse Joseph Visarionovich; study the picture of Vladimir Ilich and Joseph Visarionovich heartily shaking hands, as a smirking Trotsky stands a pace away, clearly plotting something that is never to come to fruition; browse through the American comic book in which Joseph Visarionovich is represented as a lecherous, hirsute beast surrounded by a pigtailed throng of enthralled Soviet girls; amuse yourself over the picture of Hitler (kindly provided by Kauders) in his underwear—striped shorts, reaching halfway down his flaccid thighs—standing grim, with his arm firmly erected; grip the wooden spoon given to Joseph Visarionovich by a quivering babushka wrapped in a star-embroidered scarf, who voluntarily submitted to the inevitability of collectivization; look at Dr Steiner's mezuzah, which used to be at the doorpost of a secret chamber behind a tall bookcase, bent a little, due to a misstep by a clumsy NKVD operative; and, yes, read the letter from Bukharin—Joseph Visarionovich likes to read the first sentence aloud, stressing different words; 'Koba, *why* did you need my death? Koba, why did you need *my* death? Koba, why did you need my *death*?' *Da*, there are many other things in the drawer. Joseph Visarionovich goes through some of them briskly, and some of them he ignores, never entirely succumbing to the tickling of today's delight, always leaving something for the better tomorrow.

It is Tuesday. The fire is throttling in the wood furnace, but outside it is a sunny day: the window-spine shadow is stretching languid and long on the office floor; the dust motes are twitching in the air; balloonish cloudlets are lingering over Red Square, as if waiting for an order to unload the rain; a healthy unit of chirruping sparrows has gathered over the grain that Joseph Visarionovich ordered to be procured for them. Joseph Visarionovich can hear cars revving outside, tenor doors and bass gates slamming, curt precise orders prompting curt precise answers—the revolutionary mechanism is humming along harmoniously, it seems.

He decides to go out for a ride, visit some factories and security units, see some real people. He pushes the drawer with his belly, the navel button on his uniform pings (ping!) against the edge. The drawer dutifully rushes forth, then abruptly halts with a shrill screech. Hitler's picture slides in, so now only his melonish white knees with the black socks stretched below them can be seen. Joseph Visarionovich tries to thrust the drawer forward, but it will not budge. He forces the chair back (a floor thunder) and stands up. He feels his moustache and his neck hair bristling, he glares at the desk: the Tokyo file spread in front of him; a golden pen sticking out of the holder helplessly pointing toward a remote, irrelevant corner of the ceiling; an inkwell; a dark telephone; a chessboard with a king cornered by a couple of rooks; a mug of kvass; he glares at the desk as though he could frighten it into submissiveness. He presses both of his hands against the recalcitrant drawer with all his strength, but it is as though the drawer has always been in this position. Joseph Visarionovich feels the rage swelling in his groin, then splitting in two to crawl up his sides and inflame his armpits. This time he kicks the drawer with his knee, unwisely, for a flash flood of pain zooms up and down his legs—as the desk quakes, as the king wobbles and the rooks roll across the board, stopping at the edge, as the earpiece rattles in its cradle, and as the kvass mug and the inkwell conspire to produce a tide of yeasty goo with inky spirals beginning to rotate slowly, like nascent galaxies—the pain zooms.

Joseph Visarionovich consequently employs his deep voice to commence cursing: the devil this, the devil that, fiery hell and some more hell, all the while pounding the desk with both of his palms, which rapidly redden. Joseph Visarionovich growls and pants and the room is spinning like a zoetrope, as the drawer stands immobile in its centre. But then the revolution stops and Joseph Visarionovich beholds a scrawny bespectacled man, one of those young believing bureaucrats who all look as if they were produced in the same provincial factory. He is standing in the door, bedevilled, his feet apart, his suit orderly, reliable. 'Is everything all right, Comrade Stalin?' he asks.

Joseph Visarionovich's fury is dissipated, though his knee and his palms are throbbing. He doesn't know who this young man is, but he watches him intently, for he seems to have soaked up all his rage like a sponge. There he is: a bay of baldness widening into his dark hair; glasses that have slid down a bit, exposing a ruddy impression on the ridge of his nose just above the rim; spit ardently blobbing in the corners of his mouth. He is holding a black-and-green pen lightly, as if it were a wand. 'I am Pronek,' the young man says. 'Joseph Andrievich Pronek.'

Joseph Visarionovich stretches his face into a smile, strokes his moustache comradely, first the left end, then the right, and says: 'Clean this up, Comrade Pronek.'

'Yes, Comrade Stalin,' vociferates the young man. 'Let me get some water, Comrade Stalin.' With a long stride, he disappears through the door. Joseph Visarionovich looks through the window, Joseph Andrievich's steps thudding away: the sparrows are gone, leaving no grain, the cloud balloons have not moved at all, the rain order has not arrived. He can hear the kvass and ink dripping hesitantly from the desk. He walks to the desk, stepping round the swelling puddle, picks up the phone, waits for a moment.

Moment.

He says: 'Yes. I have a cadre problem here.'

'Now,' he says. 'Yes.'

'Pronek. Joseph Somethingievich Pronek. Yes,' he says.

And Pronek re-enters, with a silvery bucket in one hand and a sallow sponge and the same black-and-green pen in the other. Joseph Visarionovich looks at him calmly, then exudes a fatherly sigh and says: 'Comrade Pronek, let me take your pen.' Pronek puts the bucket down—the water billows to the rim, peers over, but then recedes—takes the pen out of his hand and gives it to Joseph Visarionovich, who says: 'Now, clean this.' Pronek marches eagerly toward the desk, looks it over, assessing priorities, then pushes the drawer in, effortlessly, soundlessly. He sponges the ink–kvass mush off the desk, stands the rooks up on the chessboard (albeit cautiously, away from the king), and then squeezes the sponge over the bucket, producing a droplet staccato.

Joseph Visarionovich goes to the armchair by the wood stove and drops into it, exhausted. The armchair gushes with a sough, as Joseph Visarionovich leans back and closes his eyes. He listens to the fire crackling, he is quiet, breathing deeply, still holding the pen, waiting for Pronek to vanish, so he can doze off. □

THERE'S NOTHING WRONG WITH CORPORATE AMERICA.

(AFTER ALL, EVERYONE LIKES TO READ ABOUT GREED, CORRUPTION, AND EXPLOITATION.)

MOTHER JONES

THE REST IS JUST MASS MEDIA

If you're interested in what's truly scandalous in American business, then turn to *Mother Jones*. For over 20 years we've been uncovering the shoddy products, corporate backroom deals, and political shenanigans their PR folks don't want you to know about. Order a risk-free copy today. If you like our spirited brand of investigative reporting, you can get 5 more issues *(a full year in all)* for just $10. Or you can cancel and owe nothing. Either way, the trial issue is yours to keep.

SUBSCRIBE TO A DIFFERENT POINT OF VIEW. CALL 1-800-GET-MOJO.

Please refer to promotion code A120GT

The Phantom Menace
With the Cold War over, Washington is spending billions to prevent a doomsday attack by foreign terrorists. But just how real is the threat?

GRANTA

SIERRA LEONE

Teun Voeten

Sierra Leone is a small country on the coast of West Africa of roughly the same size and population as Scotland: 28,000 square miles, about five million people. Only three out of ten of its adults can read or write. Out of every thousand children born there, 164 die in infancy. The men of Sierra Leone have an average life expectancy of thirty-eight, the women forty. For these and other reasons, the United Nations Human Development Report ranks Sierra Leone 174th in its list of 174 countries. Even Rwanda and Afghanistan offer their citizens a happier, safer, more prosperous and dignified life.

There is no obvious natural or historic reason for the country's awful condition. It has valuable mineral deposits, particularly of diamonds and bauxite, and a long tradition of trade with Europe which began in the fifteenth century with the Portuguese (who named a prominent coastal landmark 'Serra Lyoa', Lion Mountain). The British arrived in the eighteenth century as slavers, but later established the present capital, Freetown, as a settlement for slaves who had been freed in Britain and North America, or seized from ships intercepted in the Atlantic. By the standards of other colonial regimes in Africa, British rule in Sierra Leone was moderately benign and typically neglectful. The country gained independence in 1961 and became a one-party state in 1978. The years since have been marked by dictatorships, rebellions, coups and counter-coups—culminating in conflicts between heavily armed and sometimes drugged gangs which have killed many thousands of innocent people and made Sierra Leone a byword for cruelty. International intervention—by ECOMOG (Economic Community of West African States Monitoring Group) and the UN—has been largely ineffective. The democratically-elected government of President Ahmad Tejan Kabbah has been shakily propped up in the capital; the rebels of the Revolutionary United Front (RUF) control most of the hinterland and its diamond mines. But that is too simple a description of a fluid conflict, in which official and unofficial armies continually change sides.

One particular species of cruelty in Sierra Leone is the amputation of hands and arms, which the RUF began systematically—as a strategy—in 1995. According to Teun Voeten, the Dutch photographer who took these pictures during three visits between 1998 and 2000, women who worked in the fields were the first victims; the RUF wanted to prevent the gathering of the harvest. During the elections of 1996, the strategy was extended to voters, both male and female; amputated voters would not be able to mark their ballot papers by the traditional method of an inky thumb-print. Child amputees are not so easily explained, though many exist. **IJ**

Diamond dealership, main street, Bo. May 2000

A mural of American rapper Tupac Shakur, who is an icon for the RUF rebels, Freetown. May 2000

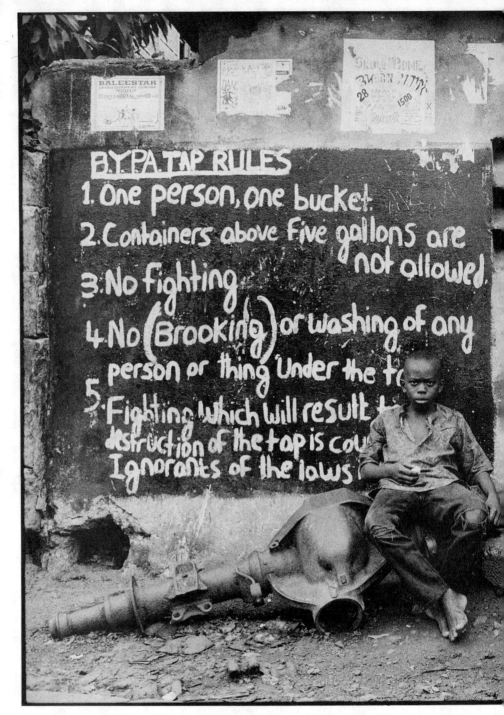

Boys at a water tap in the slum neighbourhood of Brookfields, Freetown. May 2000

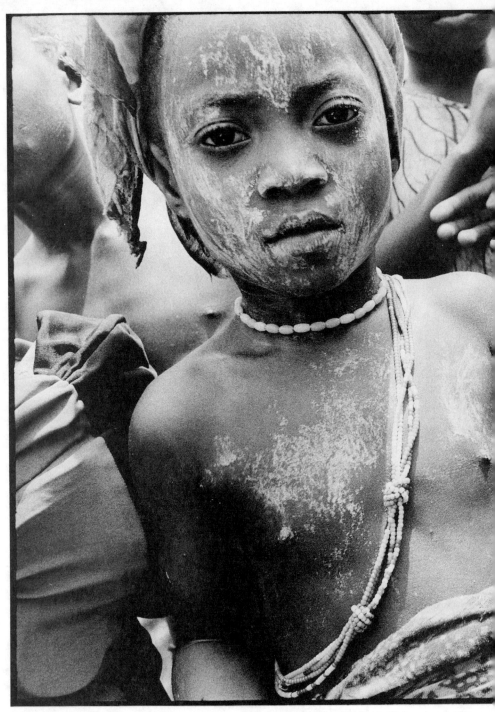

Children dressed up in ritual costume to sing and dance for money on the streets in Zimmi. May 2000

Members of the Kamajors, an anti-RUF militia, outside Freetown. April 1999

Former Kamajors, now part of the Civil Defence Forces fighting against the RUF, near Newton. May 2000

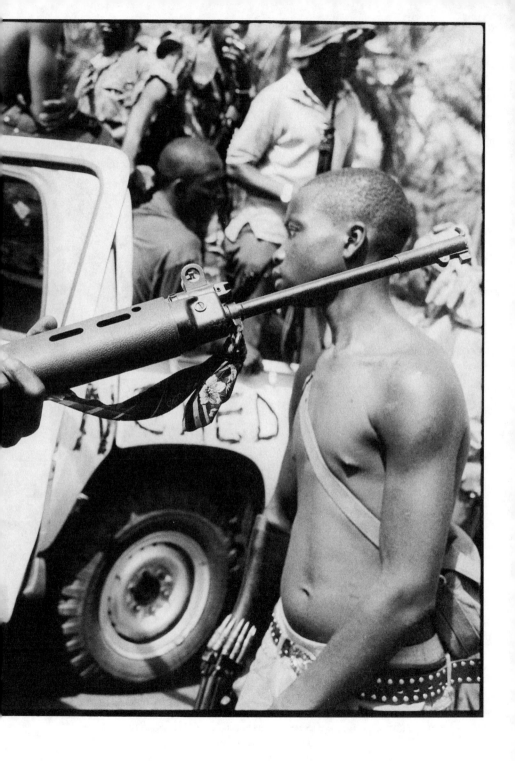

Boy dying after an ECOMOG bombing raid on Makeni, held by anti-Government rebels. February 1998

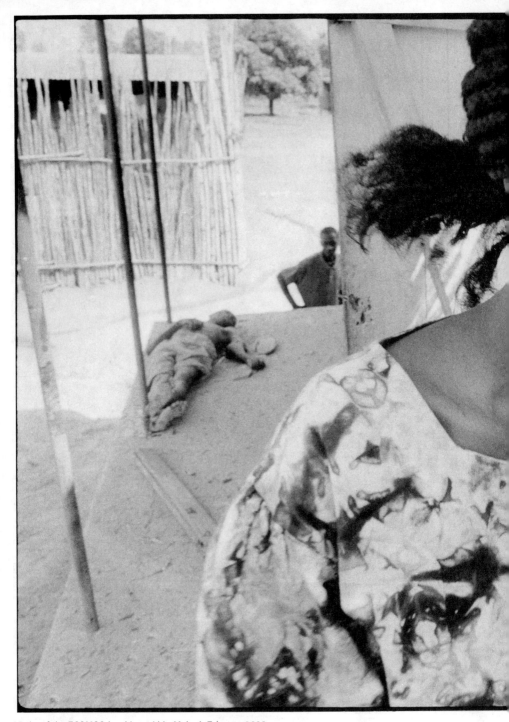

Victim of the ECOMOG bombing raid in Makeni. February 1998

Civilians in Makeni take revenge on anti-Government rebels and their collaborators. March 1998

Victims of RUF amputations at a refugee camp, Freetown. April 1999

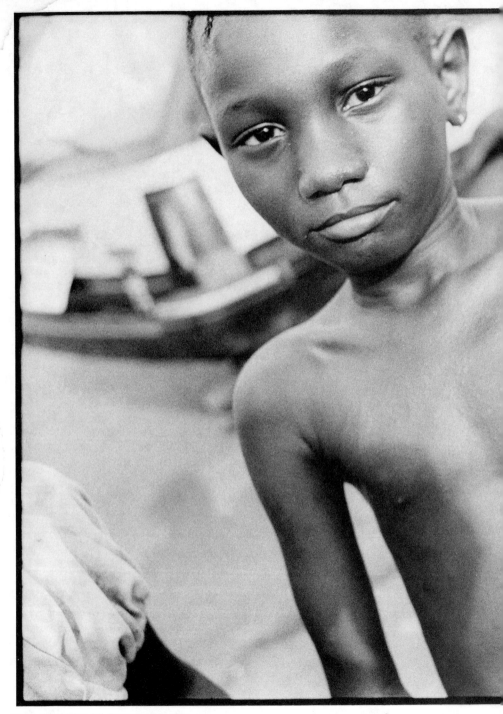

Young girl with her doll, Freetown. May 2000

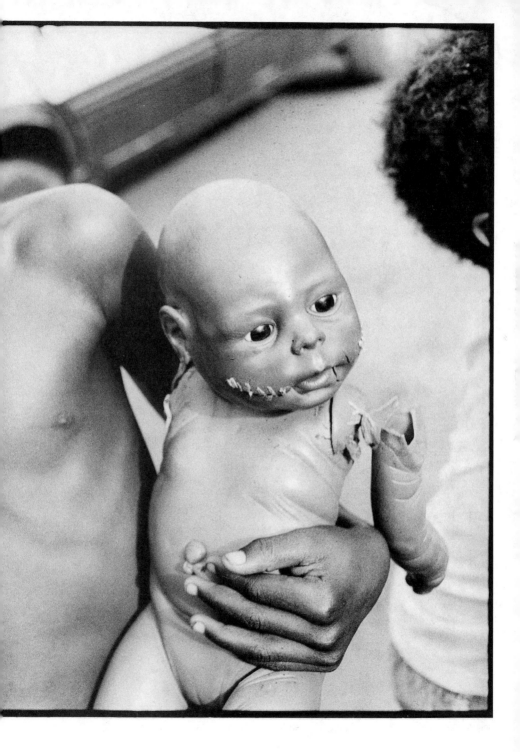

Children selling sweets in front of a poster shop in Freetown. December 1999

Woman street-seller in Freetown amid the destruction left by retreating rebels. April 1999

GRANTA

BUT RICHARD WIDMARK

Nik Cohn

Richard Widmark in 'Madigan', 1968

I ask my wife what she means by kidnap exactly, but she says never mind. We are at Pygmy's after my party where Richard Widmark never showed, and the jukebox isn't working again. All the music Pygmy's has is a boom box on the bar, playing 'Black on Both Sides'. My wife likes the bit on 'Ms Fat Booty' where Idaho potato is rhymed with Now I just can't say no.

My wife has natural wisdom; I don't. When I first knew her, I used to lie and tell everyone she was a Miss Wisconsin, but this was missing the point. And tonight I thought the point was Richard Widmark, but now my wife says No, the point was you. Whose name was on the invites? You were the big cheese tonight.

They have a house rule at Pygmy's when the jukebox goes down, they give you free salsa and chips. To my way of thinking, Richard Widmark is dead. I have an image of his obituary. HOLLYWOOD LEGEND PASSES. When Fred informed me he wasn't just living but his place was right around the corner from Fred's paper store and he came in every morning for *The Times*, I thought it was Fred being Fred. The man is an Iranian, he's not a reliable witness. His name is not even Fred. Feroudine. He makes it all up as he goes along.

No, yes, says Fred. I swear. This most distinguished person with a head of fine silver hairs comes in my store and pays cash. I think I'm knowing him from somewhere. I think this face is familiar to me. And these teeth. I think I know these teeth from somewhere long ago, but where?

Fred is a man when he has a worry in his head, it gives him no peace. Oh, this man. He'd drive you crazy sometimes. The most beautiful man in the world, and the hair on his head is so thick. Still thick and curly and once was black, I call him Woolly Bully. That's how much hair this man still has.

One day it starts snowing. The snow comes down in fat, sticky flakes, and Fred is doing the crossword. *Daily News*, it's easier. He never gets it out because the clues are all in English, but it takes his mind off his worries. Between the crossword and the snow he forgets the teeth he knows from somewhere, but where? Then he looks up and the man is standing outside the store window, bareheaded, with the snow falling white on his white head and his eyes screwed up against the wind-chill factor. He looks like an old Viking, or maybe an Indian scout. The snow drifts in his face, and he bares his teeth.

My God, says Fred.

When I tell this to my wife, she's hanging on the phone, trying to reach Visa about a charge from Frederick's of Hollywood for $1,819.82. We are not those types of people. She is sitting on a high stool swinging her leg, and her house robe has slid open from the knee. I can see the little tendril of purple vein that stands out just behind the knob of her ankle there. My wife has dark skin that gleams in any light. You're shitting me, she says. Tommy Udo comes in Fred's paper store?

That's the story, I say.

Get out, says my wife.

The purple vein has a bloom like a hothouse grape. She sits with her robe inching up her thigh and her leg swinging longer, slower, and then she laughs that way she has, makes me think of a trapeze, flying out of her mouth up high, then back in her throat down low. The Thalia, she says.

Well, of course. That's where we went to see *Kiss of Death*, the night of our second date. Victor Mature as the good family guy gone bad, Brian Donlevy as the district attorney who uses him for fish bait, and Widmark as Tommy Udo, stone killer, with the twisty wet mouth and squinty eyes and high-pitched psycho giggle. And the teeth. Big horsey front choppers that could chomp through brick or bone, and huddled Depression-time lowers. Even then I was aware that movie stars have their teeth fixed, but Richard Widmark wore his own. When he grinned his killer's grin, they filled the screen. In the big scene where Udo pushes the old lady in the wheelchair down the stairs and breaks her neck, I felt this woman I hardly knew yet start to shiver beside me in the dark. She raised up and twisted her legs, protecting herself, then she put her hand on me. And after, when we hit the street, she pulled me through a rusty sheet-metal gate into a passageway and made me the gift of herself, up against the wall, with splatters of something clammy running down the back of my neck and all the people passing, blind to us, a few feet away. She tasted of wet tobacco and whisky sours, and I kept watching the shoes go by below the gate, thinking I owe this to Udo, all this, I owe Tommy Udo for life.

According to Fred, he's one of nature's gentlemen. He drinks jasmine tea, and he's a dab hand at crosswords. He has the gift of language, he used to breed parakeets. But he won't talk about his films, not a word. You can't even say *Kiss of Death* to him, the drawbridge goes up right away. He'll chat for hours about dogs or the Dance, but try to get him on Tommy Udo, he won't give you the time of day.

Maybe, says my wife with her secret smile, maybe not. Her leg has stopped swinging, her robe is clamped tight around her knee. A man from Frederick's comes on the line, and she gives him both barrels. French-maid panties, says my wife. Red, satin, crotchless, with matching garter belt. As if. And she slams down the phone.

Come nightfall, when she logs on the Internet, she turns up eleven matching sites for Richard Widmark on Yahoo, but none help much. Born Sunrise, Minnesota, 26/12/1914. Appeared in eighty films, 1947–97, mostly thrillers and westerns, from *Kiss of Death* to *Big Guns Talk*. And that's all she can unearth. No profiles, no interviews, not even a chat room. This isn't justice, says my wife, and she types in Troy Donahue. Twenty-seven matches, eight in France alone. Can you spell travesty? she says.

Most weeks when I'm in town I go in Fred's store at least twice, but just around this time I go out on a book tour. My line of racket is bookstore readings for writers who refuse to appear in public, or sometimes they've died. Call it literary karaoke. In my time I've been J. D. Salinger, Cormac McCarthy and Robert Lowell. If I'm lucky, I manage to sneak in some morsels of my own, the odd pensée or scrap of dialogue, and nobody's the wiser. This keeps me fresh. Which I need when it's fifty days and fifty cities, and I'm Thomas Pynchon. But even this shall pass. February, and I'm back, and my wife has a new dress. A little black number, up to here and down to there, with nothing in back. She twirls in it, arms out and barefoot, like Thumbelina dancing. It's for your party, she tells me. Fred and me, we put our heads together to give you a welcome home. She is flattening dough for an apple pie with a marble rolling pin. Richard's coming, she says casually.

You asked him?

Didn't have to. Fred mentioned it in passing, and Richard jumped right on it. There's nothing he likes better than *soirées intimes*.

That's how he talks?

De temps à temps, says my wife. Right away a flush begins to mottle and spread from the base of her neck, as if I've called her a liar. There is a smudge of flour at her hairline, right where the first tiny hairs show grey above her temple. I haven't met him yet, she says, but Fred says he loves his culture. Mahler is meat and drink to him. William Carlos Williams, too. He has a nephew who works in wood, right outside La Jolla.

My Soirée with Udo? I say.

Shut the fuck up, says my wife.

That's when I know she's left me. Nights we used to spend watching Honeymooner marathons in bed with moon pies and fresh-popped popcorn we now sit in the living room, in our separate La-Z-Boys, with microwaved frozen pizza and Richard Widmark videos. *Pickup on South Street* and *Panic In the Streets* and *Night and the City, Broken Lance* and *The Alamo, How the West Was Won, Judgement at Nuremberg, Cheyenne Autumn, Murder on the Orient Express.* The man has become our lodger. He takes his meals with us, sleeps in the spare room. I look up from my morning Fruit Loops and see his wet mouth across the breakfast table, lopsided, with that loose sloppy grin. There's so much tooth in this mouth, it peels his lips back, rictus-style; at moments he looks like the Joker. But he's a good-looking man, no question of that. High forehead, raw Scandinavian cheekbones, strong jaw—in dim light you could confuse him with my wife's cousin Harold Bing that used to work for CV Collisions before he met with the accident.

One thing surprises me is Widmark's moral sense. You picture Tommy Udo and you think degenerate, but it seems that was just wild oats. The rest of his career, nine times out of ten, he was a stand-up guy, big on scruples. Just don't cross him, though. Don't presume to traverse the line, or he'd drill you a third eye, quick as blink.

My wife says it's an act. That's the way movies are, she says. Richard in everyday life doesn't even own a pistol any more. Fred asked him straight out, and he said firearms made him nervous, just give him a good book and a glass of Chardonnay. He won't even answer to the name of Widmark. Calls himself Gustafson or Gunsterberg, some Nordic whatever. But Fred isn't fooled. He never forgets a bicuspid.

When the invites arrive, they have raised gold letters in Times New Roman, same as a funeral notice. *Come celebrate*, they say. *The love you save may be your own.* This makes no sense to me. The next day when I drop into Fred's to pick up my back copies of *Autosport*, I ask him what it means. That Richard, Fred says. He lives for philosophy.

You can always tell when Feroudine's in love. His round baby's cheeks fill up like a squirrel harbouring nuts, and his vowels are wanton caresses. This man is changing my life, he says. He's showing me beauty every day. Age is no relation to him—he's still a young girl in his heart. Poetry. Parakeets. And his teeth, my God, says Fred. They are the human condition.

The night of the party, my wife wears her pearls. The hollow at the pit of her throat is deep and dark, and pearls love to nest in it. All this is yours, she says to me in her nakedness. But I know better.

Quite an evening ensues.

Nearly fifty people show up, some of them personal friends. There is wine in two colours, and vegetable sushi, and a floral tribute from the Korean grocery up the block. My wife keeps playing 'Let's Get Killed', and a couple that nobody knows who they are do a dance. Fred wears his yellow sweatshirt with the reindeer and the red fir trees. This man reads Baudelaire in French, he says. He has been to the Parthenon.

But Richard Widmark never comes.

For myself, I take this in stride. Gods have never been my personal cup of tea. In Winston-Salem one time, I was in the same diner with Cale Yarborough, and my girlfriend then, long before my wife, made me ask for his autograph. Let me just say this was ill-advised. So, no, my night isn't spoilt. It's my wife who has been betrayed. She is the girl who radiates that charm, but the taste of her mouth on mine when we slow-dance is harsh like iron filings. Richard Widmark, she says, can suck my dick. She drapes her arms around my neck and drags her feet. Robert Mitchum, she says. Now there was a man.

Sex on the Beach at Pygmy's has often helped to heal the hurt in days past, but not this time. Pearls keep trying to shelter in the dark hollow of her throat, and she keeps shucking them off. That's when she starts saying Never mind and mouthing off about kidnap.

That's not a word to trifle with, I say.

Borrow then, says my wife. Think of it as a lend.

Free salsa and chips may sound a good deal on paper, but not when the salsa is Lo-Cal fat-free and the chips have sat out for a week. Baudelaire in the French my cherry ass, says my wife.

The night outside Pygmy's is evil. We walk the three blocks to Fred's crib with ducked heads and stinging eyes, no word between us, then my wife begins to batter at the door. In time a window goes up above our heads, and Feroudine, torn from sleep, rains down Iranian curses on us. My wife has to slip off her coat to calm him, and there she stands, all bare. Richard's address? Fred says. He never exposed it to me. All I know is a walk-up on Duane, and he can see the stars from his bed. The window starts down again. He calls it his tepee, says Fred, goodnight.

Nothing stops my wife once her burner's lit. Blood fills and fattens her bottom lip, her chests push out, and her voice goes burned. Pussy boy, she calls me then. Walk me to Duane, pussy boy.

Duane these days is mostly lofts. We walk a deep pit between cliffs that used to be warehouses and manufactures before the money came and now all the windows sell extra virgin olive oil, scented soaps, gay apparel.

I don't believe my wife feels the cold, or the raw thorny whip of wind. She burrows and snouts and darts ahead, then she pulls up short in triumph. She's standing outside the Baby Doll Lounge, and its black plate-glass windows are covered in gold and silver stars. Gotcha, says my wife. She jumps in the mouth of a doorway, starts leaning on the buzzer. Who is this? says a man upstairs.

Me, says my wife. And we're in.

Sixteen years I've been loving and surviving this woman, but I have no working knowledge of her. She leads me up three flights of stairs, and a fourth. The skin of her back is covered in tiny goosebumps like braille and the scent of Sex on the Beach rolls back over me in waves. She raps on a metal-plate door with loose careless knuckles, and it opens on a chain. A sleepless old man's face peers out. Hello, Mr Widmark, says my wife.

The name's Lars Gunderson, says the man. Are those your own tits?

When my wife parts her lips, her dimples show. I have a bone to pick, she says. Why weren't you at this man's party?

I was troubled with my teeth, the old man says.

This man needed you. Fifty cities in fifty nights, the least he deserved was Welcome home. Some of the sufferings he endured, slings and arrows aren't in it. Toledo, he read for two hours straight from *Gravity's Rainbow*, and what thanks did he get?

Could mean an extraction, says the old man.

The Richard Widmark I know gets a chipmunk bulge in his cheeks when he smiles, dangerous, as if hiding a chaw of tobacco, but this man doesn't smile. You could have been there, my wife persists. He would have been there for you.

One trick she performs when she's riled is to ripple her shoulder blades, firstly gather them up in a scrunch, then roll them over and down like 'Surfin' USA'. Do that again, the man says. So she does. You'd better come in, says the man.

We enter a fighting man's room; a man who's been in the service. Metal-framed army cot, a khaki blanket, a pillowcase worn thin and grey, and a fold-up metal chair stamped NYC PARKS COMMISSION. Beside the chair stands an open quart bottle of Moose Jaw. The old man takes a small glug, not much more than a sip, and passes it on to my wife. This is my cell, he tells her. I come here when I need to be locked up.

What's your crime? says my wife.

The old man gives it a think. Age, he says.

That's no excuse, says my wife.

It's what I've got, he replies. He plops himself down on the edge of his bunk, spindle-shanks and shrivelled butt, and my wife takes one of the fold-up chairs. She arranges herself in reverse, so that the metal backrest makes a shelf for her weary breasts. Her hair is in her eyes and her mascara's smudged, and the way she licks her lips, I know that kidnap flew out the window, this man is safe. You could have sent your regrets, she tells him, but playful now.

Regrets, the old man says, I have too few to mention.

From where I stand that's a dead giveaway. What kind of Richard Widmark would quote from 'My Way'? Not the one with the teardrop dent in his hat, oozing class and menace through every pore. Flowerpots weren't his style. A man once he's died at the Alamo has no time for folderol.

That's just in my opinion, of course.

But I'm out of the picture here. The other two share a common frame—the man pushed back maybe ten degrees from the upright, as if braving a prevailing wind, and my wife pressed forwards over her breasts. Meanwhile, I'm off at the window, leaning on a gun-metal bookshelf. *The Heart is a Lonely Hunter*, *Zuleika Dobson*, Plato's *Symposium*, the poems of e. e. cummings. One time in his Iranian life Fred told no word of a lie. George Gissing and Mallarmé. So you like a good read, I say.

I do that, the man says heartily, but his eyes never leave my wife's chest. The pearls that hide in the pit of her throat send out flecks of light known as will-o'-the-wisps. Richard, she says. Does it bother you if I call you that?

Call me Bambi if it gets you wet, says the old man. He rolls himself a cigarette and starts to suck on it. Between puffs, he lets it dangle in the corner of his mouth. A homage to Tommy Udo? Could be. But I still keep seeing barracks. Something about his posture— the squared-off shoulders, the rigid neck—tells me this man in his day has scrubbed out latrines with a toothbrush.

Were you ever in Normandy? I ask.

Lovely town, Saint-Malo, he replies. My first wife painted water-colours in the harbour. The light was *sui generis*, she said. And the food. I can still taste those lobsters à l'Américaine. He takes two fast drags on his roll-up, sealing in the memory. D'you cook yourself? he asks then.

Only like a dream, says my wife.

Is that a fact? A faraway look like floating comes in the old man's eyes. In the comfort of his own home, he wears white tennis shoes with no socks, canvas pants held up with clothes line, a Navy Seals T-shirt, but he has distinction. Senatorial is the word that enters my mind. This is a man who could wear a toga and cause no derision.

Doesn't make him a good person, though. All his airs and white hairs can't camouflage the flecks of dry foam that cling in the corners of his mouth and the yellow in his eyes when he considers the flesh on my wife's upper arm that gleams in any light. Have you ever thrown pottery? he asks.

In my time, she says, and she looks at him from under her eyelashes, up and round, like she's Princess Di on TV and butter wouldn't melt in her butt. It has been known, she says.

I'll bet. The old goat gives out a honk of bottled laughter down his nose and shakes his head, ho, ho. I'll bet pottery's not all you've thrown, he says, reaching out a withered claw, and he puts his fingers on her biceps, he gives a squeeze. Strong women, he says, musing. His voice dips low, a conspirator's note, and my wife has to bend her head closer to hear him. A stray frond of hair slides over his wrist. They're intimates.

For me this is mortal, but my guess is that's the point. If I am not mistaken, the point here isn't my loss or the old man's gain, but the issue of identity. If I am dealing with Lars Gunderson, it is my right to kill him.

But Richard Widmark?

To occupy my hands, I pick up a book. The title page is *Futility*, by William Gerhardie. At the top of page forty-three, I read: 'After all, I am the mistress of this house. True, I have been thrown into the mud and trampled on, told I am not wanted, done away with, about to be thrown into the street like a dog, but while I am here, I am the mistress of this flat. After all, I am.' The rhythm in these words pleases me. I would like to read further, but my eyes are too bleary with sweat or worse, I have to look elsewhere. The old man has circled my wife's tender wrist with his thumb and forefinger. His face is turned half towards me, looking over her shoulder. I was a master baker, he says. I started out a trainee icer at Mayblooms on Jamaica Avenue. But icing couldn't hold me.

The way he delivers his words is out the side of his mouth, which Richard Widmark did, yes, but loads of other people as well, you can't prove much by that. I used to handle all the piping on the wedding cakes, he says. Half my days were spent up to my elbows in pink, it was no life for a boy, no life at all. So I joined the Marines.

My wife all this time never moves. Her head is still bent to catch his every word and her half smile says Let him tell his tales. Let him say whatever pleases him, I know what I know, let him have his fun.

Did you ever see combat? I ask. With casualties and death?

We're all casualties, he says.

The desire comes on me to whack him. It would pleasure me to blow him away here and now, but there is my wife to consider. And what about films? I say, pressing on. Were you ever in the movies?

When the old man laughs, it sounds like wind leaking out a burst balloon. That's my little secret, he says.

Oh, says my wife, full of breath, I love secrets.

Keeping them or spilling them? says the man.

I never spill anything. Not a drop, she tells him. Her wrist slips through his fingers, and she places her hand on his sunk-in chest. Trust me, she says.

I do, he says, and lowers his head to nuzzle her fingertips. I'd trust you with my life. My wife's middle finger slips in his mouth, feeding him. You're hungry, she says.

Always have been, he says.

His scalp shows pink through the frizz of his hair like a baby's and the muscles clench tight in his cheeks as he suckles. What about the films? I try again, but the old man doesn't answer, he's deafened by need.

At last a ripple like shook foil runs over my wife's bare shoulder blades, and she waggles her head, awakening. Yes, she says then, the films?

More like loops, the old man says modestly. When I came out of the service, there was no work around and I was broke, but I knew this guy in pictures, he said he could use me. So no big deal. I did one called *The Salesman's Lucky Day*, and another was *Schoolgirl Sin Slaves*.

And *Kiss of Death*? says my wife.

Instantly, the old man goes ice-cold. Never heard of it, he says, very curt, and he snatches back his fingers from her mouth. I never had no use for kinky stuff. No snuff films, or any pervert shit like that, just the old in and out. Wham bam thank you ma'am was good enough for me. He raises up off his bunk and leaves my wife to herself. Still is, he says.

No offence.

You're in my house here.

I only enquired, says my wife. She looks as if she's been struck, her face is stark white with red blotches. I never meant to traverse the line, she says. That was the last thing.

The old man picks up the bottle of Moose Jaw and takes a choke but he keeps his eyes on my wife—her head hung down, the bow-bend of her bared spine. Let 'em eat shit, he says.

She has no answer to that.

From the window I watch all the gold and silver stars that twinkle on the window of the Baby Doll Lounge. There's no air in this room. I can smell my wife in heat and pain, and I'm scared I may start weeping.

The old man picks up the copy of *Futility* and puts it back on the metal bookshelf. For the first time since we knocked on his door, he's closer to me than he is to my wife. His cheeks are criss-crossed with a fine net of veins, as delicate as lace work. Teeth are regular boogers, he says.

I've heard that, I say.

Can't live with 'em, and you can't get satisfied without 'em. He opens wide his mouth to reveal a few fangs on top, some yellow and some brown but still strong-looking, still fit for damage, and a row of stumps on the bottom. The stumps have worn through in rings like the boles of rotted trees. Just look at that, would you? the old man says, and sticks his finger in the corner of his mouth, peeling back the loose flesh to show me the root of his trouble: a molar, black and cracked, that keels over sideways at his touch. What do you say to that? he asks.

Richard, says my wife.

Her arm is around him then, dark and warm, and she leads him back to his bunk. The pearls dance at her throat and she crouches by his feet. Have you eaten? she asks him in a voice like oozing sap. You have to eat.

My cupboard is bare, the old man says.

Not for long. This man here is fit, he'll fetch anything you require. A fresh-tossed salad, perhaps, with olives and hard-boiled eggs. Or maybe you could stand to contemplate some pie.

Soup, the old man says feebly.

You got it, says my wife.

First light greys the street when I walk out on Duane. Used to be, there was a place called the Plum Blossom, corner of Canal and Broadway, served a mean dish of duck soup. But that was back in the day. Now there's just a take-out counter and the stink of Raid. What's your pleasure? the serving man asks.

Wonton, I tell him.

If you say so. The man pours a quart and throws in a fortune cookie. If you can't be wise, be lucky, the message reads. I see my wife on her knees. I see her face, blind and greedy. I hear her cry out another man's name and I start to running. The soup slops and burns between my hands, and two cops in a prowl car flag me down. What's your hurry? one asks.

Richard Widmark needs soup, I say.

Richard Widmark's dead, says the cop, but he lets me go anyway. I cross the street by the Baby Doll Lounge, I lean up against the old man's bell. Who wants to know? says his voice.

I have no words to tell him, just a noise like choking that makes him snicker. Come on up, pussy boy, he says.

My wife is waiting right inside his door. Her coat is back on, and she keeps her face turned away from my eyes. A copy of *Les Fleurs du Mal* is lying open by the old man's bunk, spine up. Take me home, says my wife.

The old man says not a word, just jumps inside the soup and starts to slurping. The sound makes my insides rebel and I have to leave the room. I'm standing at the top of the stairs, dry heaving, when my wife walks past and starts down ahead of me. I watch the back of her head till it leaves my line of sight, then I turn back towards the old man's room. His door is half open and he's sitting on the edge of his bunk, leaning forward, with the carton of wonton held between his knees. He has big hands with red knobs for knuckles, and when he feels me watching him, he raises his head, nice and slow, and looks me dead in the eye. Don't keep the lady waiting, he says. His mouth goes wet and slack, and he starts to laugh. I turn my back, plunge into the dark. Tommy Udo's giggle pushes me down the stairs.

But now my wife, she says no. It isn't him, no way. She's

standing in bright light, and she comes into my arms. The morning sun holds a faint warmth, but the woman can't stop shivering. Are you sick? I ask.

Never mind, she says. We start walking back towards Fred's store and she slips her hand inside my coat pocket. Her fingers fumble with mine, and I feel something hard against my thumb. What's that? I say.

A present, she says. So I fish it out, take a look. Forget it, says my wife.

I'm holding a molar, black and cracked. □

GRANTA

A BLOW TO
THE HEAD

A. L. Kennedy

Joseph Henry Price with his wife and daughter, late 1950s

I am looking for my dead grandfather in the British Library. Around me the new building is calm and white, a little like a hospital for books. I peck my way through layers of computer filing looking for copies of his favourite, long defunct, magazine *Health and Strength*. Here, according to the story he always told, I will find his photograph: a picture of a young man, a boxer: a middleweight before his marriage, before his daughter, before me.

I wait for the delivery of 1935 and 1936 and, without intending to, remember his scents. My grandfather smelled of Lifebuoy soap and Brylcreem and soft, soft skin. Although he was a fighter and a steelworker most of his life, his hands and feet never hardened. Each new pair of work boots crippled him. His boxing stories were filled with magical strategies for toughening his fists. When I stayed with him and my grandmother in the school holidays, I would be given the task of picking tiny metal pieces from his uncallused fingers and palms with a needle's point. I realized this was a kind of honour, he usually did the work himself, but now he was trusting me, making his hands a helpless weight in mine. The whole process made me feel sick, all the same: I knew that I hurt him.

On the desk in front of me the Reminder to Readers warns that 'Books and manuscripts are fragile objects. Please take care and do nothing which might damage them.' The living and reading are intended to be gentle when they visit, to remember that the information stored here is vulnerable, quite easy to destroy. I don't believe my grandfather ever considered his weekly bible might end its life in such sickly company. Then again, he neither liked nor anticipated his own decline into frailty.

He was, after all, a man of certainty and solutions. A tool setter for most of his life, he spent hours calibrating machine tools, measuring out their tolerances for error, refitting and modifying them to meet every conceivable demand, the trickier the better: in retirement, he mended old radios, televisions, doorbells, clocks. His unshakeable assumption that I had inherited his general physical confidence and dexterity meant my childhood was littered with unmanageable gifts: the bicycle I couldn't balance, the roller skates that scared me—I only dared to use them over gravel—and the gleaming, implacable pogo stick. We both wanted me to enjoy these things, but I never could.

Far more comforting were his remedies for likely and unlikely threats. Crouching between his shins, my arms slung over his supporting knees, I would watch old horror films long past my bedtime and we would discuss the fatal weaknesses of vampires, werewolves and monsters of all types. We knew how to finish them, every one. And he would tell me, in only the twitch and surge of television light, how to deal with any real attacker. There, with the safest man in the world, I learned how I should stamp on insteps and scrape shins, gouge eyes and chop at windpipes, or jab with the heel of my hand at the base of noses in a way which he neglected to mention might well prove fatal if it sent the assailant's nasal septum spearing back into his brain.

Which my grandfather would not have minded. It was a gently accepted fact that he would have killed anybody who harmed me, who even thought of it. These were among his quieter gifts, the ones I didn't notice at the time: his unconditional belief that I was precious enough to be so very well defended, and my certainty that I can defend myself. I have many of the usual kinds of fear, but fear of attack is not among them. I have never, it so happens, lost a fight and I have never seen the strength and size of the male body as a threat. I have had full freedom, if I've wished, to find it only beautiful. My grandfather, Joseph Henry Price, he gave me this.

When it arrives, in leather-bound volumes, *Health and Strength* has its own kind of beauty. Billed as 'The National Organ of Physical Fitness', it mingles articles on the perfect punch and sexual advice with photographs of the physically fit. Men in leopard-skin trunks and gladiator boots tense and grimace happily. A man carries a small live pony draped resignedly around his neck. Here and there, sturdy Nordic women brandish hoops or beach balls in states of noticeable undress. 'Greek' scenes are recreated in homoerotic tableaux involving a good deal of oil and sometimes fig leaves. A range of small ads offers trunks, boots and leaves, all available for convenient purchase by mail.

The effect is chaotic and hardly what I'd expected Joe Price to find comfortable—I recall him as a man who thought twice before removing his jacket and who had no time at all for homosexuals. But there is a unifying theme here, something I know he understood: the need to be admired, to be an obvious success. It's most visible amongst the amateurs: the clerks and NCOs, the shopkeepers and factory workers who once hoped to make their own fabric a thing of pride. Six decades adrift, they still look out, perpetually pale and young and keen, snapped balancing on park benches, kicking in a brief Sunday's surf. They're three years away from a world war and showing their bodies as precious things, their best assets. A Mr Harvey stands alone in 1936, braced and British and facing the desert near Cairo, naked with his back to the camera. His arms and calves are tanned, the rest strikingly white from his knees to the bared nape beneath his savage army haircut. Other articles in the same year praise 'George VI—our Athletic King' and feature, without irony, Cary Grant and Randolph Scott lounging together in trunks—'two noted Paramount stars who believe in the value of Physical Culture.' This is the promise of health and strength, the longed-for gift of physical democracy: film stars, commoners and kings all equal when stripped to the skin.

As I turn though the cheap, yellowed pages I realize how much my grandfather lived by what he found here. He left school in 1930 at the age of fourteen, walking straight into the mouth of the Depression. His family was working class with pretensions to gentility, his father a handsome man who dressed well but was violent in drink. One of four children, Joe wanted to defend what he found precious: to guarantee safety for his mother and himself, to assure his own dignity and success. It would have been tempting to believe that positive thinking and hard exercise could bring him all he wanted by acts of will. Variations on the theory were popular at the time. By the late 1930s *Health and Strength* includes more and more German snapshots: worthy National Socialist bodies, stripped and staring towards horizons bright with eugenic promise.

Joe Price didn't embrace the politics or the spurious science, but he did put his faith in the logic of effort and will. He believed that he could and must fight to build a life worth living. More an individualist than a pacifist, he would spend his war in a reserved occupation, avoiding the daily risks of steel. He once told me he thought all conflicts should be settled by champions, squaring up, the only blood shed in the ring. His idea of combat was always individual. To build a character and a future, solitary effort was the key, and the most worthy drove themselves the hardest, took the greatest punishment: the boxers. Boxing suited his philosophy, his expectations and temperament. The magazine is filled with their faces, the men who made Joe's choice and boxed. Amateur and professional, each one measures himself against the classic pose: shoulders cocked, head ducked, hands ready and high, eyes confidently alert, perhaps that touch brighter with the possibility that, 'If you do achieve success, then your fists may well be the means of your seeing the world and meeting some of its most famous inhabitants.'

The path to personal advancement through sport: it's never offered with much enthusiasm to anyone outside the underclass, the risks are too great, the rewards too ephemeral. Boxing is held in reserve for the special cases, the young and poor who might be needed by the military, who might be troublesome if they weren't given discipline early enough. The myth is as powerful today as it was in the 1930s, the thought that—as *Health and Strength* put it— 'There is no sport like boxing to develop and cultivate a feeling of assurance and self-control. It gives you an aggressive spirit, properly leashed.' Watch African American and Hispanic kids trying to knock each other's lights out in any United States amateur bout, watch every nation offering up representatives of its least prosperous groups in Olympic competition or televised professional spectacles, and you'll realize boxing remains an occupation for the hungry.

I remember sitting in a Brooklyn church gym hall, watching a young Irish fighter losing, the only white boxer of the evening. His father, a small man who had obviously led an outdoor life, was behind me, trying to smoke away his nerves—he never normally touched cigarettes. He quietly rationalized the proceedings for me. This was a chance for the boy—coming to America—he'd never even, no offence, seen a black man at home and people had been very kind and, as long as he didn't get hurt, it could all be great for him. As long as he didn't get hurt.

Another father had brought along his son, a boy of eight or nine, who was a fan of World Wrestling Federation wrestling, but was already slowly pacing and turning his fist in the air ahead of him, working through the proper motions of a punch. Weaned on the glamour and choreographed fakery of the wrestlers, this was his first time at a boxing match and he was enjoying it well enough, tolerating the lack of pyrotechnics while his father tried to make a lesson of the evening. He wanted the boy to understand how fit a boxer has to be, how hard he has to try, about winning and losing and being only a few generations away from Ireland themselves, and this somehow having to do with life's realities. The boy kept on practising his punches, hardly listening, the man looking at me now, his voice softened, his eyes making it plain that this was something too hard to say, too hard to consider all at once. Then we both looked away while I remembered that my grandfather took my mother to watch boxing bouts and wondered what it might have been that he was trying to teach her. I'd only really agreed to come there that night in case it let me feel nearer to him, edged me back towards all the things I could no longer learn.

Joe Price's aggressive spirit may not have been leashed by boxing, but it was undoubtedly given expertise. Before he was twenty, he left Staffordshire for London after a confrontation with his father. It must have been a good day for a man who liked solutions, the day he fought for himself and for his mother, for what he loved. When I was very young, I met his mother, my great-grandmother, a few times: the last in a hospital. She lay motionless in an oxygen tent, the ward around her somehow distorted by the presence of a person so near to death. My grandfather couldn't bear to look at her, or even go close. He couldn't win her back—there was nobody to fight.

In London, Joe Price was apprenticed into the steel trade, learned how to dodge molten metal when it flew, played cards with a suspicious efficiency and slept in a hostel with a knife kept close to hand, because the Queensberry Rules don't cover everything. He kept on learning how to take his lumps and, even though he'd told his mother he would stop, he kept on boxing. She realized this was the case when she opened the March 7 issue of *Health and Strength* in 1936. There she discovered him, just as I do now, standing at the edge of a group from the Corinthian Athletic Club, Stoke Newington. (My mother and I have both inherited his photographic reticence, we all lurk at the frame's edge, if we can.) I can see the slight dip in his sternum—the place where he always told me he was hit by a cannon ball, a lie we both enjoyed. He's smiling a little, a muscular twenty-year-old in neat black trunks and boots. And (I may, of course, be biased) he seems to have a confidence, a presence, that none of the other Corinthians matches. Something about his expression suggests he is standing a little apart, not out of shyness, but because he is special.

And he's right, he knows he's special: as special as human beings prove to be when given any kind of close examination. He knows, for example, that he has 'short arms'—he grinds through his opponents' defences until he can infight. In the process, he soaks up punches to the eyes, the left eye especially, and to his head. Although he only fights for something like ten years and solely as an amateur, boxing will close down his eyesight and leave him using a magnifying glass for near work, squinting at splinters of metal that he can't find in his hands. What the punches will do to his thinking, no one will really be able to tell. Joe Price, like many boxers, wasn't educated to be an intellectual and his life rarely encouraged him to lower his guard among strangers, he was a largely closed and quiet man. His handwriting was never expected to be anything more than the fiercely angular printing I recognized on envelopes at Christmas and birthdays, or on the wildly over-wrapped parcels he sometimes sent. As I write in the hush of the room, I miss his lettering. I miss him: his secrets and evasions, even the ones about his eyes.

Joe made sure until late in his life that no one he loved would be able to tell exactly how much he couldn't see. With doctors, he would be adamant his weakness had nothing to do with boxing, most particularly when they said it was. With me, he would admit his style meant he'd had to battle—that was why they'd called him Battling Joe Price. He admired Sugar Ray Leonard, marked out his life according to a calendar of all the middleweight champions, but he always had a special affection for Marvin Hagler, another infighter, another brawler.

Because Battling Joe, when I think about it, didn't fight clean. Although with me he was never anything but tender, having no son and now no grandson, he told me his secrets of victory in the ring. How to stand on your opponent's feet, how to elbow, headbutt, rabbit and kidney punch and hit below the belt, how to wet the old-style leather gloves to make them hard and how to work your fingers through their horsehair stuffing to put some knuckle in your punch. It was his own fault when he broke his hands fighting—it would have been someone else's when he broke his arm. And for the eyes, he had no mercy, because an opponent blinded by swelling or blood is no real opponent at all. The gloves Joe fought with still had separate thumbs that could gouge into sockets and untaped lace ends he could use to open cuts above the eye, just as every twisting punch he landed on the eyebrow would be meant to. He fought, as they say, 'with bad intentions'. When he acknowledged that sometimes these tricks had been used against him, he still seemed both puzzled and aggrieved. Listening to the familiar purr in his voice, I never could understand why anyone would want to hurt him, why anyone would want to punch him in his eyes.

Joe's eyes, the same blue as mine, were built in the usual way, with a lens and muscles for focus to the front and a relatively gristly exterior behind which formed an almost spherical hollow filled with a translucent gel called vitreous humour. Like the eyes you're using to read this, they were miraculous; organs of sense so delicately complex and elegant that they gave Charles Darwin pause for thought. He wondered how gradual evolution could have created something only functional in such a highly developed state. The curved back of the eye has three layers: the outer sclera, then the choroid and then the retina. Our retinas receive the images which pass through the clear cornea, lens and vitreous humour. The retina is arguably where we start truly to see. If the eye were a camera, you might say the retina was its film.

But I hope it would come as no surprise that the human retina is far more lovely than any film. Freshly dissected, it is semi-transparent with a gentle purple tint, although it quickly clouds and whitens, fading. It is, after all, a fragile thing, never intended to be exposed. Under a microscope, the retina's ten layers appear more vegetable than animal, like impressionistic wood grain. Nutrition and sensitivity combine as the nerves within the layers transmit, and their cells consume and grow, entirely interdependent for the transfer of information and nourishment. This is a balanced system, cells sometimes intertwining across layers and sometimes simply resting against each other. Which is the retina's weak point—a hard blow to the eye can distort it for a moment and split the retina's layers apart, ripping the pigment cells away from the receptors which feed them and carry the impulses to generate our sight. Rents, even holes may form. An especially traumatic blow can rupture the eye itself, allow it to lose vitreous humour, but more commonly the retina suffers. Any detached section dies and the eye becomes, to a greater or lesser extent, blinded.

Joe Price boxed at a time when ringside doctors might not be present, when referees were none too anxious to stop fights, when boxers—if they could find the matches—might fight two or three times in one night, under a false name if they had to. He took more punishment than he would today, but the laws of physics haven't changed. Multiple hard blows will do more damage to an eye, may even 'punch your man blind', but it still only takes one significant impact to damage a retina. Laser surgery can fuse the retina back into place—my grandfather was offered the option, but didn't like the sound of it. Recently, minority medical opinion even suggested that eyes repaired in this way were stronger than they had been before. This has proved, unsurprisingly, not to be the case and boxers who have suffered retinal damage or any other serious eye pathology are not legally permitted to box in Britain, or to take part in world title bouts. A detached retina effectively ended British heavyweight Frank Bruno's career. Worldwide regulations are similar, although sometimes less stringent and more easily evaded, particularly when boxers choose to change their identities. No regulations can reach the unlicensed boxing underground which quietly eats up former contenders at the bottom of their downward slope and hard men who need money more than health.

Hard men: my grandfather haunted my childhood with them as if they were entirely natural companions for a young girl's mind. In my earliest years, I suppose, he was still hard himself. I would swing from his straight-extended arm, at least as pleased as he was with his strength, but I had no cause then to consider what such strength could do. I would read the descriptions he sent me of Victorian bare-knuckle battles to the death, or the marathon bouts between giants like Jim Corbett, John L. Sullivan and Jack Dempsey (he of the lead-pipe-weighted gloves) and the carnage would seem as genuine as a World Wrestling Federation contest. Joe Price and all the ghosts were just friends. Still, I've heard the stories of the way he was as a young married man, anxious to flatten any face that stared too long at my grandmother, looking for a fight.

Joe Price met Mildred Archer in 1938 during an uninspiring period for middleweights—Al Hostak was the NBA champion, soon to be ousted by Solly Krieger who lost the rematch in 1939, the year that Miss Archer became Mrs Price. In 1940, another steelworker, Tony 'Man of Steel' Zale, was on top of the world, and the Price's first and only child was born: my mother, Edwardine Mildred.

The Prices made a tight couple, almost too tight for a daughter to fit. They wore suits cut from the same cloth and had their hairstyles matched, my grandmother sporting an Eton crop. Their arguments and reconciliations were equally close-quarter and intense. By the time I knew them, they still worked singly—my grandmother as a French polisher with spectacularly roughened hands—but otherwise they were rarely apart and seemed to need few friends. Milly would shop and Joe would cook and clean and bring her tea and magazines when she took her regular afternoon naps. Every Sunday he would dust the venetian blinds and make lunch before his wife came home from church.

For many years I didn't realize the facts upon which this intimacy rested, the reason for my grandmother's anxiety when her husband was even a few minutes late home. Her marriage to Joe was her second. Mildred Price, a woman of some passion, had courted Jack Peace and loved and married him, just as she should, and they had gone to bed on their wedding night and in the morning she had found him beside her, quite dead. He had been suffering from cancer, but had told nobody.

For a while, Mildred weathered an entirely understandable nervous breakdown. She would be eccentric all her life, but now she saw ghosts. She couldn't bear to be alone and had to be put out on a chair in the street if no one was left in the house. The family sent her to London for a change of air and this gave her a lifelong fear of the place—she never liked to hear that I was there, risking a city where she'd spent so much unhappy time. She never managed to meet

Joe in the unfriendly size of the capital, but did when they were both back home again, safe in Staffordshire.

Joe Price must have been the perfect man for Milly. He was demonstrably, tangibly healthy, more than ten years her junior and fiercely ready for anything. Joe was happy to be utterly devoted, despite his family's certainty that he was marrying beneath him, and he had that smile, that air of being out of the ordinary. Once he married, he even agreed to stop boxing—the risks would have made his wife entirely demented—and contented himself with training policemen in combat and self-defence. But he still took his wife and daughter to fights. My mother can remember attending a civic hall bout where an Irish Catholic boxer made a great point of crossing himself before the opening round. Then, in front of the almost exclusively Nonconformist audience, he hit the canvas unconscious, having caught the first punch.

My grandfather told the same story, it held another secret he intended to pass on—don't be too sure of God's protection. Never mind Providence, Joe Price believed in being personally prepared, from his indestructible parcels to his ease with a half nelson. To underline the point, he also told me the tale of Randy Turpin, a man who was thoroughly ready at just the right time. He was one of my grandmother's favourites—she liked the way he wore his initials, RAT, on his shorts. Turpin came out against the odds and beat the great Sugar Ray Robinson in Earls Court in 1951. Robinson had been overcommitted and was probably tired but was said to have been complacent, to have spent the night before the fight playing cards until the small hours. Turpin, a fine British middleweight with two equally useful hands, had arrived unawed and in peak condition. He fought the distance fluently and, by the end, Robinson was bleeding and the crowd was singing 'For He's a Jolly Good Fellow' to Turpin. If Joe Price had a dream, it must have been something like this, to slip in as an underdog and win the world.

I wasn't told that Turpin lost the title to Robinson only sixty-four days later in a rematch in New York, and never flew so high again, or that his last days were penniless, or that he committed suicide in Leamington Spa, the genteelly depressing town where I lived as a student. Robinson ended up equally poor and with Alzheimer's disease.

Depression, unmanageable anger, Parkinson's disease, substance abuse, Alzheimer's: they're among the unhappy ghosts that seem to flurry around boxing, no matter how hard it tries to be the Noble Art. John Tate: alcohol and cocaine addiction, became homeless and died in a car crash. Wilfred Benitez: brain-damaged. Michael Dokes: coke addict, now in jail for sexual assault and attempted murder. Tony Tucker: former coke addict and now religious convert. Jimmy Bivins: brain-damaged and broke. Pinklon Thomas: formerly coke addict, currently youth worker. Jerry, Mike and Bob Quarry: all brain-damaged, Jerry now dead. Oliver McCall: coke addict, jailed for assault. Floyd Patterson: brain-damaged. Riddick Bowe: currently under house arrest after abducting his estranged wife and children. All were champions once, or contenders.

The problem lies in identifying cause and effect. No matter how stunned or revolted observers were by Ali and Frazier slogging it out in the 'Thriller in Manila' in 1975, no one can definitively state that Muhammad Ali's genes hadn't always determined he would spend his later years hemmed in by Parkinson's disease.

And then there's Tyson, the poor monster, Don King's punching freak show—a money machine for everyone with the possible exception of himself. Tyson's temperament was never docile, even in the sunny days of his old coach Cuss D'Amato, when boxing looked as if it would save a ghetto kid from more jail time and an invisible, wasted life. Now the business of boxing allows him to behave badly and go easy on the sporting discipline. A truly iron Mike, after all, is bad for the pay-per-view; an out-of-shape Tyson, weakened by character defects and deficiencies in the ring, promises a positively Shakespearean spectacle. But are his flaws caused by bad character, bad company, or blows to the head? Tyson, even now, is hardly known for catching punches.

Both sides try to carve out their own moral high ground. To quote Golden Gloves of America Incorporated, which organizes America's most influential amateur championships, boxing supporters promote a sport which 'encourages a positive lifestyle for today's youth', although your average Golden Gloves competition will be heavily policed to keep all those disciplined gentlemen, and now ladies, from—possibly armed—combat outside the ring. And, for the few, we're reminded, there's the chance of fame, maybe wealth, some foreign travel. Boxing's opponents see self-destructive dupes being injured in the ring to provide promoters and ghouls with a gladiatorial spectacle. While some professionals hit the big time, in their opinion, all boxers, including juniors and amateurs, risk serious injury or death.

The physics of boxing is slightly less ambivalent. And when the will, the imagination, when thought is removed—that's what we all come down to: physics. It might be said that our lives represent an elaborate flight from the inevitable return to inanimate matter and the laws that govern it. When Ali managed not to drop before Frazier did in Manila, he proved we can buck the trend for a while, despite extreme pressure. He is, after all, the man who kept on going against Ken Norton in San Diego in 1973, even with a badly broken jaw. When Joey Gamache went down in the second round to Arturo Gatti in Madison Square Garden last spring and then sat up, looking about him—a man in bloodstained shorts with the face of a waking child— he was diminished, but on his way back from the fall. The fall, when his head met a dreadfully effective triple combination of punches, when his body dropped beyond his control—that was when Gamache was matter and nothing more, a mindless, tumbling mass. His utter unconsciousness was as plain as a tiny piece of death: as clear as— say—Tommy Hearns's knockout at Caesar's Palace in Las Vegas in 1985. Marvin Hagler had worked neatly, methodically, through three vicious rounds, one eye eventually clouded over with his own blood, while Hearns's long arms whipped in at him, increasingly powerlessly. Then, the swagger still in his shoulders, Hagler punched Hearns back into a spin, caught him with a final right and Hearns's face emptied, took on the puzzled look of a post-mortem photograph, while his body drooped over Hagler, fell without a will. Physics.

Various researchers have tried to calculate the force of a punch, placing accelerometers in punching bags, asking boxers to swing at force plates. A more realistic experiment studied the British heavyweight Frank Bruno when he punched a sixteen-pound ballistic pendulum—sixteen pounds is roughly the weight of a heavyweight opponent's head and neck. The punch travelled at a little under nine miles per second and the force it exerted was calculated at 0.63 tons. Naturally, a range of boxers would have to be tested to average out the blows for various weights and levels of ability. Still, it gives us some idea of what one punch amounts to, which is, in this particular case, equivalent to the impact of a thirteen-pound padded mallet being swung at twenty miles per hour.

In a street fight, the swing can connect where it likes; in the ring it has rules to follow, a target area for scoring blows. If the fist is correctly positioned and lands a technically proper punch to the torso or the front of the head, it is deemed 'effective'. Punches to the head, carrying with them the possibility of a knockout, or at least a knock-down, are understandably popular. What happens when the head suffers an impact depends greatly upon the physics of the skull and brain. There is a slim, fluid-filled space between the brain and the skull, which means that, when the head moves violently, the brain can literally twist on its stem inside the skull and can collide repeatedly with the surrounding bone as the skull's acceleration and deceleration fail to match that of its contents. The resultant stretching and shearing within the different structures of the brain can stress neurons beyond their tolerance. Damage to the two membranes (the septum pellucidum) that separate the two fluid-filled ventricles deep inside the brain is thought to indicate other, as yet invisible, penetrating stress. The septum pellucidum is close to the limbic lobe, an area of the brain associated with aggression. Injury here is thought to have links with violently dysfunctional behaviour. For all that the brain has a phenomenal capacity for reorganization and survival, it will always be limited by the fact that nervous tissue cannot regenerate.

A membrane, the dura, designed to hold the brain in place, can be damaged, as can blood vessels inside and outside the brain. Bleeding can increase the pressure inside the skull, even forcing the brain down towards an impossible exit, the point where the brain stem feeds out into the spinal column. Blood clots within the brain, or between the brain and skull, can cause anything from localized areas of dead tissue to coma and death. Dead tissue in the brain can, of course, affect anything and everything that we think of as ourselves: our ability to move, our senses and our personalities.

A. L. Kennedy

It's hard for anybody to imagine their own destruction. Boxers may find it harder than most, trained as they are to pare down their thinking to the moment, an eternally present tense of speed, attack, response, a sometimes self-destructive belief in the attainability of success. Their trainers and supporters surround them with uplifting lies. In Brooklyn, the young Irish kid and all the other losers heard their share as their opponents pummelled them—'Stick a jab on him when he charges', 'Punch when he punches', 'Don't feel bad, you did well', 'Even if you lose this now, you've won it'.

Win or lose, they grow from sporting teens with the usual sheen of immortality into men of certainty and solutions—because that's how they have to be, the ring would be intolerable without a mental defence. This kind of individualistic, almost magical training in faith and faith in training may be one reason why boxers, despite so many generations of uneven breaks and destitute retirements, have never formed an effective association in any country. It is always their patrons who organize. Meanwhile, alone in the ring, the boxer works in a place where self belief is all that will move a body against pain, against an opponent who is equally alone. Injury and failure are too close to consider, in case the thought might bring them on.

And the brain, in any event, is always shy when it comes to thinking of itself. Sitting in the library, I can turn my head to look around and know that I'm turning—among other things—about forty-two ounces of brain. My whole sense of myself and the world: up there in a weight I can't notice. It would fit, cradled very comfortably, in my palms, almost surrounded by my fingers. A man's brain might be three or four ounces more—either way, this seems light, considering all it represents. If I set it down on the table beside me, it would subside just a little, showing that it's surprisingly soft, vulnerable. This is what you and I carry under the scalp, above the face: the familiar coils and curves that give the organ's form a peculiar, fluid grace. Sliced cleanly through from—as it were—ear to ear, the brain looks almost like agate, the layer of grey matter undulating gently, surrounding the layer of white, the ventricles opened in twinned, seashell curves. The septum pellucidum is of an almost impossibly delicate, milky transparency. The brain makes a beautiful, unsettling study—a fascinating object with a form that gives little indication of its function. It is left unscarred by thought. I couldn't guess where, or quite how, it held scraps such as my liking for raspberries, the movements necessary for a kiss, my kiss, my past, all the memories upon memories that deal only with my grandfather's way of walking—so much I wish to be defended.

And, if I decided to enter the ring today, boxing medics would try their best to defend me. In fact, if I didn't conceal my medical history, they'd bar me immediately for the sake of my health. I have suffered serious concussion and migraines, both of which would lead to my exclusion from any kind of reputable organized boxing. The British Boxing Board of Control is arguably at the forefront of boxing safety. It submits professional boxers to an exhaustive number of tests and investigations before granting them a licence to fight. MRI scans were made compulsory in 1995. Any discovery of weakness, psychological instability, drug use or prior damage and the licence is not granted. The tests are repeated annually. There are cooling-off periods for recuperation between fights and a series of weigh-ins to pick up fighters who are trying to make their weight by dehydrating. Dehydration may slightly increase the space between the brain and the skull, intensifying injuries—it certainly weakens boxers and leaves them open to greater risk from their opponents. Participants are examined before and after bouts with particular attention paid to those who have suffered any period of unconsciousness. Doctors and an ambulance with trained staff and resuscitation equipment are on standby during bouts. Of course, safety provisions and testing for juniors and amateurs are not so extensive, although they run the same risks as professionals, without the benefit of experience.

When I asked the British Boxing Board of Control's chief medical officer, Adrian Whiteson, about the safety conditions surrounding my grandfather's boxing life, he mouthed 'appalling', as if he would rather not criticize the sport out loud. He presents modern boxing with a reformer's quiet evangelism—the professional game is conducted in a medically responsible manner, fielding boxers who are all thoroughly screened for optimum safety and psychological stability, fighting fit, chemically clean and engaged in an occupation with social benefits. In a professional boxing scene still heavily connected with organized crime, and where financial risks and pressures are high, Whiteson's portrait of the noble art admits no pressure to compromise, no lies, no evasions. The mystifying fact that Mike Tyson is able to pass a British psychological examination and gain his licence to fight here goes unmentioned. Whiteson contrasts licensed, responsible boxing with the underground scene, the legendary turf where mobster enforcers meet gypsy champions. He doesn't mention the current rise in British unlicensed public boxing—a high-risk affair with few safeguards for often poorly prepared participants—and the popularity of the even more gladiatorial no-holds-barred fighting codes such as Vale Tudo. In his, and the British Boxing Board of Control's, opinion, keeping licensed boxing popular offers the best chance of keeping boxers safe, or as safe as anyone involved in a contact sport might reasonably expect to be. Whiteson is not a member of the British Medical Association which, like its American counterpart, calls for a total ban on boxing, licensed and unlicensed. He genuinely loves boxers as individuals, loves the sport. This, many fellow medics would argue, involves him in a degree of double-thinking.

He appears absolutely sincere when he states that: 'The sport is irrelevant. At the end of the day, it's their health that matters.' He denies the existence of hard evidence that repeated exposure to head trauma produces a high chance of brain damage and points out that too few examinations of brains have been carried out to determine what a 'normal' level of damage to structures such as the septum pellucidum would be. Nevertheless, he does admit that, in such an extreme sport, it is impossible to prevent injuries, sometimes of the very worst kind: 'Not the acute brain damage, sadly no one can stop that.' Health matters, then, but boxing will continue in spite of the consequent unavoidable acute brain damage. Whiteson makes it plain that the British Boxing Board of Control's policy is to stop a fight continuing, or even taking place, if there is any doubt over a boxer's condition, because: 'One punch and he could die.' And yet he has a touching faith in the ability of an 'equally matched' fight to reduce both boxers' risks to acceptable levels.

Dr Whiteson is the kind of man my grandfather would have trusted, a proper gentleman with a Wimpole Street private practice and an OBE. Intelligent, soft-spoken and charming, he tells me how natural boxing is—that two infants in a playpen would fight over a toy. As it happens, the example undermines his point. The infants might well scrap over the toy, but then the winner would generally win and the loser would cry and that would tend to be that. Bouts of formalized, punching combat certainly wouldn't ensue. Studies show that children fighting tend to wrestle. If blows are struck at all, they are more likely to be slaps than punches and the head seems to be protected by something akin to a physical taboo. When tired or inexperienced fighters fall to clinches and slapping blows, they are withdrawing from their training into, one might say, more natural techniques. The pugilistic toddlers provide the sort of anecdotal evidence that stops comfortable people being too uneasy about less comfortable people's pain by making it a natural necessity. They have little connection with fact.

I would be the first to agree that violence exists in nature, but I also know it has nature's economy. Whether it proves dominance or provides food, it's too quick and too definitive to provide paying entertainment. Boxing exists in an artificial middle ground between death and retreat—in very human territory that encompasses humiliation, bravery, fear and the kind of sympathetic magic which creates the worship of champions. Human beings do attack each other, of course. I've been attacked and I've defended myself, once against a Parisian pickpocket and once against a Scottish drunk, but upper cuts and timed rounds didn't come into it. I did what my grandfather taught me to do, which was quick and worked. Punching someone in the head (so much a part of boxing) is an unnatural act and is often outside, or marginal to, even combative experience. Ask anyone who's stepped in the ring, or watch young fighters try to press themselves into truly trading blows—the giving and accepting of that type of pain, that particular shock, takes a lot of getting used to, no matter how much adrenalin and training lends a hand. My grandfather got used to it, he had the knack. Joe Price said he only ever lost one fight, his first, because he was frightened. He made sure he wasn't frightened again. His life had prepared him to see that as a good choice.

Go into a gym and you'll see the ones who have it and the ones who don't. Dancing and dipping through combinations, their trainers singing out, counting out, blows that will contact faster than they can be named: 'Hook, hook. One, two,' you'll realize the boxer's unopposed speed. Bodies slip and angle round each other, the presence or absence of commitment achingly obvious. Men stare themselves down in mirrors, hit the treadmill, skip and sweat, finding personal walls and breaking through them, finding and breaking through. This is where Joe Price lived, amongst the down-time tenderness of sparring partners, the small breaks of nudging play and the docile binding of hands: the willingness to let them be a helpless weight, before they take their proper place and swing, express a will. Neurological tests found one other effect of boxing, the improvement of motor functions, the increased ability to master human physics.

In training and in the ring, here is what Mildred Archer fell in love with—the flush under the skin that might be passion or pain, shame or heat. Here are the men who move with uncanny precision, even outside the ropes—soft-shoed, soft-footed men who have a constant, unusual sense of direction, a firm expression of will. When I watch old boxers—the set of their shoulders, the fix of their heads, the slightly softened mouths—I realize how much of my grandfather was burned into him by boxing. He walked like a middleweight, with that particular blend of solidity and lightness.

I've heard Tyson talk in an interview about the sheer excitement of 'being able to outsmart a man...to out-time them, to out-think them...they make one mistake and you outsmart them and then you have their wallet.' I didn't expect him to remind me of my grandfather, but he did. Joe Price was the man who would beat you every time. A burglar once decided to break into what should have been just one in a row of pensioners' apartments. But it was my grandfather's home and, even in his sixties, he was more than able to knock the intruder out cold. He was so pleased that all he could wish for was to be able to do it again. My grandfather took exception to being robbed, of course, but he also punched the man out just because he still could. Thirty years earlier, Joe Price would be the one to join you casually in a game of cards as you both whiled away a train trip, the one who would somehow manage to clean you out by the time you reached your station. That was how he got his holiday spending money. He did it because he could and you were stupid enough to let him.

At our final meeting, we got out the cards and, for the first and only time, my grandfather played as he would have against a stranger. We both knew that he was very ill and that we might not see each other again. He asked me to cut the deck whenever I dealt and named every card I cut to before I showed it. He was a man with hardly any eyesight left, with a body that was comprehensively betraying him, and he beat me soundly, thoroughly, arrogantly, beautifully. He knew what the ring was all about before he ever climbed inside: it was a place where he could win in a life where— beyond the card games—he would spend a great deal of time never even being able to compete. I know that he deserved better, because boxing rewards few and damages many—it damaged him. Boxing is not, by its nature, safe. Span your hand across the crown of your head and you'll be measuring out the greatest distance the force of a punch will ever travel, the greatest distance over which it will ever be able to dissipate. You'll be cupping your palm perhaps half an inch above the greater part of what you are. Joe Price, the little-known amateur, risked that every time he sparred, or fought, just as any world champion did, just as anyone who boxes does today. There is no audience, no manager, no promoter, no association, no doctor, no trainer worthy of that commitment.

My grandfather made the best of it, just as he made the best of an unusual marriage, of plans to be his own boss that never quite materialized, of his ulcers, his heart attacks, of the night when his wife was suddenly ill, fell asleep and never woke, of the last six years he spent as a widower growing frail. Even when it took him some effort to cross a road, he still had that air of being special, the dignity he'd fought for. If he went slowly, it was because he intended to stroll, if he leaned on my arm it was because he had decided we'd walk close. Still, make no mistake, he hated being old and unable to see. He didn't want to have lost his power, the shadow he'd always boxed, now slow beside him, uneasy in its balance. Providence was catching up with him. Used to fighting, to pushing himself where his will needed him to be, he decided to go for heart surgery, in the hope that it would free him from the problems of old age. He wanted to die on the table. In fact, the set of tests before the operation gave him his wish.

A. L. Kennedy

I thought his last gift came when he told me he was going for the surgery and gave me the chance to say goodbye. I was wrong. In researching this piece, I've discovered another. *Health and Strength* would have called me a 'brain worker' and, sifting through the Internet files and libraries, working away, I've found the secret he left for me to find.

My grandfather always called me Tiger, which is an unusual nickname in Britain, especially for a girl. It was something else between us that only we had and that no one ever questioned, although he allowed it to fall out of use as I grew up. I remember going back to his house just after my grandmother died, climbing the narrow stairs and walking into a room full of silent relatives. His chair faced away from the door, as it always had, and he turned round to me softly and said, as I'd known he would, 'Hello, Tiger', wishing us back to a time when I could still swing on his arm and his wife was alive. And now I understand why I was Tiger. Checking the middleweight champions he followed all his life, I found that the World Champion in the year I was born, 1965, was the British-based Nigerian fighter Dick Tiger. Before I even knew myself, my grandfather had made up his mind and privately christened me for a champion of the world. So now I thank him for that.   □

GRANTA

WHALE
Panos Karnezis

Whale arrived at work a little after seven with black circles round his eyes. All night his stomach ulcer had kept him running back and forth between his bedroom and the kitchen, searching every drawer and cupboard for his ammonium carbonate tablets. In desperation, not being able to endure the firecrackers going off inside his stomach, he was about to down a bottle of Mercurochrome he'd found under the sink when his sister walked in. 'Don't do it, fool!' she cried. 'Or the doctors will turn you inside out and scrub you with a steel brush!' She found his tablets in less than a minute, but by the time they had taken effect it was time for Whale to get to work.

He unlocked the padlock and raised the rolling shutters in a well executed clean-and-jerk lift learned in his amateur weightlifting days. For a few months now the shutters had been heavier and, thinking that maybe the rain had corroded the bearings, he promised himself he would grease them. Puffing and sweating, he opened the glass door to the shop and immediately felt as if he were stepping into the mouth of a sewer pipe: it smelled of rotting cabbage and alcohol. He turned round and spat in the street. The boy hadn't taken the rubbish out last night.

Whale sighed. He had to clean the place up himself before the first customers arrived. He collected the rubbish and, because the dustman had already passed, left the bins in the back. After washing the ashtrays and the glasses, he climbed on an empty beer case and lit the oil lamp next to the picture of St Barnabas. From there he inspected the shop. All in all, there was a refrigerator with a glass front, a cupboard built into the wall where his sporting cups and medals were, and seven tin tables with wooden legs, which he had made himself. The legs were standing at random angles as if they were walking towards the door.

The case swayed a little and Whale's hair brushed against the dusty fan blades above his head. Climbing down, he caught sight of himself in the mirror: the dust on his hair and last night's insomnia made him look forty years older. 'My mother was right,' he thought. 'I do look like my father after all.'

That moment the door opened and a woman came in. Whale turned round and the woman looked at his hair and raised an eyebrow. 'Good morning,' she said.

The woman, who had only one shoe on, limped towards a seat. She sat down and breathed with relief. 'I've been walking like a cripple for a mile,' she said. She held her other shoe in her hand along with a small handbag and put both on the table. The shoe was made of black patent leather and its enormous heel had come off.

'I can fix that for you,' said Whale.

'Don't bother,' she replied, but gave him the shoe.

Still out of breath, she cut every word short. She lit a cigarette and smoked it in long draws. Before she'd put it out, Whale had fixed the shoe.

'It's easier to roller skate than walk in these,' he commented, giving the shoe back. 'Here. It'll last forever.'

The woman sighed. 'Thanks. But the only thing that lasts forever is my corn.'

A car drove past outside. It was the week before the Feast of the Assumption, and the capital was empty: that was when most people took their annual holidays. A cloud of hot dust blew into the shop and Whale rushed to close the door. 'This weather is only fit for camels,' he said, switching on the fan, but the blades didn't move. He flicked the switch a couple more times but still nothing happened. Scratching his head, he opened the fuse box on the wall. The fuse for the fan had blown and there wasn't a spare.

Whale took a bottle of lemonade from the refrigerator.

'Apologies for the discomfort,' he said. 'Drinks are on the house.'

The woman took a sip.

'I'm hungry, Whale.'

'I can make you eggs. They're good for you.'

He went back behind the bar without waiting for a reply. While he fried the eggs, he whistled and hummed. 'With this heat,' he joked, over the sizzling, 'I could probably fry them faster on your table top.' With the fan out of order, Whale slowly disappeared behind the smoke coming from the pan. The woman could hear him but not see him.

'I'd give anything to be at the beach now.'

'What?' asked Whale.

'I said,' said the woman, raising her voice, 'Don't cook them for too long.'

Whale finally appeared with a plate and another bottle of lemonade. The woman ate avidly. Whale observed her for a while, as he would have observed a child.

'A day like this,' he said, 'one should be at the beach.'

'I thought the same thing, you know.'

Whale shrugged his mountainous shoulders and for a second looked out of the window in silence.

'You seem to be the only customer today,' he mused, wiping his forehead with his apron. 'We might as well lock up and ride the bus to the beach.'

'Do you mean that?'

'Sure.'

The woman put down her fork and tugged her hair behind her ear.

'Where do you want to go?' asked Whale.

'The city beach. Next to the fairground. The tickets are on me.'

'Fair enough. We can hire an umbrella there. In this heat.'

'Deckchairs.'

'And two deckchairs,' agreed Whale.

The woman ate some more from her plate and took another swig at her lemonade.

'Why not visit the rides, too?' suggested Whale. 'They advertise their roller coaster as the scariest ride next to taking a taxi in the capital.'

'And the house of horrors.'

'Sure. And the shooting gallery.'

Suddenly the woman changed expression and put down the bottle.

'Maybe I should ask Retsina first. I haven't seen him for days.'

Whale lowered his head. His hair was still covered in dust.

'I wouldn't have anything to do with a man who calls himself after a wine,' he said, lightly.

The woman looked at him quizzically.

'You're named after a fish.'

Whale blushed.

'Not fish. Mammal,' he corrected her. 'And I didn't choose it.'

They said nothing for a while. On the plate there was still one egg left. The woman picked up her fork and played with its yolk.

Then the door opened and a young man came in with a small plastic radio in his hand. He was half as tall as Whale, with narrow sloping shoulders and a face with puckered lips as if he were agonized with constipation. 'Damn! It's as hot as a kiln in here,' he said. He sat next to the woman and placed the radio on the table. He switched it on and fiddled with the aerial.

'Get me a double brandy, fat man,' Retsina said, still concentrating on the radio.

Whale went to the bar and brought him the drink.

'What is this?' asked Retsina after he'd tasted it.

'Brandy.'

Retsina smiled with contempt and turned to the woman.

'He'll soon be selling us shit for cheese,' he said.

He picked up the fork and tasted the eggs. He then produced a small comb from his back pocket. Turning round, he brought his face close to the window.

'Where were you?' he asked, watching his reflection, and combing his hair.

There was silence.

'I buy you everything you ask for,' he said, still combing his hair. 'Even the shoes you wear. And then you disappear for days.'

'It's my money,' she murmured.

'What?'

'I earn that money myself,' said the woman.

The man turned round and looked at her. She looked down.

'You earn that money yourself,' he said. 'I see. She earns that money herself.' He drank some brandy. 'Never mind me staying up all night, following you round town to make sure you don't get knifed, while you earn money all by yourself.'

When the woman picked up her fork, the man grabbed her hand.

'Let's go.'

Whale came from behind the bar.

'She has plans for today.'

'Plans?'

'We're going to the beach.'

The man let go of the woman. 'Well, well,' he said. He sat back in his chair, turned the radio down and tapped his comb against the table. 'Listen to that! Whale is going to the beach today!'

'Cut it out,' said the woman.

'He's going to play on the sand with his friends, the seal and the dolphin.'

The woman stood up.

'Leave him alone, Retsina.'

'Whale is going to go to the beach with my woman to sun his love handles.'

'Nothing wrong with that,' said Whale.

Retsina sat back in his chair and stretched his legs. Next to him, the woman chewed her nails. Inside his stomach, Whale felt his ulcer getting inflamed and bit his lip. Retsina tapped his little comb on the tin surface of his table again. His eyes fell on the framed pictures on the wall and the dusty cups on the shelf.

'Whale the weightlifter will go to the beach and eat an ice, and tell my woman all about his weightlifting days. About his medals and his cups that brought him all this fame and glory.'

He spread his arms to show that he meant the coffee shop. Whale's pain spread to his kidney. He dug his nails into the soft cushions of his palms and cold sweat appeared on his temples. He tried to forget about the pain. He thought of his sister in the kitchen. Every day at lunchtime she'd bring the pan and they'd eat in silence behind the bar.

'I'm a decent person,' he said.

'You'll miss the bus if you don't hurry, fat man,' said Retsina. 'Why don't you come and take my woman by the hand and rush to the depot?'

'Retsina—'

'Shut up,' Retsina cut the woman off. 'Whale is going to take you to the beach.'

'I'm a decent man,' said Whale again. 'There's nothing wrong with going to the beach.'

Retsina looked him in the eye. Whale stood there as if his shoes were nailed to the floor, his face turning white from the pain in his stomach.

'Look at your decent boyfriend,' said Retsina, finally. 'His face is whiter than his apron.'

'He's not my boyfriend.' The woman pushed Retsina timidly, the way one pushes another passenger in a crowded bus. 'Let's go. He must've been dreaming when he thought I'd go with him.'

Retsina looked at her.

'Are you sure?'

'I want to go. Now.'

'To the beach?'

'Home.'

Retsina stood up. He put his comb in his back pocket, picked up his radio, and turned to leave, but then stopped and came back to finish the food. 'Forget the beach, fat man,' he said with his mouth full. 'And other men's women. Learn to cook instead.'

The woman was waiting outside.

'And get some decent brandy,' said Retsina. He walked out without paying, leaving the door open.

Whale stared at the door for several minutes. Then he went over and locked it twice from inside. Walking with difficulty because of the pain, he began looking everywhere for his tablets. He couldn't find them. He picked up the phone to ring his sister, but changed his mind, put down the receiver and went and sat in a chair behind the bar. Gradually the pain became intolerable. But there he sat, with his plump hands on his stained apron, shivering despite the heat. Every now and then a customer knocked at the door, but Whale didn't move. At lunchtime his sister came with the steaming pan, but he didn't let her in either. □

Gadfly

Culture That Matters

Magazine

William Burroughs Georgia O'Keefe The
Flaming Lips William Faulkner Kurt
Vonnegut The Sex Pistols Hunter S.
Thompson Paul Bowles David Lynch Judy
Chicago Anaïs Nin Paddy
Chayefsky Tom Robbins
Louis Armstrong Keith

Subscribe Now • Save Over 40%

Haring Marilyn Monroe Alfred
Hitchcock Blue Man Group
Francis Bacon Paul McCartney John
Lennon Jean-Michel Basquiat Bob Dylan
Douglas Coupland Franz Kafka Lester
Bangs Gore Vidal Michael Herr Monty
Python Hank Williams Ani DiFranco The
Last Poets Oliver Stone Frank Zappa J.G.
Ballard Andy Warhol Terry Southern

*"Gadfly is second only to the Library of Congress as a warehouse of
American pop culture - and number one when it comes to fun reading."*
UTNE Reader

www.gadfly.org   **1.888.4GADFLY**

GRANTA

THE ASCENT
OF MAN

Joseph O'Neill

Trinidad, 1999: The Old Train Line leading to the place where Sylvia Maraj was murdered (top)

One June dusk in 1999 I found myself walking across a rice field near Fishing Pond, in east Trinidad, in the company of a game warden and a self-described naturalist-at-large sometimes known as the Turtle Man. We tramped single file through the rice field for half an hour, then came to a rickety footbridge that led into a mangrove swamp. Treading carefully, I followed my companions over the uneven planks. The Turtle Man recalled how, in the days before the bridge existed, he used to wade hip-deep through the mangroves, which as we walked in the twilight stuck up from the swamp with a stricken, Pompeiian air. The footbridge brought us to the Atlantic Ocean and a sandy beach. We headed north along the beach for a mile or two, encountering only a flock of vultures. The beach was studded with the stumps of dead trees: every year the ocean pushed the beach deeper and deeper into the swamp, and it was inevitable that the forest would in time drown in the sand. Back in the Seventies, the Turtle Man said, the beach here might have been littered with the carcasses of up to thirty leatherback turtles killed by poachers. As the authorities did nothing about the slaughter, he took it upon himself to act. He would hide his trail bike, a Yamaha 100, among the coconut trees, and, armed with a fishing gun and dressed in a khaki outfit which he hoped made him look like a game warden, patrol the miles of beaches where the turtles came ashore to lay their eggs. If he saw poachers, he would challenge them to stop. 'It was a crazy thing to do,' the Turtle Man said. 'It was the middle of the night and these men were armed with cutlasses.'

'You do it,' the Turtle Man said, 'and you don't know why you do it.' He would note the numbers of the poachers' cars and trace their owners at the licence office. Sometimes, on learning the identity of a poacher, the Turtle Man would visit him at home and warn him, pretending to be an official. Other times, he would try to frighten a poacher by dumping a turtle head in his garden. 'I became a notoriety,' the Turtle Man said. 'I finally stopped in the Eighties, when government patrols began because of all the publicity. Now the turtle beach is a top-of-the-bill tourist attraction and even I can't go there without a pass. It's tremendous.'

We reached the mouth of a small river that flowed out of the mangrove forest: gigantic seal-like creatures called manatees swam in that river, the game warden said. We stopped for a few minutes and looked around. Although oil rigs were beginning to twinkle on the horizon, it was not yet dark enough for the turtles to come ashore.

'People said that for a while there I went off at the deep end,' the Turtle Man continued as we waited for night to fall. He laughed softly at himself. It was real guerrilla warfare, he said. 'Can you believe that I would find the poachers' cars and puncture the tyres with an ice pick? If they'd caught me, I'd have been murdered. The turtle hunters were desperate people. They came at weekends, some from as far as San Fernando, way down in the south. For poor people, a turtle was a great source of food. These are giant turtles, the biggest in the world, five feet long, five hundred kilograms, maybe fifty to sixty years old. It takes a female turtle about an hour to crawl up the beach, dig a hole, and lay a bunch of eggs. That's when the killing happened. They'd turn the turtle on her back, chop off her flippers, then chop off her head.'

When the Turtle Man said this, we exchanged a look. We were both thinking about the event that had brought me—a London lawyer, not a naturalist—to Trinidad, an event that had taken place exactly fourteen years before, on the night of June 27, 1985.

On the morning of June 28, 1985, police officers based at Cumuto, a village in the Trinidadian countryside, called on the home of Ramnath 'Dread' Harrilal. They asked him about the whereabouts of his girlfriend, Sylvia Maraj. Harrilal led the officers to the rear of his shack. There a path ran to an outdoor latrine about fifty feet away. The officers followed Harrilal to the latrine. Inside the latrine was a barrel-shaped cesspit almost completely filled with fluid. 'Sylvia in there,' Harrilal said, referring to the severed head, two severed legs, severed arm, and portion of an upper torso that were submerged in the pit. Later that day, Harrilal took police officers to a spot in the nearby forest. There, in an animal feed sack, they found the missing segment of Sylvia Maraj's upper torso to which her left arm was attached. Ramnath Harrilal signed a written confession that day. He stated that, in the course of an argument the night before, he'd struck Sylvia Maraj repeatedly on the head and afterwards, using a cutlass, had dismembered and decapitated her.

In Trinidad, 'chopping crimes', such as the one committed by Ramnath Harrilal, are invariably associated with people of Indian descent—East Indians, as they're called. This prejudice dates back to the mid-nineteenth century, when the black African workforce abandoned the sugar plantations and tens of thousands of indentured Indians, mainly peasants from the Ganges plain, were shipped to Trinidad as replacements. Agricultural labour remained the defining occupation of East Indians even after independence in 1962, when the Republic of Trinidad and Tobago was governed by the predominantly African–Trinidadian PNM (People's National Movement) for decades. However, the economic revolution that followed the discovery of oil and gas in the Seventies offered new possibilities for East Indians. Many moved into small businesses which had nothing to do with swinging a cutlass in the fields. In one sense, therefore, the death of Sylvia Maraj in 1985 was a throwback, a gruesome echo of the old order. In another sense, it was a foretaste of things to come.

In the second half of the Eighties, there was a sharp increase in violent crime in Trinidad: more stick-ups, muggings, break-ins, carjackings, and a surge in homicides. By the early Nineties, up to a hundred people a year were being murdered in Trinidad and Tobago, a country with a historically law-abiding population of 1.3 million. To many who remembered a safer and more tranquil Trinidad, it seemed that the economic boom, which had stalled in the early Eighties because of the fall in oil prices and the worldwide recession, was now corrupting public morality. Many identified the trade in South American narcotics as the most potent source of the new criminality. Trinidad lies only a few miles from Venezuela, which adjoins Colombia, and by the Nineties, over 20,000 kilos of cocaine bound for Europe and the United States passed every year through the island republic. In November 1992 the PNM government took action: in defence of a society that perceived itself to be besieged by bandits and killers and hoodlums, it ended the unofficial moratorium on hanging that had been in place since 1979. Warrants of execution were once again read to prisoners under sentence of death for murder.

Predictably enough, the condemned availed themselves of every possible avenue of relief. These were plentiful, because Trinidad and Tobago, a young and idealistic state, had signed international human rights conventions disdained by older states such as the United Kingdom and the United States. From death row in Port-of-Spain, prisoners were able to petition the Inter-American Commission on Human Rights (based in Costa Rica), the United Nations Human Rights Committee (based in Geneva) and, most importantly, the Judicial Committee of the Privy Council, based at 9 Downing Street, London.

Although little known in Britain, the Privy Council has operated as a court of review since the fourteenth century, when it heard appeals from the Channel Islands. In the seventeenth century, it began to accept petitions from North American and West Indian colonies—typically involving disputes over slaves and other valuable property—and as the British Empire grew, so did the court's jurisdiction: by the 1930s, this had embraced more than a quarter of the world. Today only a few Commonwealth states—among them New Zealand, fifteen or so Caribbean states, Brunei, Gambia and Mauritius—use the Judicial Committee as a final court of appeal. They elect to do so because the court is manned by able common law judges (British Law Lords supplemented from time to time by a Commonwealth judge); because it's cheap; and because it is perceived to be incorruptible and aloof from local pressures. In Trinidad, the Privy Council always enjoyed the public's confidence—until, that is, the early 1990s, when people began to resent the quashing of murder convictions by London judges who did not have to live with the consequences of their decisions. The biggest controversy, though, was caused by the landmark case of *Pratt and Morgan* v *The Attorney-General for Jamaica*, decided in November 1993.

The appellants in *Pratt and Morgan* were convicted of murder and sentenced to death in 1979. In the years that followed, they were read the death warrant three times and three times saved by last-gasp stays of executions. The Privy Council commented in its judgement, 'The statement of these bare facts is sufficient to bring home to the mind of any person of normal sensitivity and compassion the agony of mind that these men must have suffered as they have alternated between hope and despair in the fourteen years that they have been in prison facing the gallows.' In a ruling that affected nearly all Caribbean jurisdictions, the court held that to keep a prisoner on death row for more than five years was to subject him to unlawful inhuman or degrading treatment; after five years, the sentence of death was to be commuted to one of life imprisonment. In Trinidad, where capital cases routinely took more than five years to pass through the ponderous local courts of appeal and international human rights bodies, *Pratt and Morgan* was seen as a clear attempt to undermine hanging—a penalty, it was noted, that British judges had never found difficult to enforce when the Crown itself had an interest in maintaining law and order in the Caribbean.

Meanwhile, the emancipation of East Indians had gathered a decisive, and racially divisive, momentum with the emergence of a powerful East Indian opposition party, the UNC (United National Congress). At first, the UNC was strongly critical of the reintroduction of capital punishment. But, since the rise in crime affected no one more than its voter base of commercially active East Indians, whose shops, cars, petrol stations and food outlets were ceaselessly targeted, the UNC reconsidered its position. One case, in particular, prompted this re-evaluation.

On the night of January 10, 1994 a group of men broke into a house in Williamsville, Trinidad, and shot dead Hamilton 'Teddy Mice' Baboolal, a cocaine dealer. The intruders also encountered Hamilton's mother and his recently-engaged twenty-five-year-old sister; the women were made to kneel and shot through the head—execution-style, as it's said. The patriarch, Deo Baboolal, met the same fate when he ran to the house on hearing gunfire. Some time afterwards, one of the killers, reserve police officer Clint Huggins, made a detailed confession to the authorities. Huggins implicated himself and ten others—notably, and sensationally, the island's premier drug trader and money launderer, Dole Chadee. Known as the Boss, Chadee was famous for his villainous lifestyle (sprawling high-security estate, fleet of cars, entourage of threatening 'bad john' cohorts, etc.), his gestures of charitable largesse, his killings (rumoured to number more than thirty), and his apparent immunity from the forces of justice. The authorities placed Clint Huggins in the safekeeping of the army, mindful that a previous murder prosecution of Chadee had collapsed after the violent death of the principal prosecution witness. During Trinidad's carnival, however,

Huggins somehow managed to slip out of protective custody to join the festivities. His charred body was found shortly afterwards. He had been set alight and shot several times, and his penis had been chopped off and stuffed into his mouth. To many, the killing confirmed that the drug traffickers—and the criminal element in general—had become so powerful that they threatened the democratic foundations of the state. And so when, in July 1994, the PNM government proceeded to hang a double murderer named Glen Ashby—killing him even as lawyers argued Ashby's case before the judges of the Privy Council—there were reports of people dancing in the streets of Port-of-Spain.

The UNC made law-and-order the defining issue of the 1995 election, and won; Basdeo Panday, a former leader of the sugar workers' union, became the country's first East Indian prime minister. The new government declared that, in order to maintain the rule of law and public confidence in the administration of justice, the penalty for murder had to be systematically implemented. The minister responsible for enforcing the policy was the Attorney-General, Ramesh Maharaj. Maharaj's appointment was striking in two respects: first, he had made his name as a defence lawyer and proponent of the abolition of the death penalty; second, his brother Krishna, convicted of the murder of two business rivals found dead in a penthouse suite of the Miami Dupont Plaza in 1986, faced the electric chair in Florida.

Nevertheless, the Attorney-General took to his task with great determination. Seeing that *Pratt and Morgan*, crypto-abolitionist or not, was in fact an extremely useful stimulus for accelerating the process of execution, he expedited appeals, oversaw Trinidad's withdrawal from international humans rights commitments, and argued in favour of establishing a Caribbean Court of Appeal to hear Caricom (the Caribbean Community) capital cases instead of the Privy Council.

The government's stance was highly popular. Practically the only visible dissent came from the local Roman Catholic Church and a middle-aged individual named Ishmael Angelo Samad. Samad made a nuisance of himself by standing outside the Attorney-General's office with a variety of placards bearing high-minded admonitory messages such as SLAVERY WAS LEGAL BUT IT WAS WRONG. APARTHEID WAS LEGAL BUT IT WAS WRONG. SEGREGATION WAS LEGAL BUT IT WAS WRONG. He also stationed himself outside the Prime Minister's office, outside the Red House (the parliament building), and outside the State Prison (widely known as the Royal Gaol), which was the site of death row. This last protest was inaugurated on Christmas Day 1992, the year when Trinidad revived the reading of death warrants. Every Christmas thereafter Samad staged a vigil outside the prison from six in the morning to five at night. As the years passed, his stake-out became a media event. Ishmael Samad was often recognized in the streets of Port-of-Spain. People would accost him and shout comments to him, some friendly, some hostile. Sometimes they'd call out the nickname he'd previously earned for himself: 'Hey, Turtle Man!'.

In 1998 the UNC celebrated its third anniversary in office with a rally at St Augustine, a village to the east of Port-of-Spain. Ishmael Samad attended the rally equipped with a special new placard, prepared the night before, on which he'd painstakingly stencilled a quote from Arthur Koestler's *Reflections on Hanging*. A large and animated crowd was present, and radio and television stations broadcast the event live. Samad, his placard stowed in the trunk of his car, waited among the UNC supporters for the Prime Minister. Eventually Basdeo Panday arrived and took his seat next to other ministers on the platform. When a speaker began to address the issue of the death penalty, Ishmael Samad went into action. He retrieved his placard, wandered over to a spot a few feet away from the Prime Minister's table, and silently turned his placard towards the TV cameras and the crowd.

The crowd reacted furiously. In an instant, Samad was surrounded and the placard was torn from his hands. Hands grabbed at his shirt and pushed at his chest. The rally came to a halt. As Samad struggled in the scrum, he caught sight of John Humphrey, the Deputy Prime Minister. 'John! John!' Samad shouted in terror, 'Say something on my behalf!' Humphrey, who knew Samad from public meetings in Port-of-Spain's Woodford Square, took the microphone and reminded all present that they lived in a democracy. But the assailants were too inflamed to listen to the minister. They knocked Samad to the ground and kicked and punched him. As he lay taking the blows, Samad became strangely fixated with the fate of his placard, on which he'd bestowed so much care and effort and money (seventy-five Trinidad dollars for the plastic laminate alone). My placard! he thought, as he watched people jumping and trampling on his handiwork. They're destroying my placard!

But, miraculously, the signboard stayed in one piece, held together by its film of plastic. When his attackers began to relent, Samad was able to retrieve the battered placard from under their feet and push it to safety behind the Prime Minister's cordon. Its text was still legible: THE GALLOWS IS NOT MERELY A MACHINE OF DEATH BUT THE OLDEST AND MOST OBSCENE SYMBOL OF THAT TENDENCY IN MANKIND WHICH DRIVES IT TOWARDS MORAL SELF-DESTRUCTION.

The prisoners in the condemned section of the Royal Gaol occupy cells that are eight feet by ten. There is room for a bed, a table, a chair, and a pail. Death row is a damp, claustrophobic and unprivate place. No natural light shines there. This explains why the prisoners, who are aired for one hour a day, are very fair-skinned and why their eyesight quickly deteriorates. The affliction is significant: many of the men—female murderers are held in another prison—like nothing better than to read and answer letters. For overseas correspondence, the prisoners are issued with blue air letters—sheets of paper that fold into envelopes—imprinted with the spectacular image of a long-necked, long-billed, red-feathered bird. This is the scarlet ibis, the national bird of Trinidad. The scarlet ibis also features in the standard series of stamps, which celebrates the country's renowned avian life. Should you receive a letter from a condemned man in Trinidad, the chances are that it will be stamped with the image of a channel-billed toucan or green-rumped parrotlet or fork-tailed flycatcher or bay-headed tanager.

These exotic, pathetic missives would occasionally reach London at the chambers of Mark Strachan QC, at 1 Crown Office Row, in the Temple. Although the chambers dealt principally in business law, for over fifty years it had esoterically specialized in Privy Council work. There was no ideological slant to this: it was not uncommon for a barrister from the chambers to act for a state on one occasion and against it on another. Nor was it unusual, or a problem, for members of the same chambers to oppose each other on an appeal. In the case of Ramnath Harrilal, for example, James Guthrie QC, instructed by the Republic of Trinidad and Tobago, was opposed by me.

When I received the Harrilal papers in late 1997, I had been called to the Bar for ten years. Nevertheless, I was a novice in the field of criminal appeals. I had very little experience of criminal work, and the only time I'd appeared before the Law Lords—a case concerning an oil spill in Scotland—I'd not been called on to address the court. My practice had been mainly devoted to business law and employment law. However, I had from time to time received a few random letters from death row. Written in the humble, rambling, supplicant, God-fearing genre almost uniformly adopted by death row correspondents, they begged for my assistance in respect of cloudy, near-incomprehensible grievances about prison conditions and judicial injustices. I wish that I could report a selfless, soul-searching response to these demands on my conscience and time—all such work is pro bono—but in fact I was grateful for the professional rule that barristers cannot communicate directly with a client. The letters were passed to a solicitor to undertake necessary inquiries and correspondence and, if it seemed the client might have a case, instruct a barrister to advise and draft the necessary legal proceedings. In this way, my involvement with death row inmates was limited to writing short, invariably discouraging opinions concerning the alleged infringement of their constitutional rights. The Harrilal brief was different.

The court documents told the following story. Sylvia Maraj, the mother of a four-year-old boy named Jerry, had been seeing Ramnath 'Dread' Harrilal, a twenty-eight-year-old forestry worker, on and off for around two years. It was not a secure relationship, but nor was it violent; and Ramnath Harrilal had no police record of any kind. In the early evening of June 27, 1985, the couple quarrelled. There was obscure evidence about the subject of the dispute: it seemed that Dread criticized Sylvia for drinking alcohol against her doctor's orders (she was on medication for a nervous breakdown), that Sylvia told Dread to go and bathe because he stank, and that Sylvia shouted about wanting her passport. At any rate, late in the night, things turned violent. The two 'scrambled' on the bed, and then Sylvia, who was physically a match for her boyfriend, went for him once more, perhaps armed with a bottle or a knife. Harrilal seized an L-shaped iron implement he'd fashioned for digging holes for tomato plants, and with it struck his girlfriend two or three times on the head. She fell to the ground. He tried to revive her by slapping water on her face, but couldn't. So he beheaded Sylvia Maraj, chopped up her torso and limbs, and did his best to hide the body parts. The following morning, an old friend called Tattoo stopped by and asked to use Harrilal's latrine. Harrilal told Tattoo that he couldn't use the latrine because Sylvia's chopped-up body was there. Tattoo went to the police. When the post-mortem was conducted, something odd turned up. It transpired that the initial blows with the piece of iron had merely knocked out Sylvia Maraj; it was the shock and haemorrhage of multiple chop wounds, dismemberment and decapitation that had killed her.

Ramnath Harrilal was convicted of the murder of Sylvia Maraj and sentenced to death in 1988. The conviction was quashed by the Trinidad and Tobago Court of Appeal in 1993, but in 1996, after a retrial, he was reconvicted and resentenced to death. A second appeal to the Trinidad and Tobago Court of Appeal failed; indeed, Harrilal's counsel helplessly stated to the court that there were no grounds of appeal that he could advance.

Reviewing the documents, I didn't dwell on this last fact. It is not uncommon for Trinidadian attorneys to miss points that seem obvious to their London counterparts—not so much a reflection on the competence of Trinidadian Bar but rather of the advantage enjoyed by an appellate lawyer fresh to a case. I had never laid eyes on or spoken to my client, had not participated in the trial or appeal, knew nothing about the scene of the crime or the reality of its protagonists' lives. This remoteness would have been a problem if my job had been to get to the bottom of what happened thousands of miles away on a night thirteen years ago; but that wasn't my job. My task was to take the material available and construct from it the narrative most favourable to the client, and the less constrained I was by first-hand impressions of what had happened, the better. Of course, any exculpatory edifice I built had to be founded in reality. Contrary to the impression sometimes gained in Trinidad, the Privy

Council only entertained appeals if it was satisfied that there was a real possibility that the petitioner had suffered a substantive injustice; and most petitions for leave to appeal were dismissed.

Harrilal's physical actions were clear and horrifying. But, as everybody knows, an act only acquires a particular criminal quality if it coincides with a particular mental state; and a homicide will only be murder if it is committed with an intention to kill or cause really serious injury. It was quickly clear to me that if a defence lay anywhere, it was in the killer's mind. What had driven Ramnath Harrilal, a man of previous good character, to butcher Sylvia Maraj?

Harrilal's trial lawyer had invited the jury to consider the same question. He put it to them that the deranged character of the killing indicated a deranged mind. He urged them to accept the defence of diminished responsibility—i.e., the accused suffered from an abnormality of mind induced by injury or disease—and to deliver the non-capital verdict of manslaughter. He pointed to the accused's evidence that, as a teenager, he'd been hospitalized with head injuries sustained in a bicycling accident which had caused him to suffer from dizziness, mood changes and anxiety, and he pointed to psychiatric evidence that the head injuries caused Harrilal to suffer from post-traumatic stress disorder, a condition capable of triggering sudden uncontrollable rages.

But the jury never got to consider these submissions on their merits, because for some reason the judge remarked in his summing up that there was no evidence of post-traumatic stress disorder. That, I thought to myself, was a material misdirection right there.

But it was pretty threadbare stuff. The bicycling accident had occurred perhaps thirteen years before the date of the homicide, there were no hospital records to confirm the head injuries, and there was no evidence of other episodes of uncontrolled rage. There was, I thought, a more likely story of what had happened that night. After he'd knocked out Sylvia Maraj, Harrilal had tried to revive her. Only after his attempts at resuscitation had failed did he mutilate her 'body'. In other words, he had killed Sylvia in the mistaken belief that he was disposing of a corpse—and not with any intent to kill or injure. Was this murder, or was it manslaughter?

The precedents were far from clear. I looked into a history of inconsistent decisions from India, New Zealand, Basutoland, Rhodesia, South Africa and England, cases in which the victims had been throttled then set on fire; strangled then thrown into a river (two such cases); struck on the head then rolled over a cliff; assaulted with an axe and then placed in an antbear hole; smashed on the skull with a heavy object and then gagged and dumped in an offal pit; and hit with a truncheon and then tossed into a harbour with breeze blocks attached to the legs. In all cases, the first violent act produced unconsciousness and the second produced death. In all cases the courts had difficulty in defining the exact state of mind of a murderer, a problem which in part arose, of course, from the psychological and moral impenetrability of the conduct in question. Who really knows what to make of people who commit such terrible acts?

I drew up a petition on behalf of Ramnath Harrilal. In February 1998, after a short hearing before three Law Lords, Harrilal was granted leave to appeal as a poor person to the Judicial Committee of the Privy Council.

It is something of a tradition in my chambers to make the trip to 9 Downing Street on foot. If you're brisk about it—and barristers headed for court always seem to march briskly—the walk takes no more than twenty minutes. You can go via the Aldwych and Trafalgar Square—a route which takes you past Bush House, India House, Australia House, Canada House and South Africa House— or via Victoria Embankment on the Thames. Either way, it is possible to imagine that nothing has changed since the days of Empire. On a mild day in October 1998, I took the river route with my opponent in the Harrilal case, James Guthrie. Guthrie led the way, taking the opportunity, as an obsessive consumer of dark-lit American crime fiction, to fill me in on the recent work of James Ellroy and James Lee Burke; neither of us mentioned the imminent hearing. At Horseguards Avenue, we turned up towards Whitehall where, passing the Foreign and Commonwealth Office and the Admiralty, we walked west. As usual, a group of sightseers was gathered by the iron railings that block off Downing Street. Guthrie threaded a path through the tourists and sonorously uttered the words 'Privy Council' to the police officers. The gate immediately opened.

We walked into Number 9 and climbed the stairs to the small robing room on the first floor. Boxes containing our documents and court attire, delivered by a junior clerk earlier that morning, sat on the table alongside a clutter of wig tins. We poked studs through our wing collars and adjusted our bands—in the Privy Council, judges appear in business suits and barristers in eighteenth-century outfits— and then gathered our papers and went to the antechamber of the courtroom, a sunlit wood-panelled room built in 1825 to the design of Sir John Soane. There followed the usual exaggeratedly cheerful exchange of greetings with the solicitors, the court registrar, the court reporter, and the pupil barristers who had come along for the experience. Then a loud buzzer sounded: Lords Steyn, Hutton, Hobhouse, Millett, and Sir Patrick Russell had taken their seats. The usher, a severe-looking man in a morning suit, cried out, 'Counsel!' and everybody trooped into the council chamber.

The judges were sitting around a D-shaped table only a few feet from the bafflingly small lectern allocated to advocates. I arranged my papers and then began with a few bland remarks designed to see me through the first moments of the appeal without catastrophe. As I'd hoped, Lord Steyn, the senior judge, benevolently interrupted me to indicate the direction which the court wished my submissions to take: I was to concentrate on the diminished responsibility point. After short argument, James Guthrie was asked to respond; and it quickly became apparent, from the polite probings from the bench— judges at this level rarely see the need to be abrasive—that my case was finding favour. After an hour or so, counsel withdrew to enable the court to confer; minutes later, we were informed that judgement would be reserved.

In December, I learned that the appeal had been allowed. A verdict of manslaughter on grounds of diminished responsibility was substituted for the verdict of murder, and the case was remitted to the Court of Appeal in Port-of-Spain for resentencing. Ramnath Harrilal no longer faced execution.

There was a final twist: my primary case had been that Harrilal had chopped up Sylvia Maraj because of a catastrophic, panicky misjudgement that she was dead. It seemed to me that resentencing on these grounds could well be more favourable to him than resentencing on the grounds that he was so mentally disturbed that he had chopped up the victim even though he'd thought she was still alive. I asked for a ruling on the primary case. This required a further hearing in May 1999. The court rejected my submissions and ruled that the trial judge had given adequate directions to the jury on the point. I didn't agree, but there it was. Case closed.

That, at least, would have been my normal attitude. However, something had happened to shake my professional detachment. I'd received a letter from Trinidad.

Shalom Joseph,

A pleasant greeting in the name of Yahweh to you and the rest, may these few line reach you all in the best of health, and in a joyful spirit.

Our Merciful Father Yahweh is so merciful, he see all the unjust, which take place with me, he so kind, he give you all the health and truth, to assist a poor one, and may our loving father shower his blessings on each of you, and also each of your Families, and that he keep you on his part way, as life goes a long, you all those work hard, and you all those put out the best at work's...

In life if one is willing, and get up and get things going along, things will work out with the will and power of our merciful Father Yahweh. Somebody loves you more than you ever know, and is praying this moment for you. Asking our heavenly Father, to care for and watch you all. To give you all the strength and courage, to help you all to face each coming day, And the wisdom to know is with you all, through sunshine and rain come what may. Smile.

Many many thanks to you all, in the name of our messiah.
Ramnath Harrilal

The writing-paper was bordered with green leaves and pink, sky-blue and purple petals, all hand-coloured by Harrilal. At the centre of the sheet he'd drawn an elaborate picture of an iridescent hummingbird, wings aloft, dipping its slender bill into a scarlet flower.

What had driven me, during the many days I'd devoted myself to the Harrilal case, was not a sense of virtuous obligation or my dinner-party opposition to the death penalty; it was, rather, professional conscientiousness and excitement about the challenge of the work. I had not really thought about the mortal anguish of my client. He was as distant as the defendants in the cases I'd invoked in argument, long-forgotten African, Antipodean and British individuals—Chiswibo, Thabo Meli, Moore, Church, Masilela—whose names now merely stood for propositions of law. With this letter, however, Harrilal had come alive as a creature of fears and longings; and it chilled me to think that this person, this lover of birds and flowers, had been marked for hanging. My aloofness from my client and the world he inhabited suddenly seemed wrong. What was the truth about him and the fate he'd avoided?

On June 20, 1999 I flew into Port-of-Spain, where, a fortnight earlier, nine men had been hanged in the space of four days.

The death of Clint Huggins did not put an end to the prosecution of Dole Chadee and his alleged gang for the Baboolal murders. A man named Levi Morris offered to plead guilty and testify for the State in return for the commutation of his death sentence to one of life imprisonment. The State accepted, and in 1996, after a fifty-four-day trial, the longest in Trinidadian history, Chadee and eight others were convicted of murder and sentenced to hang. Numerous petitions, motions and appeals failed to disturb the verdicts. On May 26, 1999, death warrants were read to the nine men. They were to be hanged in batches of three on Friday June 4, Saturday June 5, and Monday June 7.

The media immediately instructed the public in the minutiae of the usual execution process. Once the warrant of execution, signed and sealed by the President of Trinidad and Tobago, is read to the prisoner, his furniture (bed, table, chair) is removed from his cell together with any other potential source of injury to himself or others. Only the foam mattress and the slop pail remain. Reasonable requests for food—cow-heel soup, say, or chicken and chips—are complied with, and family visiting time is extended. No visits are allowed on the day before the execution, which is set aside for the prisoner to prepare himself for his fate. The prisoner spends his last night on earth in a cell opposite the chamber of the gallows. In the morning, he is offered warm milk but no food; the milk is usually refused. If he chooses to, the man under sentence of death can bathe. Either way, he finally dresses in brown or off-white cotton pyjamas with three-quarter length, sometimes stripy, pants. A religious official of the prisoner's choice is by now in attendance, and prayers are said. Shortly before seven in the morning, which is the customary hanging time in the case of a single execution, the prisoner is read the order for his execution. Then his hands are shackled behind his back with a leather belt and a hood is placed over his head. He is taken from his cell to the chamber of the gallows. The chamber is roughly ten feet by ten. It is situated on the first floor of section F2 of the Royal Gaol. The condemned man is led to a wooden trapdoor roughly six feet long by four feet wide. He is told to remain standing. He faces south. His bare feet are then shackled with a leather belt and the noose is placed around his neck. The rope hangs down from a large wooden beam in the ceiling. Each condemned man has a rope that corresponds to his size and height. The bigger the man, the thicker the rope. If the man is too light to be hanged effectively, sandbags, stored in a wooden chest near the entrance, are attached to his back or feet. Weights are also used to stretch the rope in the days before the execution, to make sure it's in good order. Prison officers, not hangmen, prepare the rope, using skills passed on through the generations from officer to officer. As for the hangmen, they arrive in the dark-windowed vehicles of the Ministry for National Security, wearing hoods. Nobody knows their identities. One executioner has the job of pulling the lever, the other of waiting downstairs to receive the body. Eventually the noose is fastened around the neck of the condemned man and all is ready. The door to the chamber is open to enable the hanging to be witnessed. The witnesses are the Registrar of the Supreme Court, two Assistant Registrars, the Court Protocol and Information Officer, and senior prison officers. The lever is pulled, the trapdoor opens, and the condemned man disappears from view into the airspace of the ground floor, at which point his neck is usually broken. After he has dangled by the neck for an hour, his hood is removed and his head is exposed; commonly, the eyes are open and the tongue protrudes. The noose is detached and the body is lowered into a wooden casket and taken to the mortuary. A forensic pathologist examines the corpse. He takes a blood sample and sends it out to be tested for the presence of alcohol and drugs and other substances. In due course he determines the cause of death: the injuries, he inevitably reports, are consistent with asphyxia. When the pathologist is finished, the body—which is the property of the State—is placed in a rough wooden coffin and removed to Golden Grove Prison, Arouca, where it is interred by inmates in the prison burial land known as Happy Valley Cemetery.

A predictable drama unfolded in the days before the Chadee gang's executions. A petition of mercy (signed by Archbishop Desmond Tutu and other distinguished foreigners) was presented to the President, Arthur Robinson; the prisoners maintained their innocence; politicians, newspaper columnists, editorialists and correspondents urged no clemency; Ishmael Samad held a vigil outside the Royal Gaol; and lawyers desperately pursued last-ditch applications for stays of execution, prompting the Trinidadian Chief Justice to remark that it was unacceptable for attorneys to lend themselves to the strategies of death row inmates, who used every available means 'to cheat the hangman's noose'. The Chief Justice's figure of speech was precisely expressive of a strange killing momentum that had built up. With the newspapers and television covering every twist of the prisoners' terminal struggle, the public was dragged into a drawn-out spectacle of human suffering in which the condemned and their lawyers figured as saboteurs of the righteous machinery of justice. But in the end, nobody cheated the hangman's noose. At 5.35 a.m. on Friday June 4 the news reached death row that a last-minute application to the Privy Council for a stay of execution had failed.

Dole Chadee was hanged half an hour later. Chadee walked slowly to the gallows accompanied by songs, hymns and clapping from other condemned men. According to some prison officers, he appeared calm and peaceful. By contrast (the same anonymous prison officers reported), Joey Ramiah—credited by the police with twenty-six murders—died ill-tempered and unrepentant, at 7.23. Ramkalawan Singh fainted on his way to the chamber and had to be revived. He was hanged at 8.44.

Next day saw the turn of Clive Thomas, Robin Gopaul, and Russell Sankerali. Thomas, it was said, cried and struggled and begged for a chance to live as he was taken to the gallows. Thomas had tried to cheat the hangman's noose by drinking 'soap water' the day before, but was treated at Port-of-Spain General Hospital and discharged and returned to the State Prison and hanged at 6.05. Robin Gopaul was reportedly silent and at peace with himself when he went to the gallows. Only minutes earlier he'd declared himself a Christian and asked the Hindu pundit to recite a Christian prayer. The pundit obliged. He was hanged at 7.25. Russell Sankerali shed tears but did not resist. He was hanged at 8.51. The hangman—a different hangman from the day before—left the prison at midday. His payment took the form of 1,500 Trinidad dollars (about 240 US dollars) and, if the old custom still held good, a bottle of rum. Up at Golden Grove Prison, meanwhile, convict gravediggers poured holy water into the graves they'd prepared—with the help of a mechanical digger, because the dirt was rock hard—and sang 'Amazing Grace'. When rain began to fall, sheets of galvanized iron were placed over the six-foot-deep pits to prevent flooding. The van with the corpses arrived from Port-of-Spain. The burial party wore latex gloves and masks as they handled the coffins. (There was blood escaping from the box containing Russell Sankerali, in quantities which suggested that he might have been partly decapitated.) The prisoners sang and clapped and placed wooden crosses and flowers on the graves.

Nobody was hanged on Sunday. On Monday, Joel Ramsingh, Bhagwandeen Singh and Stephen Eversley were put to death. The news was that Bhagwandeen sang 'Heavenly Sunshine' on the way to the gallows, Ramsingh sang 'Hear my blessed cry', Eversley sang 'Pass me not, oh blessed saviour, hear my humble cry'. By this time the media story was about the redemptive spiritual terrain traversed by the condemned in their last days. It transpired that even Dole Chadee had broken down, requesting that his family (he was married with five children) perform full Hindu rites for him and tearfully confessing to the prison pastor that he was sorry for all he'd done.

Then the news plunged into a tailspin of increasingly unilluminating interviews. There was a muted reaction from the relatives of the murderers' victims and keen distress from the mothers of the executed men. Prison officers stated that they'd asked for counselling. Two prisoners at Golden Grove Prison were quoted as

a high forehead, grey hair, a moustache, and a tuft of grey hair below his lips. He spoke with a soft, slightly quavering voice and possessed a remarkable facility for lengthy, orderly monologue that had been developed, I imagined, from years of ideological argument. But he wasn't, I was relieved to discover, a haranguer. Samad practised a kind of fluent openness, an out-loud musing that disclosed concerns ranging from his sadness about the massacres in Central Africa to his trouble with the Virgin Birth to the joy that filled his heart when he saw a grape-like mass of clouds tinted pink by the sun. He was thoughtful, emotional, receptive, dogged, religious and obsessive. Things delighted and amazed him.

'In spite of the barbarity, Trinidad is a wonderful little island,' Ishmael Samad said. 'Because I make my living showing people the birds and plants of the island, I perpetually see my country through the eyes of foreigners and perpetually discover new things. Take the roosting of the scarlet ibis: visitors are absolutely overwhelmed when they see the scarlet birds against the green mangrove. It's been described as the most awesome display in the avian world—and yet we take it for granted.' He glanced at me. 'We'll go to the Caroni swamp together to watch them, if you want. I'll happily take you there tomorrow.' He was, he said, a great birder. When a Jabiru stork was spotted recently in Trinidad for the first time since 1988, he had got up at five in the morning to see it in the Caroni rice fields. I made a mental note not to allow myself to be dragged into any kind of nature expedition.

'We have all been diminished by these hangings,' Samad continued. 'I have been diminished, too. Before the executions, I wrote to the Attorney-General Ramesh Maharaj saying, "If you must hang, then hang Dole Chadee and his hit man, Joey Ramiah. Spare the others." I wrote a letter to Chadee, too: "Conscience demands that you publicly acknowledge and confess your guilt and take responsibility for that horrendous crime," I wrote. "Conscience demands that you declare you are deserving of the death penalty but that the other eight men be spared so cruel a punishment. I therefore call upon you to steel yourself and bravely face your fate, cruel and barbaric though it is, but before doing so publicly request of the State that the lives of the other eight be spared. Then and only then will you be able to walk bravely to the gallows." I never got a reply. Right to the very end, Chadee refused to confess.' Samad shook his head. 'I'm disappointed in these guys. Not one of them confessed. Not one.'

We drove on for a time. It was a humid day of pale grey clouds. In the distance to our left was the Northern Range, the mountains that surround the corrugated roofs of Port-of-Spain and give the city the appearance of an enormous, brimming handful of gravel. We were on the airport road where, decades ago, Ishmael Samad and other schoolchildren would be lined up to wave at royal visitors from Britain driving into Port-of-Spain. In between advertising hoardings for Pizza Hut and Kentucky Fried Chicken, vendors of watermelons, okra, bodi beans and pineapples operated from carts by the highway. Samad gestured at the flat farmland to the south. The Caroni plain, he said, the breadbasket of the north. He confessed that he grew particularly excited at this time of year, which marked the transition between the dry months and the months of rain. Everything was turning green, insects were coming out, and the flamboyant trees (native to Madagascar, he said) bloomed with scarlet or yellow flowers. 'It's a privilege that I am able to see all this, to be alive,' he said. Staring at the road ahead, he added, 'Since those hangings, there's an intensity to my being. I cherish every moment, I try to do every good that I can do.' Samad looked at me. 'It's been a very defining moment in my life.'

We continued deeper inland. The Beetham Highway became the Churchill–Roosevelt Highway and the roadside commerce dwindled. The scenery became distinctly rural: orchards, vegetable gardens, luxuriant grasses, tropical thickets, rows of tall palms. Small bungalows and sheds and outhouses appeared in clearings. I'd been told in Port-of-Spain that people got up to no good in this thinly populated part of Trinidad, where, it was said, incest and witchcraft were common. The farmhouses were vulnerable to banditry; recently a whole family had had their throats slashed.

'Here we are,' Ishmael Samad said. 'This is Cumuto.' We had come to a concentration of detached houses and a pavement. Samad stopped the car alongside a goat, and we got out. It was hot and quiet. A burst of squawking came from overhead: red-bellied macaws, Samad said. The Northern Range was clearly visible: steam had snagged on its dark green slopes like huge wisps of cat hair.

Samad pointed at a puddle-pocked track that ran off at a right angle from the main road and continued into the forested distance in an eerily straight line. 'This is the Old Train Line,' he said. On the right side of the track was thick greenery in which moriche palms and papaya trees and parts of shacks were visible. On the left side was a dense plantation of Caribbean pines.

A man riding a child's bicycle approached us out of curiosity. We asked him about the murder and he said that he remembered the night Sylvia Maraj died. He'd been at the 'Country View' cinema, watching an Indian movie along with everyone else from the village. He knew exactly where it happened. He could take us there right now.

We followed him up the Old Train Line. The road—which was little more than a broad footpath—was covered unevenly with pitch, but back in 1985, according to our guide, it was just a gravel path. The nights were very black in those days; there was no electric lighting and the pine trees were taller and shadier. We walked for a couple of hundred of yards, passing a few small houses set back from the path. I noticed a toucan in the trees. Then the villager said, 'This it.'

Ramnath Harrilal's shack and latrine had been razed. In their place stood a small concrete cabin with a sloping roof that extended beyond the frontage of the house and, supported by two poles, formed a porch. The property was surrounded by a tall fence with improbably grand, and locked, entrance gates. At the back were a few banana trees, a vegetable garden, and some hens. The present occupants of this land, although wealthier than Harrilal had been, evidently existed on essentially the same economic plane: working in the forests and growing subsistence crops in a garden.

I turned to look at the pine plantation on the opposite side of the Old Train Line. There was an overgrown track leading to the interior of the plantation, the kind of trail—for all I knew, the very trail—down which Ramnath Harrilal had carried Sylvia Maraj's one-armed torso in a plastic sack and dumped it under the large frond of a moriche palm.

Ishmael Samad led the way through the damp knee-high grasses. 'Look,' he said, pointing at an enormous butterfly. We walked on. All kinds of grasses and shrubs and woody plants grew among the pines, and my bare arms were brushed by sticky, disconcertingly unfamiliar textures. Insects buzzed in my ears, and small black tunnels gaped in the mud underfoot: snakes? Birds called and called. Then, no more than fifty yards into our walk, the plantation suddenly gave way to a soaring wall of broadleaf trees and strangler figs and creepers and palms with stupendously large fronds, one of which became detached and fell to the ground with a thud. A thick flutter of wings came from somewhere inside the jungle. I looked at Samad expectantly. He was staring in wonder. 'This is a remnant of the primary forest,' he said. 'Isn't it absolutely magnificent?'

We headed back and spoke to a few people in the village. They remembered Harrilal, but not very well. The most detailed recollections belonged to an old fellow with an immense grey beard. He recalled Harrilal as 'a constructive man' who'd been very helpful in building the cinema (which had since burned down) and had worked very hard in the forests—harder than he got paid, the man observed. The man didn't remember Sylvia Maraj, though. He wasn't alone in his ignorance. We could only find one villager, a man who lived on the Old Train Line, who could speak about Sylvia Maraj. She was a very respectable woman, the man said.

Finally, we went to Cumuto police station, the small concrete bungalow set back from a dusty yard where Ramnath Harrilal had been taken and first interrogated. None of the policemen who'd worked on the case was still around. The only thing that the officers now on duty could remember about the case was that it had involved a woman's head being chopped off.

When we stepped outside the police station, Ishmael Samad told me that he often brought parties of birders here. The tall and rather tattered Caribbean pine that stood in front of the station, he explained, was the nesting site of a notable colony of yellow-rumped caciques. 'Take a look,' he said, handing me his binoculars for a better view, and I complaisantly looked at the zestful little birds flitting in and out of their nests. My appreciation was clouded, however, by an anxiety I'd contracted on the Old Train Line and not entirely shaken off. The scrappy, ravaged forests I'd seen here depressed me. The trouble was the ongoing struggle between man and nature, an apparently interminable conflict of hacking and chopping that had become linked, in my mind, to the crime of Ramnath Harrilal.

Before we turned back to Port-of-Spain, Samad drove me a few miles to the Arena Forest nature reserve. The trees here, I learned, included mahoe, crappo, olivier, matchwood, jereton and balata. As we walked along a trail, Ishmael Samad told me about the violaceous trogon and the glittering-throated emerald hummingbird and red-rumped woodpecker that lived thereabouts. He identified the calls of jungle wrens and woodcreepers, and alerted me to the love cries of a little hermit hummingbird. At one point he wandered off the path and pulled a handful of leaves off a tree. 'An incense tree,' he said. He crushed the leaves beneath my nose, and the forest smelled like a church.

Samad told me that, as it happened, a church had once been built in this forest by Spanish Capuchin monks engaged in the conversion of native Amerindians to Christianity. In an uprising against the colonists in 1699, Amerindians killed a Spanish priest and waylaid the Governor of the island and his party, killing all but one. A reprisal force was dispatched to Arena and there ensued a massacre of Amerindians that had never been forgotten. It was remembered, in particular, that natives who were not killed in the fighting were captured, tried, convicted, hanged and dismembered.

Two days later I went behind the tall pale walls of the Royal Gaol in Port-of-Spain. Inside the entrance, the crowd of visitors looked like a throng at a bus station. They were dozing on benches or milling around the prison store to buy cigarettes, toothpaste and snacks for the inmates they had come to see. In the meeting area they pressed against a plastic screen punctured with speech holes. A few feet behind this screen was a metal grill, which the prisoners gripped as they smiled and shouted across to their friends and relatives. It was a gloomy, clamorous room, but full of happiness. I, however, was taken to the prison guards' quarters where, behind a little table by the door, Ramnath Harrilal sat waiting for me.

He wore shorts, a thick blue cotton shirt, and yellow flip-flops. He stood up and we shook hands. He was expecting somebody older, he said. I was surprised, too: I hadn't been expecting such a youthful, good-looking man. His eyes were bright and large, and his regular cheekbones and chin were set in a handsome triangle. His hair was shaved down to a silver-peppered stubble. He had long expressive hands.

We sat down at the table together. The only prisoners I'd ever previously visited were two drug addicts remanded in custody for an attempted theft of a lawnmower from a shop in Guildford. These men were desperate to get bail, and they'd only been inside for a week; Harrilal had spent fourteen years in prison, eight of them on death row. 'I'm forty-three, you know,' he said. He seemed surprised by that fact.

He spoke in whispers; prison guards were all around us. He'd been a good prisoner, he said straight off. Although he came from a Hindu home, he now followed the teaching of Yahweh. He hadn't fallen upon his faith randomly: he'd read the Koran and scripture before accepting it. All my time on death row was with scripture and pen and paper, he said, quickly adding, in case I got the wrong impression, 'I don't hide behind Bible.'

'Where are you from?' he asked me. I work in London, I said, but I'm Irish. Harrilal brightened and said he had three penfriends in Ireland and four in England. 'We write about life and scripture. I have about fifteen or so penfriends in USA, too. I have a whole pile of letters. Last week, I get four or five letters. It lift up the spirit. It has helped me a lot. These people are nice,' he said. 'They taking me to scripture and righteousness. I asked God for help on death row, and you are his instrument.' He said that he could not describe the joy and hope he felt when he received news of his appeal.

I smiled and mentioned that I'd liked his letter with the hummingbird and the flowers. A look of surprise and pleasure crossed his face; it seemed to startle him to think that he could have done something for me. 'I draw hibiscus and buttercup,' he said.

After a little while I felt able to ask him about what had happened fourteen years ago. He seemed put out by having to talk about it. He said, 'I had a nervous condition, it wasn't me. I am sorry what I did. It wasn't me,' he repeated. He looked at me in the hope that I'd change the subject.

I asked about Sylvia. What kind of life had she led before she met him? 'I don't know anything about Sylvia's childhood or life before me,' he said. And Jerry, Sylvia's boy? What had become of him? 'My brother's wife took the child after Sylvia died,' Ramnath Harrilal said. 'Child fighting, so after he put in orphan house by social work. Sylvia drank,' Harrilal said in a pained voice, returning to my earlier question. 'She used to buy it and hide it in basket of clothes. She took medication. Affecting she. But she take good care of the house, she keeping good house, everything going all right.'

What went wrong, then? I asked.

'I can't say what caused it,' Harrilal said unhappily. He seemed at a loss. 'I was drinking at the time because of my nervousness. I had trembling hands. The nurses in the health centre told me to rest. I had sleeplessness. Too much hard working, not enough eating. Sometimes I leave at six a.m. and come back at two a.m. I work late, late. When I come here, I start to get medicine, vitamin, calcium. I improve.'

This account of his exhausted state of mind and body was new to me. I thought about asking him in terms: Did you really wish her dead, or was it just a terrible mistake? But I didn't, not because it would have been unseemly but because any answer he gave might jeopardize my theory of his innocence of murder—a theory I'd gone to great lengths to construct.

Instead, I asked Harrilal about his upbringing. He replied, 'I grew up in a decent family, with a lot of love, neighbours, everything was close.' The recollection cheered him up, and he began to talk about what he'd do when released. There would be no smoking and no drinking, he said. He would go back to gardening: 'I grow cabbage, tomatoes, bodi, coco, any kind of seasoning, sweet and hot peppers, ginger, pumpkin, figs, corn.' He said he used to do carpentry, steel bending, plumbing, and could pick it up again. 'I was not a lazy guy,' he said adamantly. 'I wasn't thief or lazy. I didn't use obscene language.' Would you go back to Cumuto? I asked. He waved his finger in the negative. He'd go back south, where he came from. His voice nearly breaking, he said, 'I love to have children, you know—growing up with lots of children in nice village with no fighting.'

I nodded. For fear of waking him from his dream of redemption, I didn't mention that I'd learned from his local attorney that he already had a child, a boy by a woman named Kamla. Harrilal's son was around eighteen now and living somewhere near Cumuto. Harrilal said, his voice taut with emotion, 'I want salvation. I want to live the life. I made mistake and I want to atone for it. Many make mistakes in life, but how many decide to turn from it? It shake me to see the people here, in this meat house. I pity them. If you knew, you would pity me too.'

He looked intently into my eyes, as he had done throughout the interview, and it finally struck me that, inevitably, Sylvia and Jerry and Kamla and his youthful self had become figures from a nightmare he'd once had. This accounted for the note of entitlement I'd detected in his attitude, almost as if he were being punished for the deeds of another man. If there had been any element of reproach in his last remark, it was because I insisted on placing him in that night of horrors in Cumuto.

I cautioned Ramnath Harrilal not to expect too much from the Court of Appeal on resentencing. There was every chance that his imprisonment would be significantly extended. Harrilal responded with a helpless shrug of his shoulders.

Our meeting was almost over. In order to extinguish any expectations on his part, I reminded him, on the subject of any future correspondence, that I was a lawyer, not a Good Samaritan. I left the Royal Gaol uncomfortable not only about the man I'd spoken to, but about the limits of my own virtue.

On June 26, the fourteenth anniversary of Sylvia Maraj's death, Ishmael Samad and I set out for the village of San Rafael, which was not far from Cumuto. Sylvia Maraj's father, a man named Reginald Girod, lived there. On the way, Samad told me things about himself—of how he'd left school aged twelve, of the places he'd worked (a bookshop, a plant nursery, a bakery, a gas station), of his time as a encyclopedia salesman (he still had three sets at home, including the Britannica's finest edition, the eleventh). He'd been born a Muslim, had converted to Pentecostalism, and was now thinking of becoming a Roman Catholic. Whereas Muslims and Hindus on the island were diehards for the death penalty, he said, Trinidad's Catholic archbishop had taken a firm stand. 'It's wonderful to be a Christian,' Samad exclaimed. 'I can claim Handel's Messiah as part of my heritage, and the King James Bible, and the Gospel of St John!'

He told me that his two formative books were *All Quiet on the Western Front* and Trevor Huddleston's *Naught for Your Comfort*. He came across Huddleston, the Anglican bishop who served in South Africa, on the BBC World Service, which he'd listened to for twenty years until his radio gave up. At home, he had 200 tapes of BBC programmes. He remembered, in particular, a television series broadcast almost thirty years ago called *The Ascent of Man*, in which Dr Jacob Bronowski traced the development of science as an expression of the special gifts that, uniquely among animal species, make humankind capable of producing the wonders of Easter Island, Machu Picchu, Newton's library, the Alhambra, the caves of Altamira. 'Humanness is a potential we must achieve,' Samad said to me as he gripped the steering wheel and now began to speak in slow emphatic sentences. 'Man is made in the image of God and possesses within himself the capacity to love. Therein lies the true measure of our humanity. We are human to the degree that we love our fellow man—even the very least of men, even a cold-blooded murderer like Dole Chadee.'

He said, 'They focus on what Chadee did. Well, that's fine. But let's look at what we're doing, too. We're torturing him, letting him agonize, letting him sing at his own wake. That's not all. We're breaking his neck and letting him hang for one hour and then taking him away in a crude box. He's a nobody, a nonentity. Which is more horrifying? The crimes committed by the wicked, or the cruelty inflicted by the good? We are very British here; we take tea in the evening, and then we hang.'

At San Rafael, it didn't take us long to find the home of Reginald Girod, who greeted us amiably. He was a tall and rather elegant man who looked athletic in his shorts and vest and bare feet. He said he was seventy-three. He'd been a great street fighter as a youngster, and then an alcoholic, though he hadn't touched a drop now for at least ten years. His skin was light brown. 'I'm of French origin,' he said. 'My father was a Frenchman, my mother mulatto.'

We sat down in his kitchen and Girod lit a cigarette and began searching through a tin of personal documents and photographs. 'Sylvia was a good-looking girl, very good-looking,' he said. 'She was my only daughter. I have one son, thirty-five years old, who is mentally retarded. Sylvia was normal.' Girod moved his cigarette between his lips while he sorted out the papers. 'Her name was Sylvia Frederica Girod. Her mother's name was Maraj, Inez Maraj—she was a Spanish mix.' Reginald Girod and Inez Maraj never married, and Sylvia grew up in her father's care. Girod passed us a couple of documents he'd unearthed. There was a birth certificate for Sylvia— born Arima 4/3/62—and a maternity and child welfare card. There was a medical card recording vaccinations and abnormalities. 'She took a photo album up there,' Girod said, resuming his search. 'I don't know what became of it.' He emptied a wad of envelopes, looking for the one remaining photograph of Sylvia that he, and probably anyone, possessed. He found an insurance policy in her name and the receipt for her burial. Then he said, 'This it here.'

Ishmael Samad and I both took a look. It was a blurry snapshot of Sylvia lounging on a double bed strewn with newspapers. She wore pink shorts and T-shirt and looked to be in her early twenties. There was something faintly seductive in her pose: her right hand touched her right shoulder and she had a drowsy smile. 'She was friendly, very friendly,' Girod said.

He returned the photograph to the tin box and lit a cigarette. 'When she was eighteen years old,' Reginald Girod said, 'she had a child. It two weeks old when she caught father with a woman making love. She got a mental depression, had to go to St Ann's psychiatric hospital. The boy, Jerry Maraj, was about three or four years old when she killed. I couldn't afford to take him, and I worked nights, as a nightwatchman. His father wanted the child in order to claim two thousand dollars out of her bank account. So I took the money and give it to Jerry. The boy spend eleven years at the orphanage before he ran away. He was very bad in school. He wanted to know his parents, about his father. He comes here sometimes.'

Reginald Girod was happy to talk about Ramnath Harrilal. 'Dread used to wear a long beard and used drugs—marijuana—and drank. I saw him in Arima rum shop, drunk. He used to live here in San Rafael and meet her here. Sylvia wanted to get away from the other fellow, who was beating her, drinking rum. Dread and Sylvia lived together up the road. Then they moved to Cumuto, where he

219

killed her. He built a shack by the line. Sylvia used to work, I don't know what. She never complained to me about him. She used to pass here and look for me. They had a falling out. I don't know the reason, but there was some Guyanese racket,' Girod said mysteriously. 'I believe that there was something he had for her but wouldn't give her. Maybe it was gold. I think she went to Guyana—with him, maybe.' Girod raised his eyebrows. 'Then she went back to him.'

Ishmael Samad asked Girod if he knew what had happened on the night she died. 'They had a quarrel,' Girod said. 'He came back from a woman, I believe. She said "go and bathe", and he hit she on the neck. He put half in latrine hole, half in forest.'

Ishmael Samad said, 'She had a very hard life.'

'I saw all the pieces at forensic,' Reginald Girod continued robustly. 'Body in one place, with a cover over it, and head showing. When I went back the next day, the head was separate. The whole head was off clean, to one side. It wasn't a pleasant sight. I cried when I saw the body.' He opined, 'I don't believe anyone of a sane mind could do that.'

I asked him whether he wanted capital punishment for Ramnath Harrilal. 'It don't worry me, hanging or no hanging,' Girod said, adding, 'although I believe that in a first degree murder you should hang a fellow.' He took a drag of his cigarette. 'I have no animosity. I come to conclusion, Well, it happened. I felt kind of sorry for him in the dock. When he shaved himself I saw he was a young fellow. Jesus Christ, I never knew he was that young.'

Ishmael Samad and I got back in the car in silence. 'I've never been able to understand why God put evil in the world,' Ishmael Samad eventually said. 'God, I sometimes say, why do we have evil in the world?'

Then he suggested a trip to see the leatherback turtles, and we drove east, to Fishing Pond.

'Look! Look!' cried Ishmael Samad. He was pointing at the sky above the mangroves, where the last remnants of daylight were disappearing into the swamp. I caught a glimpse of what seemed to be red confetti thrown up from the trees. It was a flock of scarlet ibis. The game warden, a local schoolteacher, proudly told us that a small colony of the birds, hitherto only found in the Caroni swamp on the west of the island, had recently established itself in the mangrove forest.

It was dark now, and the oil rigs glittered in the ocean like casinos. In the sky at the horizon, the glows from more distant drilling platforms showed like a series of small dawns. Presently, about fifty yards away, we noticed a blob in the water that could have been a boulder washed by the surf. Imperceptibly but steadily, like the minute hand of a clock, the object moved out on to the beach. We did not approach it—a turtle can be disturbed into retreating to the water. Looking through Ishmael's binoculars, I could see the creature paddling its flippers and schlepping itself uphill over the damp, packed sand. Finally, the leatherback reached the higher part of the beach. She began moving in a circle, flinging away the soft sand in a kind of breaststroke, and then wriggled her body down into the depression she had made for herself. Then she began to dig with her rear feet. Now we approached. She was immense. Her carapace—leathery and ridged and oval—looked like the keel of an upturned boat. The turtle's rear flippers dug and dug until there was a hole about one foot wide and two feet deep. Then the eggs began to drop from the rear of her belly. They fell steadily, soft glistening white spheres like snooker balls. She laid about a hundred in all. Then she buried them with sand flipped by her rear legs, occasionally panting and sighing, revolving and splashing in the sand until the eggs were hidden from predators. Ishmael Samad softly patted her enormous head, with its beaked bill and lachrymose eyes.

She lugged herself back down towards the sea. The moon was out now, and the clouds dispersed by the breeze. She entered the luminous foam and slowly swam out, ready to eat jellyfish. It had taken her an hour or so.

Opponents of capital punishment often argue their case pragmatically: for example, that the death penalty has no real deterrent effect; that because guilt can rarely be established with total certainty, innocent people are sent to their deaths. But the fundamental position of many of them is that no matter how terrible the offence, or conclusive the evidence, or pardonable the urge for retribution, it is wrong to execute a human being. Why this should be so is almost beyond persuasive articulation: but not, I realized as

Joseph O'Neill

I walked up the beach towards the mangroves, beyond revelation.

I left Trinidad at the end of June. A few days later—on July 9, 1999—Ramnath Harrilal was sentenced to a further five years in prison. On July 28, 1999 a mechanic named Anthony Briggs was hanged in Port-of-Spain, but as I write, in October 2000, there have been no further hangings in Trinidad and Tobago. However, the Attorney-General of Trinidad is again promoting the idea of a Caribbean Court of Appeal which would replace the Privy Council in London and so prevent condemned prisoners from challenging, delaying and consequently escaping their executions. The Attorney-General is also gearing up for the forthcoming elections. Preparing to contest the Attorney-General's parliamentary seat is the Turtle Man, Ishmael Samad. □

STATEMENT OF OWNERSHIP, MANAGEMENT, AND CIRCULATION
1. Publication Title: Granta
2. Publication No. 000-508
3. Filing Date: September 29, 2000
4. Issue Frequency: Quarterly (4 times per year)
5. Number of Issues Published Annually: 4
6. Annual Subscription Price: $37.00
7. Complete Mailing Address of Known Office of Publication: 1755 Broadway, New York, NY 10019-3780
8. Complete Mailing Address of Headquarters of General Business Office of Publisher: 1755 Broadway, New York, NY 10019-3780
9. Full Names and Complete Addresses of Publisher, Editor, and Managing Editor: Publisher: Rea S. Hederman, 1755 Broadway, New York, NY 10019; Editor: Ian Jack, 2/3 Hanover Yard, Noel Road, Islington, London N1 8BE; Managing Editor: Sophie Harrison, 2/3 Hanover Yard, Noel Road, Islington, London N1 8BE
10. Owners: Granta USA LLC, 1755 Broadway, New York, NY 10019; NYREV, Inc., 1755 Broadway, New York, NY 10019; The Morningside Partnership, 625 N. State St., Jackson, MS 39202
11. Known Bondholders, Mortgagees, and Other Security Holders: None
12. Tax Status: Has Not Changed
13. Publication Title: Granta
14. Issue Date for Circulation Data: Fall 2000
15. Extent and Nature of Circulation: Average No.Copies Each Issue During Preceding 12 Months
a. Total No. of Copies: 78,157
b. Paid and/or Requested Circulation
1. Paid/Requested Outside-County Mail Subscriptions as Stated on Form 3541: 29,682
2. Paid In-County Subscriptions as Stated on Form 3541: 0
3. Sales Through Dealers and Carriers, Street Vendors, Counter Sales and Other Non-USPS Paid Distribution: 30,484
4. Other Classes Mailed Through the USPS: 1,797

c. Total Paid and/or Requested Circulation: 61,963
d. Free Distribution by Mail
1. Outside-County as Stated on Form 3541: 0
2. In-County as Stated on Form 3541: 0
3. Other Classes Mailed Through the USPS: 238
e Free Distribution Outside the Mail: 291
f. Total Free Distribution: 529
g. Total Distribution: 62,492
h. Copies not Distributed: 15,666
i. Total: 78,517
j. Percent Paid and/or Requested Circulation: 99%
Extent and Nature of Circulation:No.Copies of Single Issue Published Nearest to Filing Date
a. Total No. of Copies: 70,445
b. Paid and/or Requested Circulation
1. Paid/Requested Outside-County Mail Subscriptions as Stated on Form 3541: 29,723
2. Paid In-County Subscriptions as Stated on Form 3541: 0
3. Sales Through Dealers and Carriers, Street Vendors, Counter Sales and Other Non-USPS Paid Distribution: 28,942
4. Other Classes Mailed Through the USPS: 297
c. Total Paid and/or Requested Circulation: 58,962
d. Free Distribution by Mail
1. Outside-County as Stated on Form 3541: 0
2. In-County as Stated on Form 3541: 0
3. Other Classes Mailed Through the USPS: 251
e Free Distribution Outside the Mail: 292
f. Total Free Distribution: 543
g. Total Distribution: 59,505
h. Copies not Distributed: 10,940
i. Total: 70,445
j. Percent Paid and/or Requested Circulation: 99%
16. Publication of Statement of Ownership will be printed in the Winter 2000 issue of this publication.
17. Signature and Title of Editor, Publisher, Business Manager, or Owner: I certify that all information furnished on this form is true and complete. Rea S. Hederman, Publisher

GRANTA

THE TROUT OPERA
Matt Condon

1.

On the veranda of the Buckley's Crossing Hotel, reclining in dimpled leather armchairs, Judges Carrington and Thorpe observed in silence the giant trout shuffling across the bridge. It was almost dusk, and the two elderly men, nursing malt whiskies after a day's fishing, said nothing of the apparition, just as they would have said nothing in their courtrooms back in Sydney on the hearing of evidence. They lived in silence—it made them fine fishermen, by the by—and their identical blankness of face at the appearance of the outsized trout indicated there was very little in the world that surprised Judges Carrington and Thorpe.

A light breeze pushed up from the river bringing with it the tinkling of the trout's scales. Both men heard it, tangled in the roar from the Snowy, and if the slow-moving trout, rocking on the points of its tail fin, had disturbed their recollections of the day's fishing—the loop of silken lines, the shape of the stones beneath the soles of their boots—they did not show it. Watching it, they felt a chill rise up from their feet and through their legs from their memory of the early morning wading. As inexplicable as the sight of the tin-and-hessian fish was, they could not help recalling the icy waters of the river. They had been discussing Henry Jones & Company's fish canning operations out of Hobart when they first noticed the trout moving towards them along the dirt road into Dalgety. Both, surreptitiously, had glanced into their whisky glasses. As it kept approaching, both concluded that this was, after all, the twentieth century.

'As for canned trout,' said Carrington.

'Preposterous,' snorted Thorpe.

'An insult.'

'With no trout shape,' said Thorpe, 'there is no trout.'

With that, and the apparition defining itself as it hobbled closer to the bridge's western approach, the judges—almost brothers, really, and law school chums—each recalled the respective specimens they had mounted under glass in their chambers back in Sydney. Two rainbows, caught on the same trip, transported in ice and preserved against a hand-painted river-bank scene with the same loving care and attention by Mr Smiggett Junior of The Rocks. (Poor Smiggett Senior, dead not a year from arsenic asphyxiation.) Two rainbows, high up on the wooden walls facing their desks. Two rainbows, in which the men often lost themselves, dreaming of clear streams and distorted stones, when they should have been dismantling the great and complex machine of the criminal mind. If only the truth could be pulled from the water as readily, and mounted, they often said. How much less complicated their lives would have been.

The dinner gong sounded inside the hotel, yet the two judges were loath to leave the veranda and the spectacle of the giant trout, now clambering with difficulty on to the wooden side rail of the bridge. Encased in the hessian trout was Wilfred Lampe, aged six, who finally, after a few false starts, managed to balance on the rail's middle rung and peer over into the swift-running river. He slipped down into the suit momentarily, the mouth-opening rising above his forehead. Yet once firmly balanced, he tugged the head down and had a clear view through the padded, velvet-lipped slit.

They must be there, he thought, the water roaring. They must be there, facing upstream, waiting for the fall of white moths. He knew them better than anyone in Monaro. Had names for them. Talked to them, for heaven's sake.

But what would they have made of him now? This giant trout, one of their own, yet not, looming over them high up on the bridge. Suspended in the sky—out there, in the dryness, in the mirror world that was both life and death for them—where there had only ever been the descending stick legs of their prey, a madness of flying ants and dragonflies, or the exotic, often brilliantly feathered morsels that fooled so many of them. But this! Its huge eyes wild and googly and tenuously attached to an ill-shaped head. The flanks vibrating. The tail ragged. The side fins abnormal. This, some god of trout. A king of trout. Watching over them.

In an hour Wilfred Lampe would take the stage of the Imperial Hall as star of *The Trout Opera*. He had known his lines off by heart now for a fortnight. This, he realized, would be his last rehearsal. Gripping the rail tighter, he leaned over even further and told them: *I am King Trout of the Monaro. I am your guardian, your protector, here to ensure that your spirit will forever travel through the rivers and creeks of this country, into the lakes and the pools and the hollows.*

He was distracted by the special string of light bulbs at the front of the Imperial Hall which suddenly crackled to life. He momentarily lost his lines, thinking of the bulbs. *Oh yes,* he said, addressing his shadowy audience again. *However many of you may disappear from the waters, however many of you are lifted into heaven by the pretty fly, there are multitudes more who will grow older and older, and pass on their secrets, and, and...*

There was a bell ringing deep inside the hotel. He squinted again into the darkening waters of the river. Are you there? He thought he saw a flickering movement, a scissoring of trout shapes across the constellation of stones. At this time of day, at dusk, you could not be sure of anything. He liked to think they were always there somewhere, just as clouds continued their business easing across the sky while he was asleep.

They had told him not to go into town so early. To wait for the cart. But he had shuffled off anyway, down the track to the gate, and on to the road into Dalgety. He could hear the rumble of the river even as he started off. (Like the ocean, he imagined, having never seen the ocean.) His scales of tin-can lids occasionally caught the setting sun, sending discs of orange light through the lucerne stalks. He slipped once in a cart rut and fell with a clang into the dust. Inside the suit he felt so much bigger than he was—this narrow boy with his elongated torso and broom-handle arms and spectacular splashings of freckles across not just his face but his ears and eyelids as well. They had always called him Trout anyway. And here he was, Wilfred Lampe, aged six, looking over the bridge rail for his obedient subjects. *Me lady,* he said croakily. *Me lady.* But the lines had gone from him, lost in the sighs from the willows and the sharp honking of frightened ducks that exploded into the air at the river bend.

The giant trout finally came down off the rail and progressed towards the hotel. Suddenly, horses and carts began arriving from all directions—the cricket oval, the blacksmith shop, the police station and lock-up east of the town. The giant trout, disoriented, had almost stumbled into the path of one, the horse shying.

'My word,' said Carrington, enjoying the show.

'Bound to be an accident with a big fish like that allowed to wander freely,' said Thorpe.

'The litigation would be terribly complicated,' Carrington added.

The traffic was of the most extraordinary kind, and it would be something the judges would recall fondly—in the confines of their courts, even in their sleep on occasion—for the rest of their lives. For in each and every cart and sulky were children dressed in costume. Whole transports of frogs and birds and insects. (One particular flying ant, on passing, had waved vigorously and emitted a distinct 'G'day'.) There were trout flies, drab in the torso but bearing spectacular tendrilled headdresses. There was an entire flatbed dray of muddy browns, rocking with the gait of a Clydesdale, not to mention an assortment of yabbering bulrushes and reeds. A single flame robin, alone among a cluster of crows, wailed inconsolably.

Wilfred Lampe continued his slow progress up the rutted road in front of the hotel, his wide trout eyes spinning wildly through a veil of dust, his small freckled fingers occasionally emerging from a gill in recognition of the shouts of his school friends. His excitement was now so great he felt for a moment that he might faint. He stopped, leaned against the railing of the hotel, and caught his breath.

The judges observed him and took pity on the hot and heaving fish. 'May we be of assistance in any way?' Thorpe enquired, his glass empty. A muffled voice said through the gill: 'No thank you, sir.'

'Are you sure?' asked Carrington. 'A little water, perhaps?'

'Thank you all the same,' the boy said. 'I must be getting on.'

'Very well,' said Carrington.

With that the trout shuffled over to the Imperial Hall, watched paternally by the judges, and entered the skittering maelstrom of plant and fish and horse and parent and dust beneath the sagging string of lights. Through yellow light the judges could just read the sign attached to the wall of the hall: DECEMBER 12, 1906. DALGETY SCHOOL PRESENTS THE TROUT OPERA. ONE PERFORMANCE ONLY. AN UNFORGETTABLE EVENING.

Only the judges could hear the hotel dinner gong being struck with some urgency.

'I believe it is Trout Amandine this evening. With a sauterne.'

'Very well,' said Carrington.

Outside the hall the children poked and prodded Wilfred Lampe and rattled his scales and shouted, 'Trout! Trout! Trout!'. He turned repeatedly on his heels but found it difficult to recognize anyone through his thick velvet lips.

Finally it was time, and the cast of *The Trout Opera* waited behind the heavy curtains at the front of the Imperial Hall, tittering and whispering and waiting for their cue—the slow lilt of a violin. It came at last, the note as thin and graceful as a freshly-cast silk fishing line. He heard his queen, Her Majesty the Lure, clear her throat beside him, her feathered rainbow headpiece reaching up towards the wooden ceiling of the hall. The muddied browns muttered incessantly despite a repeated 'Ssshhh!' from the wings. And the willows, ahead of time, had begun their ghostly humming.

Wilfred Lampe started to sweat inside the hessian. The sounds of footsteps and the barking of chairs echoed through his suit. The single note of the violin sailed through the heat, through perfume and hair oil and a trace of cow dung and the whole sticky breath of the Imperial Hall. Then the curtains opened.

2.

Wilfred Lampe sat with his mother during the making of the trout suit.

On a stool beside his mother's chair was a white china plate, and on the plate a brown trout, caught by his father on a whim at the deep hole up from the Dalgety bridge. As she cut and stitched, glancing at the trout as she worked, he marvelled at how she recreated the fish from the pile of hessian brought from the general store. At first he had little confidence. This rough shapeless sacking, sliding across her knees, as dun-coloured as the paddocks that stretched out from their woodslab house. And she, taking instruction from the rotting fish, its greying body arced at head and tail from the heat of the day. Wilfred Lampe tried to avoid its shrivelled eye.

After ten days he was required to try on the suit, slipping into its dark cavity, scratching his arms on its scaffolding of wire and kindling. He could see, through its incomplete mouth, his mother's brow creased with concentration, her own mouth spiked with bead-headed pins.

'Is he almost finished, Mama?' He had lost count how many times he had asked this.

'Patience,' she said through the pins.

Later, when his father came in from the property, the boy,

standing silently inside the hessian during the attachment of the scales, would hear him washing his hands in the tin bowl on the veranda, his heavy boots entering the house, and the clicking noise he made with his tongue that signalled his homecoming. 'He's a good fifty pounds, wouldn't you say, mother?'

And the sniggering of his three sisters would scratch around him like mice. Everything that he thought he knew—the voices of his family, the chiming of the old clock on the wooden mantelpiece decorated with carved chickens, the spit of the fire, the gunshot cooling of the boulders out in the paddocks—became fresh and new and trembled with a strange vigour inside the body of the trout.

'He's just about good enough to eat,' he heard his oldest sister, Astrid, say. 'Shall we get the pan out?'

Each night as he went to sleep on his cot out on the veranda that summer, he recited his lines from *The Trout Opera* and regularly rose from his pillow to make sure it was there—the suit—standing in the corner. Once he'd been afraid to sleep alone on the veranda with its encasement of ragged fly wire punctuated here and there with the husk carcass of a fly or wasp. But now, with the dark shape of the trout nearby, he felt at ease.

On a clear night he could hear the river from his cot and he thought of the families of trout sleeping in their hollows, and of his trout, the guardian trout, forever awake and vigilant and looking over not just him, Wilfred Lampe, but all the trout of the Snowy, all the trout nestled in the great river that wound its way past the hulls of grazing cattle near the cricket oval and the Chinaman's vegetable patches of cabbage and rhubarb that ran in neat lines almost to the water's edge.

Sometimes, when the river rumbled so loud that it herded sheep to the far corners of paddocks and made the old clock on the mantelpiece chime without respect for its thin black arms, he closed his eyes and imagined the source of the river, high up in the mountains where he had never been. He saw himself diving into a narrow rivulet in the trout suit. He would ease through giant walls of gums, glide over lichened rocks, eddy and swirl in the intermittent pools, until he came out at Dalgety. There he would pass scores of fishermen on the banks of the river and they would wave to him and he would slip under the bridge and through the mountains and finally enter the sea, where he would sail the currents of the world.

He would be approaching Madagascar, or ogling a giant iceberg in the Antarctic, when he would be shaken out of sleep. 'C'mon, boy. Time to get up.' And still coconut trees and white beaches and blocks of ice would be with him as he stumbled around the property in the blue light before breakfast, helping his father.

Wilfred Lampe, aged six, was beginning to see the shapes of the world out there, of ancient church spires and clock towers, of pyramids rising from the desert, of ocean liners and the plumed hats of horsemen and Chinese junks fat in the water and volcanoes, distorted as they were, translated from picture book to mind, his memory shimmering with the disconnectedness of it all. But it was still his own world that reflected back to him and through him so powerfully. All the little things that constituted the universe of a boy— favourite tree, deepest waterhole, secret cave in the monolithic clusters of boulder, patch of bulrushes, collection of pink granite stones like jewels in the hand under water, stub of toe, bumps and dips of the dirt road into town, the personalities of marbles, crack of fresh laundry from the copper—were a part of him. Were him. All that, and the polished round spectacles of school teacher and principal Mr Schweigestill, the lenses so thick his eyes appeared huge, huge, like some fish dragged on to the bank and fighting, heaving, for life.

Mr Schweigestill was tall and stooped and disappeared when he turned sideways (or so said Wilfred Lampe's father). His clothes billowed around him like the coat and trousers of Chin's scarecrow in the vegetable patch by the river. The skin on his face and hands was stretched and white, almost translucent. His fingers were spidery, the bones and knots of cartilage and veins so unpleasantly near the surface that some of the children pulled back from them, leaned away as the fingers skittered towards exercise books and ink pots and the backs of chairs. He had no lips—his mouth a quick gutting with a sharp fishing knife—and, as far as they could tell, no teeth, or none to speak of. On top of his narrow, elongated head was a small thatch of oiled black hair divided down the centre by a parting so exact and so brilliantly white, even compared to the rest of his whiteness, that it hurt to look at it. Everything about Mr Schweigestill was loud. The thud of his boots around the granite block schoolhouse. The tapping of his pointer. The snapping shut of a book. His voice was even louder than fat Mr Eale, the last schoolmaster, whom they'd buried not long ago in Berridale. He'd simply died on the spot, dressed in his hat and suit at the fair on the oval in Dalgety, amid spread blankets and wicker baskets and shattered eggshells from the spoon races. They thought he was sleeping, and there he stayed, his hat tilted over his face in the shade of a gum, for the rest of the afternoon. Wilfred Lampe himself, dripping with river water after several leaps from the new bridge, had passed the resting figure and bid him a good day.

They had all liked Mr Eale. Meat and potatoes, Mr Eale.

And even before his funeral (no big deal to young Wilfred, really—what's death on the land?—his days already punctuated with sheep ripped and torn by the razor teeth of foxes, the bloated ships of drowned cattle etc.) had come Mr Schweigestill. A committee of parents and the local constable had greeted him on his arrival from Cooma, had witnessed the angular difficulty of the suited stranger extracting himself from the carriage like some giant insect emerging from a cocoon.

'Guten Tag,' he had boomed, forgetting himself, this foreign utterance so at odds with the spring air thick with dandelion heads and the perfume of eucalyptus sap and crushed ants, that it had stamped him, indelibly and for all time, as just a visitor to the Monaro.

In the first few weeks his every move was scrutinized. That he received, once a week, foreign sausages and pastries by post, did not escape a single person. That he read books in the corner of the Buckley's Crossing Hotel, sitting for hours, hours mind you, on a single ale, somehow told the community all they needed to know about Mr Schweigestill. Oh yes, he's the gentleman of the books and the sausages.

In class, he had opened an atlas on his desk and pointed out to the children where he had come from and they had crowded around him carefully avoiding the hands and there, at the tip of his long index finger, just over the perfectly manicured nail, was the small town in southern Germany, a dot of ink, beside a thick river. It meant nothing to most of them, this tiny green mark on a map. What was a dot compared to this, their place, warted with thousands of granite boulders and criss-crossed by fences that disappeared over hills that gave way, eventually, to the shoulders of the Snowy Mountains? Wilfred Lampe saw, by looking at the map, that the two of them would get along. They both knew about great rivers.

They could never pronounce his name. They just called him Mr Ssshh. One Saturday, downriver, Wilfred Lampe had come across him wading knee-high in the cool shadows of a buttress of lantana and blackberry bushes. The boy had almost missed him through the tangle and amid a thicket of bulrushes, their sausage-like heads brushing against the teacher's thighs. Mr Schweigestill had a look of such strained concentration, almost of desperation, that Lampe did not disturb him. He could hear Mr Schweigestill humming a tune as he flicked a rod back and forth, and on the bank he could just see the teacher's neatly placed leather satchel, a camphorwood fly box, a book and a pair of polished, ankle-high laced boots. Mr Schweigestill appeared to be praying to the fish.

On the Monday Wilfred Lampe presented to his teacher a tobacco tin of flies made by his father. Sitting at his desk after class, Mr Ssshh examined each fly, turning them over reverently with his spidery fingers, bringing them almost flush with his thick spectacles. Again, that same look of agonized pleasure came over his face.

'Ohh,' he said, studying the flies.

'Keep them,' said Wilfred Lampe. 'I got plenty.'

After the gift of the flies, Mr Schweigestill started attending evenings of card games at the Buckley's Crossing Hotel. He abandoned his dark woollen suit for variations of tweed, and was observed strolling with difficulty in a new pair of boots with elasticized sides. Local graziers were frequently startled by him wandering across their paddocks, seeking out farmhands and jackaroos for a friendly chat. He attended a working bee at the Imperial Hall, and lost a fingernail trying to nail up some loose floorboards. And he started wearing, out of nowhere, a large tan bushie's hat, its shade as big as a cartwheel.

The sausages and pastries stopped coming through the post.

Mr Schweigestill had started landing trout with Wilfred Lampe's flies. So many, in fact, that on his domestic errands he distributed them, wrapped neatly in newspaper, as gifts to the people of the town. He would leave them on bar counters without a word, beside the glass cabinets in the general store, anonymously on verandas and front steps, and in the garden box of Miss Emelia White, the only single woman in town under thirty, who had been the recipient of many gifts from suitors all over the district—from flowers and lace doilies through to a bull, tethered early one evening to her front gate—but never trout, lovingly smoked and gently placed among her dahlias.

He would whistle now as he walked. A strange, complicated tune too rich and ebullient to be carried by his breath and absence of lips. He twittered and tweetered, and the notes, by virtue of their thinness, would be carried away by the slightest puff of breeze as soon as they had escaped from him. Still, Wilfred Lampe could not help but think that his father's black and grey flies had snagged something deep within Mr Schweigestill, and brought it into the open air. Could not help but think that the thick ribbon of the Snowy now stretched all the way to Mr Ssshh's river back home in Germany, that the two rivers had joined, and the trout the teacher so fondly remembered in his other life had now connected with trout here, on the other side of the world, and swam freely with them, and that this had made Mr Schweigestill extremely happy.

It may have been the tobacco tin of flies, too, that gave birth to *The Trout Opera*.

That summer, six weeks before the holidays, Mr Schweigestill informed the class that their annual Christmas pageant, an institution in Dalgety as fixed as the birth of Christ, would on this occasion be something 'a little special'. That here, at the beginning of a new century, the boys and girls of Dalgety would celebrate the Federation, would perform a ceremony—an opera, no less—that commemorated the birth of a nation. Here, on stage in the Imperial Hall, thirty-seven children would tell the story of Australia and its future. It would be an evening, he said, his gaze drifting out of the small window, that would be remembered and spoken about for generations.

The class had no idea what he was talking about.

Wilfred Lampe tried to explain the nature of the pageant to his parents.

'The bloke's cracked,' his father said, preparing trout flies at the kitchen table.

'What about the baby in the manger?' asked his youngest sister,

Emily. 'No baby in the manger?'

Wilfred Lampe shook his head uncertainly. He wasn't sure what 'opera' was.

'I'll tell you one thing,' his father continued. 'No baby in the manger come concert time and they'll toss him in the river.'

Wilfred Lampe felt sorry for Mr Schweigestill and wanted to warn him about the dangers of staging the opera. It would be the end of his Saturday afternoons fishing for trout, his wooing of Miss White, his card evenings. It would be the end of everything. But Wilfred had no opportunity. At first rehearsals for *The Trout Opera* he discovered that he, Wilfred Lampe, was to have one of two starring roles. He would be King Trout of the Monaro alongside his Queen Lure— Maggie Corcoran. He. Wilfred. Or Herr Lampe, as Mr Schweigestill had referred to him since the bestowing of the tin of handmade flies. He. Right beside Maggie Corcoran, inches taller than him, daughter of the town's second largest property owner, the only child in the district picked up and returned to school each day by sulky. Within days, the boy noticed, Maggie had taken her regal manners from *The Trout Opera* outside the class, and stepped into and alighted from her carriage with a previously unseen delicacy and confidence. But Lampe. He felt embarrassed rehearsing the imperious gestures of King Trout of the Monaro. He was a boy with manure beneath his nails. A boy of nettle wounds and fence post splinters and dust on the rims of his freckled ears. He peed behind trees and broke wind.

It would change later, once he was inside the trout suit itself. Yet on those many afternoons when it was so hot in the hall that children fainted and Mr Schweigestill became so pale you could almost see the shift of his muscles and organs beneath that tissue skin, Wilfred Lampe saw only disaster, and the minutes became hours, and he could picture nothing of his teacher's grand opera, just the waterhole down from the bridge which, the second rehearsals ended, he and several others raced for, tripping in their haste, rolling in dust, discarding their clothes on the run, piece by piece, as they approached the willows, then dived into, disappeared into, washing away all thoughts of violin and dance, harmony and waltz, losing all sense of history, losing the oppressive heat of it, as they paddled deeper and deeper to the stones and sand of the Snowy river. □

GRANTA

WHEN I WAS LOST

James Hamilton-Paterson

Lowly creatures that are watched for a time often seem purposeless in their movements. Time-lapse photography and pheromone detectors can, however, reveal that slugs dash about on explicable courses, criss-crossing their fellows' trails and apparently able to meet or avoid suitors and predators. An analogous overview can equally come to someone passing his fiftieth birthday. On looking back he can see similar patterns emerge from the ostensibly random comings-and-goings of his life so far. In my own case I am unable to ignore the significance of all those unmade roads down which I have chosen to live. The tarmac stops and gives way to a track leading into a forest where, after a mile or two, some paths intersect, one of which heads towards an abode from which no neighbours can be seen. This has been as true of a hill side in Italy as it has for a forgotten province in the Far East. I must recognize that in a trivial sense, at least, I have a need to become lost.

Judging from most accounts, whether in psychoanalytical texts or travellers' tales, to become lost involuntarily is a frightening or unpleasant experience. Being lost in the desert with a dwindling supply of water is a reasonable cause for fear, but mostly the circumstances of becoming lost are not life-threatening. Yet the distress caused seems out of proportion to the temporary inconvenience. Control has failed, vulnerability increases... One wonders at people's feeble grip on their sense of self, that their entire ontology can be so easily eroded. Suddenly one has an impression of the great energy they must expend daily in order to hold themselves together, an energy which if challenged by unfamiliar surroundings swerves at once to produce rising panic. I note this with curiosity, being by nature rather the opposite: not only content to live in some degree of isolation but on occasion revelling in finding myself stranded in strange territory and out of touch with the rest of the world. This seems to be the one consistent pattern that has emerged from years of slug-like meanderings about the globe.

In fact it is not at all easy nowadays to become physically lost to the extent that one's position cannot be known or one's presence detected. Sadly, the days are pretty much over when travellers could vanish on expeditions with faulty maps and broken compasses, when confronting fate demanded self-reliance and stoicism. A little GPS

(Global Positioning System) instrument that tucks into a rucksack pocket will place you anywhere on the planet's surface to within fifty metres; a radio beacon will bounce that position up to a satellite which relays it to emergency services, or else a mobile phone will enable you to swap banalities with your family from the middle of the Gibson Desert. It is the sudden recent spawning of mobile telephones and their babble that eloquently testifies to a deep general insecurity, to a yearning to remain constantly 'in touch'. From all this it is clear that being truly lost has to do with a more than merely physical state; but becoming physically mislaid is a good place to start. I shall not easily forget the exhilaration of a few years ago when for a couple of hours I effectively vanished from the known universe, having fallen through all technological safety nets and being quite beyond finding or rescue.

This happened in 1995 on a dive I was making in a Russian manned submersible, one of the twin MIRs deployed by the research vessel *Mstislav Keldysh*. These were the same MIRs used in filming the *Titanic*: two of only four submersibles in the world rated able to descend 6,000 metres (the other two being French and Japanese). I was part of an expedition searching for the Second World War Japanese submarine *I-52* that had been sunk off the coast of West Africa in 1944 while ferrying—among other things—raw opium and two tons of gold from Japan to Occupied France to aid the German war effort. Our expedition had lapsed into the routine of slow sonar searches as it looked for the wreck: days of ploughing up and down in mid-Atlantic on tightly controlled courses, gradually mapping a likely swathe of the ocean floor in a technique jocularly known as 'mowing the lawn'. Each evening the printouts of these scans were examined and possible targets identified. No one knew whether the submarine had reached the bottom intact or as scattered debris. The sea at this point averaged 5,000 metres in depth. Sonar resolution of any object smaller than ten metres long was unreliable. Every few days the *Keldysh* would heave to and prepare to send the submersibles down to see if these blips on the printout were seabed features or pieces of Japanese submarine.

Sending three people in a tiny MIR down into that lightless and crushing pressure five kilometres beneath the ship's keel required careful preparation. At such a depth and distance from help there is really no hierarchy of priorities. Anything from a dozen different kinds of mechanical failure to becoming entangled in wreckage could have fatal consequences. The MIRs had been beautifully designed for full mobility and independence. No wires or cables connected them to the *Keldysh*. Once they had been launched, they were entirely in the hands of their two Russian pilots. Externally they resembled the fuselages of little helicopters, the 'cockpit' being a titanium pressure sphere two metres in diameter into which the three occupants fitted like spacemen of the Sixties surrounded by dials, controls and life-support systems. The rest of the 'fuselage' consisted of mouldings of syntactic foam (a buoyant material which would supposedly always bring the MIR to the surface) and directional motors whose propellers gave the craft complete manoeuvrability. It was this self-contained independence that also gave the MIRs their inherent ability to become lost. The first of the preparations, therefore, was for the ship to drop a pattern of transponder buoys to enable the submersibles to navigate in their dark and unmapped world. These buoys were each tethered to float a hundred feet or so above the seabed. After the dive was over a signal would be sent to them to trigger a release mechanism that would jettison their pig-iron ballast and they would come back up to the surface for recovery. When deployed, each buoy sent out its own signal at a distinctive frequency. The MIR's onboard computers would then interpret this net of signals three-dimensionally so that provided they were within range the crews would always know where they were in relation to the buoys. That, at any rate, was the theory.

Three hours after the hatch had closed on a blue, tropical sky *MIR 1* reached the end of its silent descent, having fallen five kilometres to a precise point on the planet's surface that no human eye had ever seen. This is a strange and wonderful sensation, rare in these post-explorer days. Seen through a porthole in the small circle of light cast by our external lamps the Atlantic bed was a reddish-grey rolling desert. But it was certainly not a lifeless world. Everywhere the dunes and hillocks were scarred with holes and casts that testified to the worms and other biota living in the topmost few feet of the sediment. Shrimp, copepods and occasional rat-tail fish were attracted to the MIR, swimming in and out of its illumination; but whether they were drawn by its lights, its sounds or its faint mechanical smells was anybody's guess. The submersible must have been the noisiest thing to have alighted in those parts since the ocean's formation—or at least since a dying Japanese submarine had sunk there almost forty years ago, its last watertight spaces imploding under the pressure and leaking all manner of sonic energy as well as heat and oil, blood and opium. We were planning to search down here for twelve hours, after which it would take a further three to ascend. Having worked out our position from the transponder buoys, we set off towards the spot where, if the *Keldysh*'s GPS reckoning was correct, we would find the first of the targets we were scheduled to investigate.

As the hours went by and each of the targets was revealed as nothing more than an outcrop of pillow lava or a small dune, our gliding progress a few feet above the seabed became more dreamlike and felt less and less like anything as purposeful as a search. Occasionally our navigator became confused, and we would set down to recalculate our position. Sometimes our slug-like meanderings took us across our previous track and we either saw the marks of our own skids or else passed through a cloud of reddish silt we had disturbed. It was the colour of the Sahara, the sand having fallen there from the winds that blow out of Africa westward across the Atlantic and which often deposit the same desert dust on Florida. I stared and stared through the thick perspex plug that was my window on the primordial world outside, sunk into my own thoughts with an alertness that was attuned entirely to this unknown place into which I had fallen and not at all to finding a piece of military wreckage. Our cramped spherical chamber, around whose icy surface my body was bent on the observer's couch, unaccountably seemed to expand until it became roomy, far too large for the eyeball into which I myself had shrunk. The growing sense of majestic isolation was helped by problems of communication. In an immediate sense, I couldn't converse much with my two crew mates since I spoke no Russian and they scarcely any English. But our difficulties turned out to be more radical than that. During the descent the pilots had been in intermittent voice contact with the *Keldysh* as she basked in the sunshine somewhere miles overhead. Water is, of course, an excellent conductor of sound, though a poor one of radio waves. The MIR's communication system was therefore not based on radio. Instead, it converted ordinary speech to a higher frequency, amplified it and broadcast the sounds into the water column. Far away the Keldysh received them, converted them back to the frequency of normal speech, and could hear our crew's voices. Likewise, we could hear Control. Any nearby creatures such as fish or whales would have heard our speech as a shrill babbling squeal. As we were going down our shipmates' voices had become more and more faint and distorted as the gulf between us opened up. Now, nothing so intensified the feeling of having landed on an unknown planet beyond all human reach as the occasional ghostly voices of our friends speaking from brilliant tropic air. Gradually, their remarks became unintelligible, the vestiges of syllables echoing away into the limitless deep that encased us. I remember a story by Ray Bradbury that used to affect me very much as a teenager. There is an explosion aboard a spaceship not far from earth, and several of the crew are scattered into space in their suits, each helplessly propelled on his own trajectory away from the others. For as long as they remain within range of each other the doomed men talk over their radios, their voices growing ever more distant until one by one they fall silent. Before they do, they variously try to bring about hurried reconciliations or are amazed at the grandeur of their fate. One is swept up in a cloud of asteroids to be carried along for eternity in their orbit about the sun. Another is captured by earth's gravity and knows he will burn up on re-entry. The story ends when at dusk somewhere in Illinois a child looks up and sees a shooting star. Some residue of this tale inhabited me on the bottom of the Atlantic as the voices of our shipmates faded. The MIR had drifted into a complex of valleys formed by high dunes. Suddenly, no external sound was breaking the loudspeaker's soft hiss. At the same time, the transponders' navigation signals were likewise blocked.

From this moment we became lost to the world, lost to humanity and to the twentieth century. We had fallen off all known maps. We were as out of touch as a space capsule passing behind the moon, our presence no more than inferred from our last known position and supposed trajectory. The two Russians lay imperturbably as we hummed along, the pilot gazing through his port and his colleague fiddling on a borrowed laptop computer. They munched peanuts and from time to time exchanged a comment I couldn't understand. I had never felt more alone, more at the mercy of natural physics, more exhilarated. How many times in my choirboy days on that far-off planet earth had I sung the words *'Justorum animae in manu dei sunt'*? The souls of the righteous are in the hands of the Lord. I was not righteous; I did not think I had a soul; I did not believe there were any merciful hands out there where our halogen lamps shed a crawling speck of light on creation's primordial darkness. Indeed, it seemed probable that creation had yet to take place fully. Despite the occasional fish and the ubiquitous signs of other life being lived at a pressure of 500 atmospheres, the world beyond our titanium sphere was somehow pre-Genesis. The Garden of Eden was yet to come. I was an anachronism, a time traveller, non-existent. We were more than lost: we were expunged from the record. And yet I felt secure.

One need not have read Anna Freud's paper *About Losing and Being Lost* to sense that this state is not a simple proposition, either psychologically or philosophically. To take her example of a child becoming separated from its parents in a department store: the boy might have found a toy in which he is engrossed, while his parents who can't see him fall into a complete panic, at once imagining all kinds of horrors have befallen their child. From the boy's perspective he is not lost at all until the toy no longer distracts him and he begins to miss his parents. In other words one is never lost until one feels lost. My first remembered experience of this prosaic oddity was during the Festival of Britain in 1951. My parents had taken me, aged nine, to the South Bank Exhibition where I was having an interesting time looking at the Dome of Discovery and the Skylon when suddenly I became aware of loudspeakers. As soon as I heard them I realized I had been hearing them on and off for the previous ten minutes, repeating the same message which I had ignored. The message they were repeating was my own name;

followed by instructions on how to find my parents. The news to me was not only that I was officially lost, but that I hadn't recognized my own name when it was spoken by a public address system because public address systems spoke only other people's names. I was me, myself, the world; but I needed no public identity. It was only then I felt suddenly alone amid the swirl of strangers, the lights and noise. When we were finally reunited my father was, inevitably, furious in a way that seemed to me entirely unjust. After all, he had lost me, not I him.

Such things came back to me more than forty years later aboard *MIR 1* as we and our mother ship became lost to one another. I began to muse about the pleasure I was taking in our predicament; about how I didn't feel lost, had never really felt lost in my entire life, only disorientated in a strange place. At this moment I was merely out of touch, which I experienced as a form of being freed. What made others panic was for me a solace. The echiuroid worms beyond the porthole were endlessly fascinating. Everywhere were hillocks of sand with a hole from which little puffs of sediment were emitted from time to time, like smoke signals telling of absorbed life processes going on inside. It was as if the whole burden of my previous life—friends, loves, pleasures, interests—had been shed like a lump of pig iron and I was free to roam forever in this pre-Genesis landscape in a kind of weightless trance. Many hours later, when I had been restored to the upper air and the late twentieth century, I was amazed that I should ever have contemplated sacrificing my identity for permanent communion with that dark and primitive dimension. And yet enough of the experience's pungency lingered— lingers still—to remind me that I had been neither hallucinating nor anoxic but had briefly crossed a threshold that led to a world whose profound interest to me depended on neither thought nor desire. I would never have believed such a thing possible. In some way it approached a state of complete satisfaction, which certainly threw an ironic cast over our mission in the MIR as well as over the entire expedition.

For down there in the eternal chill of blank and fathomless water we were looking for a lost object, a Japanese submarine; and anyone who has dipped into Freud (or Zen Buddhism) will know that the search for lost objects is always doomed because they can never be found. The Lost Object is the outcome of the structure of desire, and being party to this is the lot of all mortals. Unbelievably, it is a form of loss that can even precede possession, as witness ultrasound scans showing infants in utero sucking their thumbs as a substitute for the breast they have yet to encounter. As adults, of course, we can satisfy our wishes imaginatively if sadly, summoning back our dead or fantasizing ourselves rich or erotically triumphant; but such attempts do not depend on reality. Needs and urges can be fulfilled; desire, never. I had plenty of time in the weeks aboard the *Mstislav Keldysh* to speculate about this expensive search for the *I-52*. Whenever I wondered about what it was we were really looking for, our professed target seemed to give a smart sideways jump. It was like trying to focus one's eye on a piece of retinal debris. We were looking for the submarine, of course. Only no; we were actually looking for the two tons of gold she was allegedly carrying. But nobody really wants gold, the stuff itself, which is useful only for being locked in vaults as dark as the one it was currently lying in. What one wants are the things it stands for, the things it can buy. But the things one can buy with it are never quite what one thought one wanted, and themselves stand for something else... And on and on it skids, pursuing itself relentlessly around the desire that can never be fully satisfied. The one thing people believe they most long for, and then get, always carries within it a tiny seed of disappointment. Even a Nobel turns out to be a second prize after all. No one ever gets their hands on complete fulfilment. Thus desiring and losing turn into a single topological figure that chases its own tail. There is no lost object without desire; there is no desire without the lost object. The circle cannot be broken. But for a strange long moment it can perhaps be sidestepped, as when I stared out of *MIR 1*'s porthole on to a world that was not lost, and which I was not finding, but whose busy physics and skeins of phosphorescence underlay things much as the galaxies and nebulae of the night sky overhang life on dry land.

Our expedition never did find the Japanese submarine, as it happened, but a subsequent expedition did. Ah, it might be said: surely those others found the thing they were looking for, the object that had been lost? But no. They found the submarine all right, but to date they have not found the gold. Not a single ingot. Not even enough to make a pen nib. Given the accelerating costs of deep-sea recovery and the diminishing price of gold, it may no longer be worth launching another expedition. Besides, dark rumours are circulating of top-secret wartime hoodwinking that hint the gold was perhaps no longer on board the submarine when she sank. The desire goes on, but sometimes the pursuit has to be dropped from sheer weariness or inanition and a new goal fixed.

For almost two of our seventeen hours' dive *MIR 1* remained lost to the world, threading the maze of dunes in silence, searching without success for our third target. At last our pilot took us up above the sedimentary hill tops, and there we once again picked up the far-off pinging of the transponder pattern. The world had returned to us. The instant our onboard navigation equipment began buzzing and winking and resetting its coordinates we re-entered the dimension of normality. Where we next investigated, a mile or two away, the terrain was gently undulating, like Home Counties pastureland done in ochre. There were the same echiuroids, the same little crabs, starfish and holothurians; but now they could be assigned a position. Now, too, voices began ebbing faintly back through the loudspeaker. 'They are asking how you are,' the co-pilot told me in halting German. Once again I had failed to recognize my name over a PA system, although there was some excuse this time since the speaker was Russian and the mournful echoes were bouncing around the water column as though we were being addressed at the bottom of the world's deepest well.

So what of that world among the dunes where for a while we had been truly lost? Had the same vast tonnage of ocean that had cut us off from all signals and voices from the upper world also attenuated desire and rendered meaningless notions of loss and being lost? It had certainly felt like that: a dimension so different as to abrogate the norms of the human psyche. (It must be said, however, that the human body had remained cheerfully unaffected, inconveniently asserting its desire to pee, its pleasure in eating peanuts, and its susceptibility to the cold that penetrated the sphere.) It could only be called a lost world in the sense that it had never before been found. Its fascination for me was that it nevertheless felt like something familiar after which I had always hankered, and which I would now safely carry with me to the grave.

In the three chill hours as we slowly ascended like a bubble rising in a tower of oil, I wondered how it would be to have done the trip alone, to have found oneself alone and cut off on the ocean floor: a fantasy that was always punctured by sharp actuality. The whole experience had only been possible because of skilfully manipulated technology. If I had never felt fear it was surely because I had complete faith in the capsule and its pilots, despite all the pre-trip warnings and disclaimers of responsibility, and despite accepting that the chances of catastrophic failure or a trapped death from oxygen starvation were always there. However often the *Keldysh* deployed her submersibles it was never treated as a humdrum or routine matter. It was a solemn thing to visit the roots of the sea. No MIR ever went down without two highly qualified and sober pilots. The only imaginable way in which I might have found myself alone on the seabed would have been if both pilots had been struck down simultaneously by fatal food poisoning or something, in which case merely being lost would have been the least of my worries. In order to examine the true implications of getting lost one obviously needed to discount all those cases where one's life was in real danger, when fear was justified. Actually, the only interesting component of getting lost was irrational fear, and I was now sure this was something that happened to other people rather than to me.

The best thing about the end of our dive was that we came up well after midnight, so we were not greeted by blinding sunshine and rows of faces lining the decks. It was a more private affair. The necessary crew and a few colleagues were there beyond the puddle of light cast by the deck lamps on the black and rocking ocean. This grateful darkness helped the transition to the everyday world in which one was going to have to do the rest of one's living. The MIR was winched up, swung inboard, and deposited gently on its cradle. The hatch was popped and we emerged, a little stiff and breathing in the fresh Atlantic breeze with pleasure after so many hours of canned and recycled air. The mother ship seemed not inclined to be punitive about its precious child having strayed out of contact for so long. Instead, we were congratulated on our safe return and commiserated with over our failure to find the submarine. Submarine? Oh, that submarine... I had completely forgotten about the pretext for our dive, our search for the lost naval object. Well, yes, I said; that was a bit of a disappointment. But it wasn't, of course. The entire experience had been so amazing I had scarcely given the *I-52* a thought.

I carried with me back to my cabin a bottle of pee and the knowledge that I had been well and truly lost, but had never felt it and now knew why. Or at least, I knew it was a consistent and lifelong quirk of mine never to be completely lost, despite having no sense of direction and a laughable ability to have no idea where I am. But that is not being lost, and it seldom produces in me more than minor irritation and quite often a serendipitous pleasure. A secure sense of one's identity does not depend on geographical whereabouts, after all. Anna Freud seemed to think the children she studied felt lost largely because they had not been securely enough loved, and promptly *got* lost to prove it. I note that a recent report by the University of Maastricht on primary school children's fears cites the commonest of these as spiders, blood and getting lost, which suggests phobias rather than something more rational. Global positioning systems cannot help orient the psyche, and for the susceptible there is an awful lot of Elsewhere in the world. Luckily for slugs they don't get lost. Maybe the trick is to find your surroundings so engrossing, so diverting, as to be unaware that anyone is missing you. The chances are nobody is. □

GRANTA

AGAINST
TRAVEL WRITING
Robyn Davidson

Shortly after its publication in 1980 I was surprised to learn that I had written a travel book. I knew nothing about literary genres then, but felt an instinctive recoil, as if my intentions had been misunderstood. I had indeed walked alone through the deserts of my country, Australia, and I had used camels to carry my gear—a pragmatic solution to lack of cash. But the geographical distances and the means by which I covered them were not, I thought, the important thing.

The book's success had bizarre and unexpected consequences.

Firstly, magazine editors and tour companies offered to send me to holiday destinations in order to describe them to people 'back home' who might wish to vacation there but who, it seemed, wished to experience my experience before they felt confident enough to experience their own.

Secondly, publishers pressed me to produce another book, as similar as possible to the first. But the journey had been the unique outcome of singular causes—that was the *point*. To seek to repeat it would be to render my own life kitsch.

But once the world sticks a label on you, it takes great effort to resist conforming to it. Reality takes on the shape of a fish trap and if you are not constantly vigilant, down the funnel you go. Ten years after *Tracks* was published, I yielded. I went to India, lived with nomads. My intention was genuine enough—I was interested in transhumance and I did want to write something resembling ethnography. I would select one group, live with them over a long period of time, study them in isolation from their wider context. When it came time to write it all up, I would edit myself out of the account.

That intention was rendered ludicrous from the word go. There is no such thing as a disinterested observer (I carried my concepts with me, through which I interpreted what I saw), just as there is no such thing as a community isolated, spatially or temporally, from the greater society in which it is embedded. I also carried my own time with me—post-industrial time. I could get into a jeep and in a few hours be in a telephone booth, or in a large city—a journey which would take my companions weeks, and involve them in many physical hardships. It was not possible for me to live with them in the way I had envisaged, because I embodied that other version of time.

Both the experience and the attempt to describe it honestly confirmed my view that the accepted models of travel writing were compromised to such a degree that the best one could do was subvert a decadent genre.

But commerce has its own laws. If the book that came out of my Indian experience, *Desert Places*, didn't fit its category, *Desert Places* would have to be retailored. The book was packaged according to the exigencies of the market—exotic travel: subsection, female. (But I shall return to the assets and liabilities of sex in the field of literature a little later.)

I found I could not pass the travel section of bookshops without feeling obscure irritation towards the browsers I saw there, and sorry for various books I knew were stranded in the stacks, like guests fetched up at the wrong party and forbidden to leave. Nor was I alone in my aversion. There were grumblings of denial from writers you would think represented the very epicentre of the genre—Bruce Chatwin for example, and Paul Theroux. Even Claude Lévi-Strauss, in his arresting introduction to *Tristes Tropiques*, confessed to hating travel books, before writing one that is literature of the highest order. To the best of my knowledge, no other genre has suffered this weird allergy to itself.

And yet the vast piles of books written by people who leave home that I have devoured during forty years of literate life have given me, for the most part, deep pleasure—a seeming contradiction which begs the questions: what is travel writing, and who gets to say so?

All taxonomies are fuzzy sets. That is, boundaries imposed on what is really a continuum—and in these postmodern days of genre bending they are getting even fuzzier. Literary borders are permeable; books migrate. But this tendency to escape standard classification is countered by a more powerful restraining force, as if ambivalence—the space in which we can make up our own minds—is antithetical to the laws of the marketplace. Readers (or rather, buyers) are encouraged to use the travel section much as tourists are encouraged to experience holiday destinations—herded along the usual routes, all wilful peregrinations discouraged.

Take a glance around that section and you could be forgiven

for thinking that the genre is so capacious as to lack meaning. Maps, tourist guides, yachting almanacs, photo essays, rock climbing manuals, a few hoary classics and shelf upon shelf—a staggering plenitude—of contemporary travelogues, all commissioned, published and usually written with the intention of satisfying a market. It's not that such books don't deserve a place here, nor that they may not be well written and entertaining, it's that they have come to represent the genre as it is generally conceived—that is, a literature to accommodate a longing for the exotic, in an increasingly homogenized, commercialized and trivialized world.

But the literature of movement covers a richer and more complex range of experiences, and far from being capacious, that section of a bookshop is impoverished by omission. Out in the genre's fuzziest borders, away from its predictable destinations, you can come across all kinds of characters you would never think of as travel writers. Berlioz setting off in a stagecoach with his pistols in his lap, for example, or Nadezhda Mandelstam facing Siberian exile. Clara Schumann sledding her way through Russian snows to perform her husband's music; Kafka made queasy by the sight of naked men playing leapfrog in a nudist colony. Rousseau crossing the Alps; the Buddha setting out for that most elusive destination of all—this moment, here, now. And what about the less fortunate travellers, tugged around the world by circumstances over which they have no control—slaves, soldiers and the victims of war? You would not catch them at a travel writers' party, yet their stories all fit an acceptable definition of travel writing: non-fiction works in which the author moves from point *a* to point *b* and tells us something about it.

What makes them different from the commissioned traveloguers is that they set out because of an inner compulsion to do so, or are driven by some form of necessity, and their tales therefore have the power to reconnect us with the essential. Virginia Woolf said that the art of writing 'has for backbone some fierce attachment to an idea…something believed in with conviction or seen with precision and thus compelling words to its shape'. If we accept that view, then it has to be said that most contemporary travel writing is pretty spineless.

Describing what lies beyond must be one of the oldest compulsions to storytelling. Certainly it was already there at the inception of writing, and the prototype must have existed since human self-consciousness began. The metaphor of the journey is embedded in the very way in which we conceive of life—a movement from birth to death, from this world to the next, from ignorance to wisdom. In Aboriginal philosophy its metaphorical possibilities extended to include the earth itself—Australia *is* a travel narrative. The desire or necessity to move on has given and continues to give our world its shape.

Each epoch has reinvented its means of and reasons for travelling, and each has its own distinctive way of speaking about it. From pilgrimage to package holiday; from the eighteenth-century grand tour, available only to the upper classes, to Thomas Cook and Baedeker, caterers to the masses; from the Homeric mixture of fact and fantasy, to the Enlightenment's project to collect rigorously accurate information about the new world: all have created characteristic accounts of Elsewhere.

But whatever its varying motivations and styles, the value of the literature of restlessness is located as much in the sociological—the unique insights it affords into the disruptive, restructuring activity that is history—as in the literary. This perhaps goes some way to explaining why even its best representatives seem to lack the canonical weight afforded to the classics of other genres. (Flaubert thought it a 'low form of literature' and 'the same as news items'.) But to compare Apsley Cherry-Garrard's *The Worst Journey in the World* with *Madame Bovary* is a fairly meaningless exercise. Each aims for a different kind of truth, and achieves a different greatness.

The genre's most recent apogee—its great age, if you like—was the century that ended in 1914, the high years of Western imperialism. Classics occupy the centre ground of a genre, and writers such as Cherry-Garrard, Mary Kingsley and Euclides da Cunha threw a long shadow across their territory. These days, things look pretty slumped and irrelevant there at the core. Bill Buford, in his introduction to the first of *Granta*'s travel editions in 1983, said that recent travel writing reflected a 'wonderful ambiguity, somewhere between fiction and fact'—a sad manifestation of the confusion of our times, in which veracity is less important than the need to show off. Bruce Chatwin is often cited as exemplifying this new trend towards fibbing in the traveller's tale, which seems a little unfair, given that he insisted on calling *Songlines* a novel. But whereas Chatwin could fib with charm, erudition and elegance (he was a born fabulist), lesser writers just fib. Nothing happening out there in travel land? Make it up! What could be more postmodern?

There are exceptions of course. (V. S. Naipaul refers to his travel writing as the 'writing of enquiry' and he so dwarfs even the best of his peers that he almost deserves a category of his own.) But perhaps they are so prominent because of the lowlands surrounding them.

There are many complex reasons for this decay. The slaughter of the First World War shattered confidence in Western civilization. Cherry-Garrard's chronicle of Scott's Antarctic expedition is profoundly moving, not because of his descriptions of the sufferings he and his companions endured, but because of what he reveals to us of the pre-1914 mind—a species lost to time. *The Worst Journey in the World* was the last great work arising out of the heroic ideal, and it marked the beginning of the decline in the classic travel book form.

A more uneasy traveller emerges after that. Anxious, self-reflective. One begins to hear a tone of lament, for lost places, lost times. Ways of life that were thought primitive by the Victorians were now seen to possess their own validity, might even be sources of moral or spiritual regeneration. They were being threatened by the corruptions of the twentieth century, and there was an urgent need to record and preserve them before they all went down the drain of modernity. The empire was ending, scientific rationalism was being questioned, and there was a gathering awareness of the political implications of who gets to describe the 'Other'.

To quote Lévi-Strauss again: 'The first thing we see as we travel round the world is our own filth, thrown into the face of mankind.' He wrote that sentence when ideas of here and elsewhere, self and other were less fraught with anxiety. Now, in a world in which African nomadic camel herders use mobile phones, we can no longer pretend that our time hasn't penetrated every chink of previousness.

Tourism is often blamed for the reduction of difference in the world (masses obliterating classes) and for the rise of its commodification as a series of theme parks. But it seems to me that tourism is a symptom, not the disease. The word itself dates from the late eighteenth century when people headed for the Lake District, following in the footsteps of the Romantic poets. But it wasn't until the Second World War blew the old orders apart that the democratization of travel really began—one of the most significant episodes in post-war life. It is an irony that just when the ability to both travel and publish has penetrated the boundaries of class, race and sex, there should be nowhere left to 'discover'.

Today's tourism is likely to take the form of a transferral of 'here' to 'there'—chunks of home chopped off and deposited somewhere under a foreign sun, yet happily divested of foreigners.

Meanwhile 'abroad' is now situated at the very core of the familiar. Why go all the way to Egypt to see a souk when there is a perfectly good souk just down a London high street? The people in the London souk will be polyglot—immigrant citizens of the new city, as well as its older residents. In this souk, it is no longer the white man looking at (and describing) the Other. Here, the Other looks defiantly back.

Yet all that social upheaval, the mixing and moving, crossing and re-crossing, has been little reflected in travel writing. It's as if the genre has not caught up with the post-colonial reality from which it springs. One would think it should collapse under the weight of its paradoxes, but quite the opposite is happening. There is a passion for travel books harking back to a previous sensibility, when home and abroad, occident and orient, centre and periphery were unproblematically defined. Perhaps they are popular for the very reason that they are so deceptive. They create the illusion that there is still an uncontaminated Elsewhere to discover, a place located, indeed, somewhere between 'fiction and fact'.

The nineteenth century also saw the entry into the genre of women, who co-opted it for their own purposes—usually an exultation in a new-found freedom. Before that, there were very few women who could move about as they liked, even fewer who had the education to write about what happened when they did. The new conditions of the Victorian era allowed their numbers to increase exponentially, like mammals at the end of the dinosaur age. They set the tone for what came to be seen as a strongly bounded sub-genre, raising the still contentious question: is women's travel writing different from men's?

Robyn Davidson

A woman sets out into a world whose public domain is organized by and for men. How far can she claim a freedom of action taken for granted by her male counterparts, knowing that she is always, and everywhere, potentially prey? Isabelle Eberhardt solved the problem by dressing as a man when she travelled through the Sahara. Others waited to reach an age when their sex was no longer so desirable, when they could become, as it were, honorary men. Some took companions or servants with them. Most just took their chances. But it is internalized fear that is most crippling to spontaneity—the necessary reining-in, the ceaseless attention to modesty, to the body and, therefore, to the self. It is perhaps because of this self-consciousness that women's travel writing is often concerned as much with inner states as with outer objects. At its best, it can create a richness and intimacy lacking in the more so-called objective texts. But there are far too many exceptions to prove any rule. Plenty of women have written in the objective mode, just as plenty of men have used the subjective. An individual's sex will be just one factor among many in the uniqueness of his or her perceptions. Certainly as anthropologists, ethnographers and travellers, women have helped to reveal the hitherto hidden half of human consciousness, but they have not been able radically to transform the genre, or to revivify it.

Travel literature was always predicated on privilege; it may always have had at least one of its roots in a desire to escape the real world rather than apprehend it better, and it has always reflected the movement of world history as seen from the perspective of the centre. But surely never before has it risked floating free of its own ground.

At the moment the 'travel' sections of our bookshops are swamped by books written by a Centre describing its Antipodes. However, already the Periphery is beginning to describe itself to itself without reference to the Centre, and it will eventually journey to what was once the hub and describe that too. This about-face of the Other may well be the one social phenomenon powerful enough to revitalize a clapped-out genre.

But whether it survives as a coherent category or not, as long as we are all travellers in 'this wilderness of the world', we will need to find authentic ways of telling each other what we discover there. □